JESUS FREAKS

Dear Jude,
Thank you for supporting me!
It means so much ♡

SUKI HOLLYWOOD

love, Suki Hollywood

Text copyright © 2023, Suki Hollywood
All rights reserved.
Printed in the UK in 2023 by Mixam
Typeset by Liina Koivula
Cover art copyright © 2023, James Fenner

This is a work of fiction. Names, characters, business, events and incidents are the products of the author's imagination. Any resemblance to actual persons, living or dead, or actual events is purely coincidental.

Content warnings can be found on the last page.

This novel includes quotations from *Dictionary of Angels: Including the Fallen Angels* by Gustav Davidson (1967). References are provided throughout.

www.sukihollywood.com

*Dedicated to everyone who knows
their hometown wants them dead.*

a man named Lazarus was sick

the same one who poured perfume on Jesus and wiped his feet
So the sisters sent word to Jesus, Lord, the one you love is sick

When he heard this, Jesus said, This sickness will not end in death.

Our friend Lazarus has fallen asleep but I am going there to wake him up

Chapter One

The graveyard lay just outside the broken wall, so they drove through the gate, the stone arch thick enough to cast a shadow over the green car passing underneath. Dana couldn't remember the last time she'd drove out this far, but she didn't have time to look around. Not only were they running late, but Brussels was low on gas.

10:51am. If she made it in and out of the Dale's Gas Station in five minutes, they might still make it. Besides, she was wearing her uniform: 'police business' was a one-size-fits-all excuse.

She took a sharp left, pulling over to Dale's. 'Welcome to Lake in the Woods!' a sign beside the pitstop proclaimed. It faced outward, looking towards the open gates which marked the town's official limits. Underneath the welcome, a cartoon evergreen tree gave the reader a thumbs up, grinning.

Beside the sign—about 15 feet high and 7 feet wide—was a white wooden cross.

Gary turned away from the car window to glance at Dana. The grey polyblend suit he wore was fresh. It had been a gift from their father for his High School graduation, something to wear to job interviews. He pulled back his sleeve to check the time on his digital watch. Unbuckling her seatbelt, Dana ignored his performance.

'It's almost eleven,' he said.

His dirty fair hair was floppy in the heat, combed back behind his ears.

'It's fine.' Dana replied. 'It's like five minutes.'

She got out of the car and instantly regretted it. As weak as Brussel's air conditioning was, it provided some relief from the solid stickiness of the day.

Dana gave Gary a crumpled twenty-dollar bill and sent him inside to pay while she filled the tank. She watched him through the dust-streaked window as he greeted Mr Dale. Gary's job at Dale's Gas Station was a recent achievement and the novelty of earning his own money hadn't worn off for him yet: he looked happier to see his boss than Dana had ever been to see anyone.

She was waiting in the driver's seat when he emerged with a bouquet of red and white flowers. Condensation still clouded their cellophane wrap; they appeared fresher, more alive than the sad collection on offer outside, stems limp and drooping.

Gary handed Dana her money back. 'Mr Dale wouldn't take it.'

She rolled her eyes and put Brussels in gear: it was 10:58am and she did not have time to argue.

When they arrived, the service had already begun. Luckily, the funeral home had been optimistic in the amount of fold out chairs that they had provided, and the two of them easily found seats at the back. Towering evergreen trees, sweet with sap, pressed in on them. The grass underneath the chairs was brown and burnt, and they looked on to concrete car park. With nothing to shade them from the sun, the heat bore down on her like the eyes of an angry god.

A man stood by the grave, his eyes sweeping over the Fishers like a searchlight that was not searching for them. Though it wasn't the town's preacher, the faded black suit and tastefully sad expression he wore indicated that he was a professional, rather than recreational, mourner. They had caught him mid-eulogy, but he was still on the early years. Though, Dana thought, when you die at twenty-three, your life is all early years.

'In life, Ariel was known to many as a kind girl who always had time for others. In school she excelled. As a high school graduate, her dedication to her town remained unwavering, and she took pride in her role as a cashier...'

Dana let waves of his speech roll over her as she studied the small congregation. She was the only person not wearing black, but as a trickle of sweat ran down her lower back, she couldn't quite bring herself to be embarrassed about it. Vague recognition tugged at her. Hilary, the editor of *The Declaration*. The manager of Green's Groceries. His sister, Shelly. She'd changed her hair. Last time Dana had seen her, it had been the colour of cocktail cherries. Now it was black. It didn't suit her.

She couldn't see her dad. Or any of Ariel's remaining family. Including Gary and herself, there were, at most, twenty people present. A poor show for someone whose smile 'lit up the room'.

A sniff drew her attention. From the corner of her eye, she looked at Gary. His eyes were red. Evidently, something about Ariel's particular 'zest for life' had tugged his heart-strings.

Dana looked away. Her eyes landed on Hilary, who was also dabbing at her wet eyes.

Was everyone going to start crying? Would it be weird if she didn't?

'And if the congregation will now stand.'

Dana nudged Gary up. The speaker gave a stage magician bow and stepped to the side. No songs or speeches to elongate the service, two men in boots and wifebeaters began to lower the coffin into the waiting hole.

The men were unfit, faces red. Dana had a hysteric vision of their strength giving out. The coffin hitting the ground with a sudden *crack*, Ariel's body sprawling like spilled milk.

As the congregation edged towards the grave, Dana hung back. The eulogist handed the closest attendee—the High School's retired biology teacher—a small, decorative hand trowel. Inside the ostentatious spade was a modest pile of earth.

Unsure, the man holding it looked at the eulogist as if for reassurance that this was the correct procedure, before twisting his wrist to upturn the dry earth into the grave. It hit the wood with a smatter, like vomit. He received a nod and a smile from the eulogist to confirm that he had performed correctly.

In Lake in the Woods, good people got cremated, so burials were unfashionable. Ariel's was the first that Dana had been to. No-one had left without putting earth in the grave. Dana didn't want to do that, but maybe she had to?

Gary looked at Dana, uncertain. She walked towards the open mouth of the grave. He followed.

The other mourners had places to be, people to see. The two of them were the last ones there.

'I'll, uh, give you a moment,' Gary said. He pushed the chrysanthemums into her hand. As he walked away, she could see him wiping his eyes.

Dana had barely known Ariel and Gary hadn't known her at all, but teenagers were like that. Every loss felt unbearable, until you grew up and bore it.

Ariel Enckles, 1986-2009.
Beloved Daughter and Sister.
Born and bred in Lake in the Woods.

The flowers that Gary had given her were still limp in her hand. Dana wasn't sure what to do with them. In the movies, they put flowers on top of the soil, underneath the headstone, but Ariel's coffin was still uncovered. Dana wasn't sure where they were meant to go.

The eulogist had gone, but the two other men stood nearby holding shovels. One of them drew his hand, clad in a workman's glove, across his forehead. He was sweating, and he wanted her to know about it. Dana felt certain that they were impatient to get started. Get milk. Change your tire. Bury Ariel Enckles, 23. Tick.

Dana wasn't about to rush just so these two could clock off early. To kill time, she tried to reminisce. Think back to when they were kids, she and Ariel and ▇.

But Dana didn't have a good memory. Instead, she stared out into the woods and wondered if she'd be buried here herself, some day.

Something moved in the trees. A person was standing in the shadow of the woods, facing her. Leaf filtered light turned them green, and vague. They were far enough away that Dana couldn't be sure that they were there for the service. But then, why else would they be here?

All Dana could see was that whoever it was wore dark clothing, and that they were looking at the open grave where she stood. No, that wasn't right. They weren't looking at the grave. They were looking at Dana.

Dana looked behind her. The workmen had wandered away. Even Gary had gone back to the car. She was alone. Unsure what to do, she realised that she, too, had been staring at the person in the trees.

They were probably just wondering why a cop was at a funeral—or maybe they had been late like her.

Either that, or they were hiding—ashamed to be seen at here.

Dana refused to be ashamed. She lifted her arm and waved.

Almost simultaneously, the person in the woods lifted

their arm as well. They waved back, then turned and walked away.

I see you, Dana thought. You want to hide, but I see you.

Dana put down her hand. She threw the flowers on top of the headstone to die. The workmen reached for their shovels.

Chapter Two

> Our town was founded on perfect land. Lake water sweet, grass lush, woods serene: an Eden for the new world. Some say it is surprising that the fertile forest on which the town was built was uninhabited. I prefer to accept the miraculous.
>
> *Lake in the Woods: A Complete History of an American Miracle*, Francis Fisher, 2015

Melville, the sheriff department's latest intern, was manning reception when Dana arrived to work.

'Officer Fisher, hi!' Mel said, shoving the copy of *Christian Youth* that he'd been reading under some paperwork. She watched the moment he remembered that this morning was the funeral play out across his face in real time. 'How are you?' he asked, voice soft and special.

'I'm fine, Mel.'

'Do you think you'll be up for Deputy Boldry's gig later?'

'Maybe,' Dana said, opening the door to the office.

'Something to look forward to,' he said, then louder, 'The sheriff wants to see you!'

The fire escape door was open but the ceiling fan, was the only movement inside the office; circulating the same air. Though smoking within the building had been illegal for six years, the smell of stale tobacco clung to the thin carpet. Admittedly, this could be because of her partner Stan, who spent most of their working hours out the back with a lit *Natural American Spirit*.

The door to the sheriff's office was open. Dana knocked, before ducking her head around the door.

'You wanted to see me, sheriff?'

Sheriff Wormwood looked up from his desk, mouth working over a piece of gum. 'Yep. Come in, close the door, take a seat.'

He tapped on his mini desk fan while she sat down.

'So? How was it?' he asked, looking up to regard her.

People sometimes described the sheriff as mild-mannered. It was true that he cultivated a constantly calm persona, but she could never bring herself to describe him as mild. To her, he was polite in a way that made it impossible to tell how to best please him. Still, she respected him. He was one of the few black people who lived in Lake in the Woods, maybe the only one who had ever served the town in any official capacity.

'The funeral, sheriff?'

'Yep.'

'It was fine,' she said. Thinking about it gave her a feeling of faint embarrassment. 'Really fine, actually.'

'Poor turn out?' he speculated.

'I guess,' Dana said. For Ariel's sake, she was reluctant to admit to the sheriff just how poor. The person in the woods came to mind. 'Some kept their distance.'

'Was the mayor there?'

Dana thought. The stranger had dark hair and looked around the right height. It could have been Michael. But she doubted it.

'Not sure. Don't think so. To tell the truth, I didn't see any family there.'

The sheriff nodded, as if he had expected as much. 'It's a shame,' he said.

The day they found her, he'd said the same thing to her down the phone. Damn shame.

He took his gum out, folding it up in a post-it note. The smell of spearmint lingered. 'Nice girl. Seemed too bright to go and do something stupid like that.'

'Well, you never can tell,' Dana said.

'That's true enough,' Sheriff Wormwood replied. His eyes bored into her, steady, sure. 'I realised that in all the commotion, I forgot to say, I'm sorry for your loss.'

Her gut response was to dispute the grief. Say that she hadn't really known Ariel, they'd been friends a long time ago, that Sera had been their only real connection. But Dana made it a habit not to argue with the sheriff. Not because she was afraid of him, but because he was usually right.

'Thank you,' she said, scratching the nape of neck. 'Officer Wu around?'

'He's at the school. He'll be back soon,' Sheriff Wormwood said. When Dana raised her eyebrows in question, he continued, 'Frank called this morning about some vandalism.'

The officers of the sheriff's department were frequently called to the high school to deal with everything from chaperoning prom to scrubbing graffiti off the bathroom walls. *Miss Blake is a whore* in the boys'. *Miss Blake is a dyke* in the girls'.

'Should I go out and give him a hand?' Dana itched, she had to do something.

The sheriff shook his head. 'It's nothing to worry about.'

He turned back to his papers: she was dismissed.

♦ ♦ ♦

'It was probably a ghost,' Stan said, when she finished describing the stranger.

'Spooky,' Dana said, after a beat.

She didn't know much about ghosts. Halloween was not celebrated in Lake in the Woods, the exceptions to the rule as sporadic as they were unsuccessful. Two years ago, a couple teenagers had put carved pumpkins out by their porches, inspired by some movie. The pumpkins had been found the next morning, butchered by unknown assailants.

'Not really,' Stan said, unperturbed by her scepticism. There wasn't much that rattled Officer Wu. 'Ghosts are just people, you know? It's nice that they get to visit. Sort out unfinished business, tie up some loose ends...'

'Very practical,' Dana agreed. She could never tell when he was being sarcastic.

'Yeah,' Stan continued, squinting behind his large glasses. 'I mean, sometimes it's less returning books to the library and more vengeance orientated, but depends on the ghost. I like to think that when my Nai Nai comes back for a visit, she just complains that I haven't got married yet.'

He was trying to make her laugh now, so she obliged. Rolling down the window, she kept one hand on the steering wheel, one eye on the cool, suburban streets. They were halfway between the church at the town's centre and the trees. Even with the windows down, the smell of hot leather was nauseating.

'I don't think it was your Grandma. Whoever it was looked pretty solid to me.'

There was a car blocking a drive-way. She wasn't in the mood to ignore it. They pulled over, and Dana took great pleasure in writing up a ticket.

Stan took a fresh pack of cigarettes out of his breast pocket, unzipping the plastic wrapper and flicking the bottom. He offered the lucky one to her, as always. She declined, as always.

'Who do you think it was?' he asked, cigarette balanced on his bottom lip. In the sunlight, the smoke was blue.

Dana thought. It hadn't been Michael in the trees: he did nothing quietly.

Since her husband passed, Mrs Enckles was only ever seen in church, and always with her son on her arm. She was too small, too fair.

If it was anyone in the family, Joe was the likely suspect. He still lived in the Enckles' white house, the house that was becoming emptier with every year that passed. Dana wasn't sure what he did for a living, but it seemed to involve money and power and business trips. Once, years ago, he'd seen her replacing Sera's missing persons poster at the Grocery Store, gave her a look of pity and said something like, Don't you think if she was still here, you'd have found her by now?

It was probably Joe.

When in doubt, it was the boyfriend. But far as Dana knew, Ariel had never had one, not even a high school sweetheart: more interested in church than boys. The Enckles were religious types.

It could have been a friend. People liked Ariel, she was the smiliest check-out girl at Green's Groceries. She asked every customer how they were and, what's more, it always sounded like she'd genuinely wanted to know.

Dana could have been Ariel's friend, if she'd wanted. Coulda, woulda, shoulda.

'What was up at the school this morning?' Dana asked, instead of I don't know.

Stan squinted behind his glasses. He tapped the ash out the window. 'Some kids just messed with Ariel's photo. The one in the foyer.'

Dana knew the one. Framed in gold, with a plaque that read 'Class Valedictorian, 2004', her smile bright, her hair shining. Not gold, not red, but strawberry blonde, a shade that blushed. No one else had hair like that.

'What did they do to it?'

He took a drag. He breathed out. 'Just some graffiti. I took care of it. Don't worry.'

Stan had called her the morning Ariel was found, right after Dana had got off the phone with the sheriff.

I was there when they took her out, he'd said, voice sleepless. I can tell you any details you need to know. If it'll help.

This time, Dana found that there was only one detail she needed to know.

'Were any of the other pictures vandalised?' she asked.

Stan shook his head. 'No. Just hers.'

In moments like this, Dana felt like Sera was sitting between them, still seventeen. She flexed her hand on the steering wheel, trying to shake off the memory's weight on the conversation like a dog trying to wring the river water from its coat, like throwing salt over her shoulder to banish the devil.

'That's good,' was all she said.

There was nothing that was worth saying. Mentioning Sera made people awkward. Dana tried not to bring her up. No need to dwell on it, make them both feel bad. But if she was being honest with herself, the list of other people who still felt sad about Sera Enckles was short. With Ariel gone, shorter. Any day now, she wouldn't be a tragedy anymore; she'd be a ghost story.

♦ ♦ ♦

Dana spent longer than usual in the shower, scrubbing work and sweat away, washing and conditioning her hair. Afterwards, she combed it, gently squeezing—not tugging—the moisture out of it, as a hairdresser had once advised her to. Her hairdryer was in the back of her wardrobe. Most days, she just used a towel. Denim *Levi* shirt with white popper buttons, frayed at the cuff, dark jeans, a two-dollar brown mascara. She'd bought it before going on a first date with a construction worker last year. There hadn't been a second date. Dana spat, turning on the tap to wash the mint foam and saliva down the sink. There was a slip of red in it where she'd worried her bottom lip.

It was then that she remembered Ariel was dead.

Mrs Trieger waved at her from her porch, reclining on her swing chair. Its palm tree pattern was almost obscenely corny.

'Off to meet a friend, dear?' she called. At her feet, Dusty the dog panted.

'Yeah,' Dana called, but she didn't slow her steps. She was never in the mood for a Bible passage, but she thought hearing one right now might tip her over the edge.

'Good for you,' Mrs Trieger said. She winked. Dana reeled. 'Make sure he treats you right.'

The church hall was busy, at least twenty people there, and only four of them in the band. Sloppy Sal was at the mic, doing a decent job of 'All Along the Watchtower'. Though the doors were open, it was as hot outside as it was in. Against the near-night blue, the fluorescence was obscene.

Over by the stage, Shelly Ackermann met Dana's eyes. She smiled.

Dana looked away. She wanted it to be quick enough that her rude fear would be excused as ignorance, but she knew it hadn't been quick enough.

Stan waved her over to where he was sitting with Mel and the other officers, Jacob and Coops.

'What took you so long?' Jacob asked. Not waiting for an answer, he got back to his story.

Stan handed her a room temperature beer from the BYOB stash under the plastic topped table, though he was drinking Coke himself, and gave her a nod. There was no room to talk, with Coops and Jacob already competing for airtime.

Jacob was kind of a dick, but Dana hated Coops. She hated the way he called Stan 'Officer Woohoo', hated that he didn't talk to her at all. She was pretty sure Stan felt the same way, but he was a more forgiving person than she was. He usually gave Coops a ride home when he was too drunk to drive.

Mel was nodding along, nothing to contribute, laughing at the right parts. Dana tried to follow his lead, tried not to regret being here at all.

Michael Enckles was across the room. His top button was undone. It was the weekend after all.

Above his loose tie, she could see his silver cross necklace. Ariel had worn one just the same. In her head, Dana rehearsed things she could say to Michael that could be construed as innocent and angry at once. I must have missed you at the service this morning.

Limp cheers announced the band taking to the stage. Len pushed up his glasses and grinned. He was the lead singer of Creedence Lakewater Revival. He'd began as a one-man act, The Lenny Rodgers Experience, but after his fiftieth birthday last year he'd decided to start taking music more seriously.

They stood up to crowd round the makeshift stage. Len opened with 'Fortunate Son'. Light beads of sweat stood out on his forehead, and his glasses had steamed up.

Across the room, Michael was tapping his toe. Beside him, Father Thomas was nodding along to the music. He had known Ariel too, hadn't he? She'd taught Sunday School. But here they all were.

Working at the label on her beer bottle with blunt fingers, Dana wondered how many songs she was obligated to stay for, how long it would take before David Ackermann would break out a bottle of the family moonshine, how long it would take for this feeling to pass. Earlier she'd been fine. But when she closed her eyes now, she saw a red water bath, tasted salt.

Dana opened another beer, she felt hot. It had been a long time since she'd been to a funeral. They hadn't had one for Sera, just a family day at court to declare her dead—in the legal sense. No longer missing. Dana had always hated that word, anyway. Keys went missing, a shoe or a piece of gum, but people weren't misplaced like household scissors. They always existed somewhere. Maybe lost, or stolen, or dead, but somewhere.

The final chorus of 'Have You Ever Seen The Rain' finished. Dana jolted herself into mute applause. She congratulated a beaming Len. Everyone agreed that it was Creedence Lakewater Revival's best gig yet, the sheriff would be sorry he'd missed it, beer caps hit the wooden floor. The Mayor came over to clap Len on the shoulder. Stan excused himself, heading out for a cigarette, too quick for Dana to offer to go with him.

'Sorry for your loss, mister mayor,' Mel said. In an instant, the laughter was cold.

Michael smiled. His eyes were bluer than Ariel's.

'Thank you,' he said. 'I know she would have wanted us to have a good time tonight.'

How convenient, Dana thought, for that to be what Ariel wanted.

Len's face was pickled with sympathy. 'At least she's with your father now. And your sister, Lord rest her soul.'

It was only after Len spoke that he seemed to realise his mistake. Michael's lips thinned. He smiled, clapped Len on the shoulder once, and moved on.

In the ladies room, Dana sipped moonshine from a red cup. It tasted of thin plastic.

Ariel had died the slow way. Committed. None of the euphoria of drowning, or impulsiveness of rope. When you're bleeding out, there's time to realise you've made a mistake, to press your hand on the wound and hold on to your life as it's pooling outside your body. Time to be saved. But Ariel hadn't turned back. She'd waited. Who was to say it wasn't what she'd wanted?

Sera would want you to move on. She couldn't count the number of times she'd heard that. The truth was, no one knew what Sera had wanted. Even Dana had always been guessing.

The open mic night was slowly dying, just a few stragglers holding out with the band. Father Thomas was becoming more insistent, hovering around the door. Anyone who wanted to stay out past eleven had to go to Nyx, or to the woods.

Father Thomas had been the preacher for three years, but he was still 'the new preacher'. Father Thomas had made some things, like a friendly beer and vacations, acceptable again, if not holy.

Some considered him soft touch, including Mrs Trieger, Dana's neighbour. If Michael had become preacher, as he should have been, he wouldn't allow this backsliding. Stan and Dana agreed that Michael didn't need to be the town's preacher to hold the position in all but name.

Dana wanted to say goodbye to Stan, but she couldn't see him. Coops might know if he'd already left.

Back to her, he was describing something vividly to a small audience, his beer splashing on to the pale floor as he moved his hands.

'They spray painted two crosses over her eyes and a noose...' he demonstrated, sticking out his tongue. 'And all this satanic shit.'

'Hanging,' Jacob sighed. 'What a way to go. Doesn't make a lick of sense if you ask me.'

'She didn't hang herself. She slit her wrists in a bathtub and bled to death. They didn't find her until morning,' Dana said. 'Tell Stan I said good night if you see him.'

♦ ♦ ♦

Dana wasn't ready to go home, to have to see her dad and discuss the tired facts of the day, so she drove around drunk but rolled the window down. She kept turning over her conversation with Sheriff Wormwood this morning in her mind, kneading it like bread. She'd said the wrong thing, she was sure. When someone sneezed, she knew to say bless you, or she knew to say you're welcome when she was thanked. I'm sorry for your loss seemed the kind of thing to have its own conventional response and what she'd said hadn't been it.

She drove out of town, to see if Gary wanted a ride home. By the time she reached Dale's Gas Station the place was shut, windows dark and quiet like candles on a cake that had just been blown out. Gary had probably gone home hours before, so she couldn't explain why the sight of the empty gas station disappointed her.

Michael had responded in the same way. *Thank you.* Even if he couldn't be trusted in any other regard, he could be trusted to be polite.

It had been ten years, and the feeling had not changed. Dana still pulled out her phone, then realised she had no one to call. Did it really get better, or were these just life's conditions?

The graveyard car park a little down the road was the easiest place to turn. If she kept going, she'd just get further and further from the town.

She checked herself in the rear-view mirror and stilled. The gates to the graveyard were open. Not just ajar—wide open, one of them sagging slightly to the side.

Dana turned off the engine. She reached for the glove compartment, putting her badge in her pocket. Her flashlight was there too, along with her gun. She took the flashlight in one hand and her keys in another, their jagged edges woven through her fist, just in case.

She ran the yellow light up and down the seam where the hinge was. It was not broken, but warped in some way. As if it had been bent. Had someone hit it with a car? Maybe they'd reversed too deep in the dark.

But why would they have left the gates open?

Her torch light bounced off headstones and trees. There was no one there. Probably some weirdo tourists had been snooping around earlier, had banged into the gate with their car on the way out. They were long gone.

Dana walked towards where she thought Ariel's grave should be. The closer she got, the more certain she became. It was the right grave, but there was something that looked wrong about it—what were the black masses lying on either side?

She walked a little faster, closer, until she could reach out and touch them. Her hand pressed on something wet, and spongy, and came back black. Dirt.

Dana looked at the grave itself, where she had seen them

lower in her coffin this morning. She put out her hand to touch the grave. She pulled it back, astonished, when it met nothing but air.

Empty. The grave was empty.

Her heart pounded. Dana patted down her pockets—call the sheriff, call Stan, Dad—and something appeared at the edge of the forest, about twenty feet away.

She scrambled backwards, reaching now for her non-existent gun. Whatever it was began to move closer, rapidly, running. Unsure how, Dana got to her feet, and began to run, zigzagging through headstones, making herself a harder target to hit. Someone was calling her name, but she would not turn around; her foot hit something soft and damp and she fell.

All of her hit the ground except for her other leg which dangled, impossibly, in empty air. Ariel's grave was not the only one empty.

Dana pulled her leg out of the grave as if it had been burned, getting to her feet and running. It hurt her foot to run and Dana prayed it wasn't broken, because the person chasing her was gaining, yelling for her to stop and she knew that voice.

Chapter Three

> I remember one occasion—it was winter and getting dark—returning home, I had cut across an unfamiliar field. Suddenly a nightmarish shape loomed up in front of me, barring my progress...The next morning I could not be sure whether I had encountered a ghost, an angel, a demon, or God.
>
> *A Dictionary of Angels (Including the Fallen Angels)*, Gustav Davidson

Into Google, Gary typed 'how to tell if someone is alive'. In the recommended searches, 'how to tell if someone is alive **or dead**' appeared. He pressed enter.

Reading through the step-by-step guide, Gary deduced that he could probably skip step one ('ask firmly if they are playing dead') and two ('gently prod the person to initiate a physical response'). However, he did decide that a few of the exercises might be helpful and went to acquire the necessary tools: a torch and a mirror.

Gary's bed was a relic from his childhood, now dwarfed

by his adult height. However, for the body perched on the edge of it, looking at the wall through partially decomposed eyes, the bed was just right. Its hands lay on its thighs, tips of the fingers curled inwards like paws.

Gary shone the torch into the body's eyeball. He noticed the light illuminated hints of the formerly blue iris, hidden under grey film. The pupils did not constrict. The body's left eyelid shuttered closed.

'Sorry, um, was that too bright?' he asked. 'Sorry. I just want to—is it okay if I...' he held his Dana's compact mirror up. The body's left eyelid sprung open once more. Go ahead.

He knelt in front of the bed and held the mirror under the body's nose. This position brought him almost face to face with it. It did not smell bad, or of anything, really, only the barest hint of salt. Gary knew by the quietness in the space between them that the mirror would be unclouded by condensation, but he checked anyway.

He went back to his computer.

Dead but conscious

Dead but walking

Finally, he typed

How to know if you are dreaming???

Gary turned around on his computer chair. It was not looking at him, but through him, black dirt trapped in the corner of its eyes and underneath its fingernails from where it had clawed its way out of the ground—

'Is this a dream?' Gary asked it.

It looked at him.

'Well, even if this is a dream, we might as well kill some time,' Gary said, narrating to a unresponsive audience. 'What do you think?'

The body made no reply. Gary took this as agreement. He made his way to the bathroom. Turning on the taps of the bathtub, he rooted about for the strawberry scented bubble bath he kept at the back of the drawer. It was his Secret Santa gift from someone at school and Gary was fairly sure that it had been intended as a gag, but he liked it all the same. Alternating between checking on the body in his room and agitating the bath water to make bubbles, he drew out the inevitable for as long as possible.

After shepherding the body into the bathroom Gary felt a little anxious. Maybe it didn't want a bath?

'Do you want to get in?' Gary asked.

It edged slightly closer to the bath tub, but made no move to undress.

After several minutes fumbling, Gary managed to find the zip of its dress and pushed the body's arms up so the garment could come off over its head. He turned to hang the dress up on the radiator, and when he faced the body again he found that it had kept its arms in the raised position. He pushed them back down by its sides.

The body was not wearing underwear, meaning the 'Y' stitched into the front of its torso was unobscured. Gary tried to ignore it as he helped it into the tub, step by step.

Finally, the body was reclining in the water, partially submerged in the pink bubbles. Its greenish pale arms rested on the side of the bath, the underside facing upwards to reveal wounds.

Gary dipped a cloth into the hot water and began to wash it. He started with its hands and feet, scrubbing until the beige cloth was brown.

He touched the wounds gingerly, watchful. On the right arm, the wounds were long and vicious, like an animal attack.

As he cleaned away the dirt on the left arm, he realised the wounds were much more careful. Thin lines, swooping curves, almost like words, as if the forearm was a page.

But the time Gary set the cloth aside they all shone white: unhealed and bloodless.

It gazed greyly forward as Gary massaged the olibanum scented shampoo through its hair. The scalp needed to be shampooed and rinsed with the shower head twice before its coppery hair colour was really visible.

Evidently the hot water had helped with the body's mobility. After slipping out for a minute to retrieve some old pyjamas, Gary came back into the bathroom to find the body standing in the centre of the room, dripping. What before was brown and grey was now luminously white and crimson.

He was a little irritated at the body's apparent inability to move—as well as its brazened nakedness—but, irritation would get him nowhere, so he began to pat it dry, averting his eyes when he reached its breasts and pelvis. Repeating his movements from earlier, Gary lifted the body's arms up and pulled the top down over the head. After anxiously considering how best to get the bottoms on, he led it back into the bedroom and pulled the trousers on with it sitting on the bed, again averting his eyes.

At last, the body sat there in the same position as before, hands again curled up on the thighs. Although the skin was soft and clean, it was unearthly in its whiteness and the body's eyes were still covered in grey film. Its hair was causing a damp spot to darken the shoulders of the pyjama top, so Gary sat behind it on the bed, delicately combing through the hair to form a lumpy plait.

Hearing his dad's car approaching, Gary left his bedroom, guiltily turning off the light and leaving the body once more alone in the dark.

Gary waited for his dad to finish grace. He'd told Gary and Dana his decision to convert over dinner a few years back. I won't make the choice to accept Jesus for either of you, he said, but I'd be lying if I said it wouldn't make me happy to see you at church.

Gary was thirteen at the time and hadn't given god much thought. He looked to Dana. She'd been crumbling a piece of bread between her fingertips.

They're never going to ask you to join the council, dad, she'd said. No matter what you do.

Where was Dana? Gary didn't know. Any jobs? Mr Dale said if he kept working hard, he could be assistant manager. What about real jobs? What about your future?

It didn't grate on Gary like it usually would have. As long as his Dad was talking to him about what a loser he was, he wasn't talking to him about the funeral, and Gary knew that if he started thinking about the funeral, he'd have to think about what was in his bedroom.

Once the plates, one scraped clean, one half eaten, were cleared away, Gary began to do the dishes, keeping his eyes on the stairs. It was Friday, so his dad turned on the television to watch *Escape From Bethlehem*. The crime show was set in a gated town in the U.S.A, in the forties before legislation made such religious communities illegal. Gary wasn't sure if his dad actually enjoyed watching it, or just enjoyed pointing out the historical inaccuracies.

This week's episode saw them once again joining *Escape from Bethlehem*'s hero, Jack, as he investigated yet another of the gatekeepers' villainous schemes.

'I think I've seen this one before,' Gary said after ten minutes.

'You can't have. It's brand new.'

His dad's favourite character was Jack, but Gary preferred Maria, a mysterious femme fatale, origins unknown. Dana never seemed to enjoy the show.

During an advert break, Gary excused himself to the bathroom and went into his room, half dreading, half hoping it would be empty. His laptop was open, the white glow of it bathing the room in half-light, illuminating the body where it lay on the bed. It wasn't breathing, but its left eyeball twitched under the lid. Like that, in the pyjamas, with its plait coming undone and one arm curled up around a pillow, the corpse looked almost like a girl.

But it wasn't. It was a thing.

Gary closed his laptop and put a blanket over it, shutting the door quietly behind him. The web browser shut down, erasing its last open page:

iut his hekk? Is yjis hell?

Showing results for out this hell? Is *this* hell?

Chapter Four

> [2] the Lord will come ▓▓▓ like a thief in the night.[3] While people are saying that everything is peaceful and safe. Then suddenly they will be destroyed ▓▓▓ they will not escape.
>
> *Thessalonians 5:2-3*

It was strange to be in the sheriff's office without Sheriff Wormwood. Even stranger to be in there alone, now that Deputy Boldry had left the room. Dana wrapped her hands tightly around the cup of coffee he had made her. It was hot and weak, the sugar in the bottom heavy and unstirred.

Regret. Should've taken the shock blanket when the sheriff had offered it to her. She'd turned it down out of principle, as she was not in shock, either emotional or physical. She just couldn't stop shaking. Shivering, not shaking. It was before sunrise. She was cold.

Deputy Boldry came back into the room with the station's only recording device, smiling at her wetly, his eyes magnified behind his glasses.

'Usually, we'd do this in one of the rooms, but it's warmer in here. A bit, anyway. We can move if you want...'

Dana nodded, not listening, wiping her hair away from her forehead. There was a small, swollen graze on her temple. It wasn't bleeding, but she couldn't stop touching it.

'Let's just do it.'

Stan and his dad arrived half-way through her statement. Len paused the recorder. Dr Wu was broad, with a salt and pepper moustache and closely cropped hair. Dr Wu explained, as he shone a small light in Dana's eyes, that he used to be a radiographer before he got qualified and was offered a job in Lake in the Woods in the seventies, and could she look up for him, atta girl.

'No concussion,' Dr Wu said. 'Does your head hurt?'

'No, it doesn't. My ankle does, though.'

'Well, that's an easier fix than a head injury, so count your stars. What did you cut it on, anyway?'

'I, uh,' Dana swallowed. 'I don't remember.'

Gingerly, Dana eased her right foot from her boot and stripped off her damp and clammy sock. The outside of her ankle was swollen, the skin a faint green yellow. Deputy Boldry hissed in sympathy. Dr Wu's fingers were thick, but he touched her delicately.

'Does that hurt?'

He moved her ankle slightly. she felt as though she would pass out.

'No, not really,' Dana said.

'Got you,' Dr Wu said, winking. 'You'll live. Nothing a Tylenol, a whiskey and a good night's sleep can't fix.'

'That sounds like a good idea, dad,' Stan said. 'How about I drive you home? This isn't anything that can't wait, right, deputy?'

Boldry looked embarrassed. Before he could open his mouth to stammer his way through telling Stan that, in fact, this wasn't something that could wait, Dana said, 'it's okay. I just want to get it over with.'

Dr Wu bandaged her ankle and gave her a painkiller, telling her to call him if she needed anything. Stan waited outside while Dana finished telling the deputy about finding empty graves, how she'd panicked, tripped, fallen.

She hadn't seen anything. Yes, she was sure.

It was easy to lie, when you had to. The truth was, Dana had seen someone. When she shut her eyes, she could still hear their voice, calling her. But it couldn't be. Dr Wu had missed something; she must have hit her head. It was impossible.

Once the deputy had finished taking her statement, he suggested that she go home and rest. Dana didn't want to rest. She doubted she'd be able to. Everyone else was at the graveyard—that's where she should be.

Stan and Deputy Boldry shared a glance.

'I'll drive us,' Stan said. 'Do you want to wash up first?'

Looking in the bathroom mirror, Dana was surprised at how normal she looked. Her hair was a mess, and there was a smear of dirt across her forehead, but otherwise she looked the same as she always did, if whiter than usual. She reached up to wipe the mud away, and it was only then she realised how dirty her hands were. Looking down, she saw that her jeans, too, were splattered with soil.

♦ ♦ ♦

The uniform Dana borrowed from the department was too big for her, but she was far from being the only one who looked a little worse for wear in the morning half-light of the crime scene. Mel, in his desperate rush to be helpful, had not changed out of his pyjamas. Even the sheriff, his uniform pressed, had a slight five o'clock shadow.

Yellow tape hung, half-hearted, around each of the opened graves, like banners at the birthday party of a child who knew the other kids wouldn't show up. Jacob was pointing a camera at one of the open graves—Dana was sure it was the one she had almost fallen into. The camera still had the lens cap on. The forensics specialists were not there yet. The nearest lab was a four-hour drive.

The sheriff was standing a little away from Mel, with Mayor Michael and a paunchy man Dana recognised as chief of the town's volunteer fire department. The three of them looked almost casual, like dads standing around at a BBQ. Maybe that was because of the unfashionable blue jeans Michael wore. Dana had not seen him in jeans since they were teenagers.

Three search parties were formed: Boldry and Michael,

Coops and Jacob, Stan and the chief. Dana would stay with the sheriff and Mel.

The sheriff asked Dana to tell him what she had seen and where. An hour passed. Mel handed the phone to the sheriff once or twice. He had been put in charge of informing the families of all the deceased that their remains had vanished. The search parties returned. Mel handed out coffee in Styrofoam cups. The chief and the sheriff were about five minutes into a debate over how many torches the search party would need when forensics arrived. The search parties would take a break.

None of the forensics guys wore hazmats. Dana told them what she had seen and where she had seen it, and then again. She sat on a headstone, one that still had a person underneath it.

Civilians began to arrive soon after, congregating in the parking lot. First, just a handful. Then more.

'What are they doing here?' the man asked, pressing Dana's fingertips into ink, so firmly they blanched.

'That's Martha Dorhamer, I think,' Mel said, following his gaze. 'Anthony Dorhamer's widow. She was pretty upset when the sheriff spoke to her this morning. Oh—and there's his sister...'

'You already called the families?' he asked.

Mel nodded dumbly. The man raised his eyebrows but said nothing.

After an hour or two, forensics were finished. As they jostled their way through the people in the parking lot, Dana realised she hadn't called her dad, to explain why she hadn't been home. Her phone was where she'd left it; stuffed in Brussels' glove compartment, parked behind the department. She looked out at the faces. Hilary from *The Declaration* was there. If her dad hadn't heard already, he would know soon: Ariel Enckles' body was missing, along with four others.

♦ ♦ ♦

Until the people from the forensics lab found something more, there was nothing to do but clean up, and start searching.

'You want us to fill in the holes, boss?' Coops asked. 'I can ask my brother for shovels.'

The sheriff looked at him. 'Officer, I'm hoping we'll be able to put the bodies back in before we fill them again.'

Mel began to hand out the tents which he had been sent to the department to get: long wooden poles and white tarpaulin. Dana recognised them from last year's Community Cook Out.

In pairs, they were each assigned a grave to erect the tent around. Coops and Graham took Ariel's. There were odd numbers of officers, and Stan was on guard duty by the entrance, so Dana began to put up her tent, alone. She didn't look at the headstone. She didn't want to know their names, to work out how she knew them.

The coffin was still there. It had sustained minimal damage, the lid cracked in half where it had been prised open. It was only half-uncovered. They would have had to pull the body through the top of the coffin and drag it through the tunnel they'd made in the earth.

Ariel's coffin was worse. Broken and splintered, edges of it still hanging in shards. The cuts to the wood were not clean. Rather than an axe, brute force and a blunt object had been used. Forensics would know.

Her ankle throbbed and her head pounded, the morning sun beating down on their backs, but none of them dared stop. Besides, the soft, springy earth was calming, like shut eyes before sleep. Dana felt tempted to drop the pole she held, crawl into her half-filled grave and pull a blanket of the cool earth over her.

'Dana?'

Dana looked up—Mel was hovering, a phone pressed to his ear. It was clear he had said her name more than once. She grunted.

'The sheriff needs you back at the office,' Mel said. There were dark circles under his eyes, and Dana felt a rush of guilt. He was barely older than Gary.

'I don't have my car,' she said.

Mel nodded, repeating what she had said to whoever was on the phone.

'I'll drive you,' he told her, after he had hung up. 'My car is here.'

His car was in the parking lot. They'd have to walk through the crowd. Because it was a crowd now. One middle aged woman, crying and loud, was holding centre stage.

'I want to talk to the sheriff!' she said to Stan, face pulsing white, then red. 'Where has he gone? What's going on?'

Her voice became sharper with every question she asked,

an arrow hitting the spot behind Dana's eyes.

Stan was calm. 'Ma'am, I know you're upset, but the sheriff is doing everything—'

'What the heck do you know?' Her words rang out as sharp as a slap. 'Where's my son? What have they done with him?'

The crowd around her parted. Michael was there, suddenly at the woman's side. She turned to him. Her face, dark with fury, crumpled when she saw his. She became small.

'My boy,' she said. 'My beautiful boy.'

Michael embraced her. Stan stood by the gate, his face carefully blank as Michael held the woman, and repeated everything he had just said.

♦ ♦ ♦

'Do not be afraid'. That's what the note said, on a slip of paper he found underneath the door of the custodian's closet.

It could be for Frank. It could be from Frank, though that would be curveball. But something told Jerome that it was for him. He put it in the breast pocket of his boiler suit and pulled out the waxer.

It was probably from one of the senior girls who crushed on him; the ones who thought he was a Satanist, therefore forbidden, therefore attractive. Jerome didn't find it flattering. Being one of the only guys at school who wasn't old enough to be their dad or young enough to be their brother was enough for these good girls. Everybody in Lake in the Woods was Christian when the lights were on, church on Sunday and Jesus Saves.

But the ones who liked him tended to be the ones who were like his foster mom, the ones who genuinely saw it as their sacred duty to cure his sickness and save him from Hell.

Because I love you, she liked to say. I only say it because I love you.

Jerome wasn't convinced that was what love was meant to be like. Love was that time they'd broken into the locked-up pool and gone night swimming naked. With the lights off, the only thing that kept them from drifting into the dark water was their warm skin beside each other. That was love.

After the school was closed, he waited at the bottom of their tree. It was cute that they had a tree, even if the tree itself was kind of disgusting: a bulbous growth sprouted off all sides of it like a cancer. Frankly, it smelled. He sat on the forest floor, back against the trunk, legs folded into his chest. His denim jacket didn't do much to keep out the cold, so he was wearing his boiler suit over his T-shirt and sweatpants.

Jerome blew into his cupped hands, chapped from winter and bleach. He unfolded the note.

'Do not be afraid'.

Put it in his pocket. He ran his hands through his hair, pawing at it until it was greasy. He waited.

At midnight he scratched a line into the bark and left.

Nights like this, Jerome tried not to be mad. Family shit happened, he got it.

Nights like this, Jerome wanted to obliterate himself. He wished he could let this go, get it through his thick skull that whatever was between them wasn't forever, that he should get over it before he was left behind. Sometimes, he thought if he could find that broken bit inside, wrap his fingers around it and pull, all this shit would come rushing out and he'd be himself, the person he was meant to be, healed. But he could never settle on where the crucial damage lay. Inside, he was a dilapidated house. Each time he worked out where the damp was, his foot sank into another broken floorboard.

As he lay down and drew up his knees to his chest to sleep, he thought of the note again. Do not be afraid.

Nice, but kind of intense. Christians were like that, even the ones who wanted to be your friend—especially the ones who wanted to be your friend.

♦ ♦ ♦

Someone was calling her.

'Um, Dana?' they said. 'Dana. Dana.'

'Mmm?' she asked. Her eyes were shut. She didn't want to open them. She was very comfortable.

'Dana, sorry, but the sheriff needs to see you...'

Someone was touching her.

Dana opened her eyes and sat up, body caught by the seatbelt.

She was in a Chevy Pickup, a little newer than Brussels, though not as well maintained: the floor was littered with twigs and crumpled fast food containers.

Mel's car. The person who had touched her on the shoulder was Mel. He had stopped immediately, but his guilty hand was still in the air. They were parked behind the department, where Stan went to smoke.

'How long was I asleep for?' she asked. Her neck felt stiff. The sun was lower in the sky.

'An hour or so. Maybe a little more. Sorry. You looked like you needed it.' He scratched the back of his neck. He was red. 'Sorry.'

The sheriff was in his office, speaking to Deputy Boldry and with the door ajar. Dana knocked on it and entered. The two of them turned to look at her, falling sharply silent. Deputy Boldry excused himself, shutting the door behind him. The sheriff sat down, gesturing to the chair in front of his desk.

'Was there a problem with my statement, sir? Did the forensics guy have more questions?'

'No, Dana, it's not about that,' he said. Despite the day they'd had, he looked energised. 'Look, there's no easy way to say this, so I'm just going to come out with it.' His eyes met hers. 'It's Sera Enckles. We found her. I know she was a close friend of yours.'

'Oh.' Dana blinked.

It must have been one of the search parties. In her mind she saw Coops coming across Sera's body, uncovered by a landslide. Look what I found, he'd say, excited. What a catch.

She had to say something. 'Where did you find her?'

The sheriff's was watching her.

'She found us, actually. Turned up here earlier today.'

'Turned up? Did someone just—just leave it here, or—' the image of someone leaving her on their doorstep, like a present from a house cat, made her feel sick.

'Dana, I'm sorry, I've not made myself clear. Sera has turned up alive.'

Dana stared. 'What?'

The sheriff didn't quite smile, but there was an almost feverish glint in his usually steady eyes. 'Sera Enckles is alive. She's here, in the building, and she wants to speak to you.'

Chapter Five

> 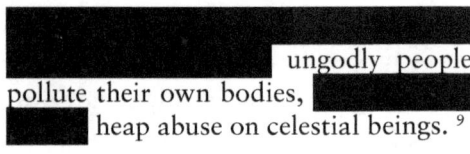 ungodly people pollute their own bodies, heap abuse on celestial beings. [9]
>
> *Jude 9*

It was the whiteness she saw first, visible between the gaps of the trees like the shock of exposed bone. Dana walked out of the woods towards the driveway, tall grass swimming around her bare legs, and marvelled. Even in the sun it was crisp, as if the paint on it was fresh, though Dana knew the Enckles' house was old as the town or older. It wasn't the mansion the kids at school made it out to be, but it was still the biggest house she had ever seen; perched on the edge of the lake, like a boat about to set sail.

With each step towards the porch, towards the front door, the sound of woodsmoke laughter on the wind got louder. Everyone was here already—she was late. It was her own fault. He'd offered to pick her up, but she'd insisted on walking.

Her knock on the front door came out like a question: *am I doing this right?*

'Come in!' a voice called from inside.

The hallway smelt clean. Not clean like fresh air, but clean like laundry detergent. The walls were white, the floor a dark wood that Dana couldn't disguise her steps on, each one sharp and present. Her plastic bag crinkled in her hand. Her dad had told her it was polite to bring something and given her a bag of off-brand *Cheetos*.

'Be with you in a sec,' Michael called. The high ceiling lent his voice a melody. The words bounced down the steps of the staircase to land at her feet, *be with you.*

The door was open, so Dana looked into the living room. Music played from a small stereo on the couch, but there was no one there. In family photographs, they all wore matching sweaters. A small table sat to one side, on it was a green telephone, the old-fashioned kind you wound with your finger. There was a piano, lid closed and hushed. Everything was beautiful.

Above it was a mirror. Dana tugged at her new skirt: denim, short, rhinestones flashing in the light. It was the kind of thing a girl with a boyfriend would wear.

♦ ♦ ♦

School was over for summer. For Michael, school was over forever. The majority of that year's graduating class lounged around on the brown sand lakeshore. Besides an inflatable ball that being tossed around, the 'beach theme' was present only in plastic leis and dry bikini tops a few of the more daring girls wore over their skirts and shorts, and the hum in the air.

The back of the house was perched on a sequestered inlet of the lake, the tall green trees at its edge making it feel private, like a pool. The shore led to a small jetty, the two rowboats tied on still.

Ed Spinner, captain of the football team, had magnanimously presented a thirty-six pack of beer for everyone to share, and it sat untouched in the middle of the circle like an object of worship. Dana spent most weekends communing with the television, and she didn't know how to enter the conversation. So, she pulled out a bottle to give her something to do with her hands. Prising off the cap with her house keys, she took a lukewarm gulp. It was flat and savoury, coating her tongue like plaque. She tried to hide her disgust.

Across the circle, Michael was busy hosting, cup of soda in his hand. He wore shorts and t-shirt, barefoot. Dana had never seen his feet before. One of the girls had offered him a red and white lei, the string of synthetic flowers dangling from the tip of her finger. He ducked his head to accept, grinning, and then he looked over at Dana. She looked away, but not before she caught a flash of his blue eyes, saw him take in the beer in her hand. Michael had promised her dad that this evening would be *good, clean fun.*

Michael left them and came towards her. Sitting beside her on the deck chair, he took the lei off and put it over her head.

Dana was pretty sure Michael wasn't her boyfriend, but they'd held hands in front of his friends twice now. Two weeks ago, they'd made out in her kitchen, Gary in the next room eating pizza. It had just happened once, so she didn't know if that meant it would happen again, if she should expect anything, but she knew enough to not ask, to be cool.

'Don't your parents mind you having this party?' Dana asked, taking a sip of her beer and pretending to like it.

'They're out of town seeing my Aunt Hanna. What they don't know won't hurt them.' Michael grinned. 'Or me. I hope.'

'They left you and your sisters on your own?'

'Well, almost,' he said, 'My cousin is here to watch us.'

He pointed. A girl in a yellow bikini was on the jetty with a dark-haired boy.

'She's very…' Dana thought for a moment. 'Blonde.'

Michael looked where Dana was staring and laughed.

'Oh, no,' he said. 'That's Shelly Ackerman, his girlfriend. She played Mary three years running, remember? Some people get a job after High School, some people go blonde. Joe is my cousin.'

'Oh,' Dana said. From the shore, Ed Spinner threw the beach ball at Shelly. It bounced off her chest and Joe laughed. He laughed with his head thrown back, like Michael did.

Dana had heard of Joe. Heard that one of his eyes was green, the other brown; that he was born out of wedlock, but his Uncle Joshua had taken him in; that he was mixed-race, though it was considered impolite to directly reference this.

Girls liked him almost as much as Michael, some more

because he was *different*. They didn't stand a chance though, because he was Shelly Ackermann's now and that probably meant forever.

Michael was distracted. Shelly and Joe, hand in hand, ran to the edge of the jetty, cannonballing into the water.

Dana watched as the bubbles on the surface died away, counting. It took under a minute to drown.

Shelly breached the surface of the water, her hair plastered over her eyes, Joe beside her, a grin on his face and a twig in his hair.

Michael saw her staring. 'Do you want to go in?'

'No,' she said, too fast.

He raised his eyebrows. 'Wouldn't have taken you for the superstitious type.'

'I'm not superstitious,' she said. 'I'm not a strong swimmer.'

Michael drained his cup. He took her hand and pulled her to her feet.

'Come on,' he said. She was reluctant, but he smiled at her. 'I know where the shallows are.'

♦ ♦ ♦

She hadn't brought a swimsuit; she didn't own a swimsuit.

'You can borrow one of Sera's,' Michael said, leading her upstairs. 'She's about your size.'

It was quiet on the upstairs landing. The party felt very far away.

'That's her room,' he said, opening the door. 'You can change in there. I think she keeps them in the top drawer.'

She paused, remembering that moment when he leaned over and kissed her by the fridge, smelling of boy, of fresh sweat and clean-cut grass. What would happen if she asked him to come in with her now? Inside her, was something thrummed like a shook-up can of soda: she wouldn't be able to tell if it was excitement or fear until she opened it.

Michael leaned against the wall of the hallway, arms folded. 'I'll wait here.'

Immediately, Dana felt relieved.

'I'll just be a sec,' she said. She closed the door behind her.

Standing in front of the full-length mirror, Dana examined herself in the businesslike black one-piece she'd picked from the drawer. She turned to the side. Stripes of light dappled over her thighs, her chest, her stomach. Black was slimming, black was cool. Shelly's yellow bikini popped into her head. Maybe black was just dull.

In a locked cubicle in the girl's bathroom, she'd overheard senior girls, Shelly among them, saying that Michael had taken a vow of celibacy until marriage, that he'd only ever kissed his ex-girlfriends, and even then with no tongue.

'What a waste, right?' one of them had said.

'You are so *bad*,' her friend had hissed, giggling.

He was waiting for her outside. She sat on the bed, strict navy sheets crumpling. The room was so neat. Rather than the cheap perfume and CDs Dana hoarded, the desk housed stacked schoolbooks and sharpened pencils. Above was a calendar with no pictures. On each day that had passed was a tick: a task completed.

On the bedside table were more books. She ran her finger over their cracked spines. How many Bibles could one person possibly need?

The floorboard outside the bedroom creaked. Dana wasn't ready to go back yet.

She pulled out one of the Bibles, flipping it open on a whim.

There were two strange things about this Bible. The first was that it wasn't written in English, or even with letters that Dana recognised. Russian, maybe?

The second was that even if she'd shared this language with Sera Enckles, most of the verses had been scored through with thick, black lines, the butchery sparing only the occasional white-rimmed word.

♦ ♦ ♦

None of Michael's friends would go in with them. Tourists swam, and some townsfolk would fish, but the people of Lake in the Woods would rarely go into the water. It wasn't just a superstition, her dad had told her more than once. The lake was miles deep. Dana must promise him she'd never, ever go in.

She tucked her folded clothes underneath a tree, it's roots half in earth and half in sand. The shouts of the others were becoming louder: someone had pulled out an acoustic guitar, and she could hear singing.

'Come on, Dana,' Michael called. He was already standing ankle deep.

He walked backwards, until he was submerged to the knee. In the sunlight, the water was transparent, and she could still see his legs underneath the surface.

'If you're scared,' he said, holding up a small bottle, full of faintly green liquid, 'I have some liquid courage.'

She stepped out from underneath the tree. The sun warmed her skin. She pointed her foot, and let her toe touch the lip of the water. *I'm not scared*, she wanted to say. *I'm not scared, I'm not scared.*

'I'm not a great swimmer.'

'It's okay. I'll look after you,' He held out his hand and, not taking his eyes off her, he moved further into the water. 'Come on.'

Before Dana had decided what to do, she'd stepped in. The sun had warmed the top of her foot, and the sudden coldness of the water was such a shock that she almost pulled it out again. Gritting her teeth, she walked, the bed of the lake strange, sharp sand mixed with soft mud. It became slicker further out, the mud nosing its way between her toes, changing from cold to cool to soothing.

'It's nice, isn't it?' he said, when they were both submerged to the waist.

Away from the trees and the green light beneath them, it was bright. Michael was glowing beneath it, warm and right there. Their legs touched underneath. The water moved a little around them, reflecting the sky and the trees in flashes.

Tiny insects caught the light in their wings as they buzzed over the surface. The water looked like Michael's eyes, sparkling and so blue. Dana flushed with embarrassment, as if she said the thought aloud.

Michael took a sip and offered her the bottle. 'What do you think?'

'It's beautiful,' she said. She meant it. Taking a swig, she struggled not to cough.

'That's good shit,' she said, handing the bottle back.

Laughing, he took her hand and held it underwater. The water lapped against her upper arm, the plastic flowers he'd given her floating on the surface.

'Do you guys swim in the lake a lot?'

'All the time. Since we were little.'

Dana was surprised. She'd heard the stories.

'Have you ever,' she stumbled over her words, her tongue numb, 'I don't know, seen anything?'

Michael nodded seriously.

'I've seen some pretty strange stuff. Like just earlier...' he stopped to look at her. 'I didn't want to say anything. But I saw something. It was black, shapeless,' he pinged her swimsuit strap. 'Oh my goodness, Dana! It's got you right now! It's swallowing you whole!'

Laughing, she shoved him. His eyes widened as he lost his balance, and grabbed her arms, the bed of the lake slipped under her feet, the two of them plunged under the surface.

Dana kicked her legs out, feet straining for the ground, but they just met water and more water. She opened her eyes and all she could see was greenish brown, with no up or down, and yet she was falling, and Michael was nowhere. Her heart pounded but she felt frozen. One thought asserted itself: I am going to drown.

Hands wrapped around her shoulders and pulled her backwards, and her eyes were dazzled by the day. Michael's arms were wrapped around her torso, holding her securely. Underneath her, his strong legs were kicking, keeping them afloat. Breathing heavily, Dana's head flopped back, cradled in the crook of his shoulder. Her heart was still pounding, and her head was spinning, but a euphoric calm bubbled up inside her—all she could do was laugh.

Michael brushed her hair away from her face, one arm wrapped around her waist.

'Told you I'd look after you,' he said, voice close to her ear. Dana shivered. She was ticklish there. Michael kept them afloat, the only thing tethering her in the endless water.

The inflatable beach ball hit the water in front of them with a smack.

'Mike, you playing or what?' Joe called.

♦ ♦ ♦

Joe's rules for his made-up game seemed to dictate that missing the ball meant taking a sip, getting hit with the ball meant taking a sip, hitting someone else meant taking three. The rules had dissolved in Dana's memory, so she just drank when Michael told her to until the bottle sunk to the bottom of the lake, empty. Beer brave kids from school had splashed out to join them after a while, and Dana felt a little dizzy and pleasurably silly. The sun was just beginning to set.

Michael wrapped a towel around her as they sat by the fire, and Joe passed her a piece of barbecued chicken. The tip of her nose was squashed against the warm meat as she took a bite.

The sky was turning purple, and someone put on music, passing a wine bottle back and forth on their way to the bathroom. Shelly was confident, as if she knew her way around.

'I'm leaving town,' Shelly told her, lips loud, but eyes whispering, *it's a secret*, wet bikini bottom pooled round her feet as she peed. 'I'm going to Los Angeles, to make it in the movies.'

Dana laughed, rubbery and unstoppable. Dana danced with Shelly, until she disappeared into the trees, still wearing her yellow bikini, hand in hand with Ed Spinner.

Michael took her hands to dance with her. It was dark now, and the bonfire was the only thing keeping them warm. On his bare, tan back, she could see a birthmark, like a thumbprint. She wanted to press it.

'Where are you taking me?' she asked him, laughing.

Michael's grip on her hand was firm as he pulled her through the trees, keeping her steady as the forest floor shifted underneath her. Laughter echoed through the trees, bouncing off the bark; it was a moment before Dana realised it was her who was laughing. Michael looked back at her, his eyes lost in the dark. 'Shh,' he told her, pressing a finger to his lips.

The lake water was black. 'Lie on your back,' he told her, as they sat on the bank. 'Close your eyes,' he said. Dana shut her eyes. The stars were still dancing behind them, but they were upside down, and she was looking at them from under the water, she reached out for Michael, but this time he wasn't there, her hands met air, she couldn't breathe.

Chapter Six

> Angels, like human beings, were created with free will, but that they surrendered their free will the—moment they were formed. At that moment, we are told, they were given (and had to make) the choice between turning toward or away from God, and that it was an irrevocable choice.
>
> *A Dictionary of Angels (Including the Fallen Angels),* Gustav Davidson

Dana closed the door behind her.

Sera looked up. Her eyes widened. Dana was relieved. She hadn't realised it until that moment, but she had been afraid that Sera would not recognise her, or that she wouldn't know Sera.

She knew her.

Sera was sitting in an armchair. This was the room they used to interview victims, or the recently bereaved, and the slanted back of the chair encouraged people to sit back and relax. Sera was perched on the end, her long legs bent because her feet were tucked under the chair, and arms holding her elbows.

She was staring at her, but hadn't moved. Neither had Dana.

Dana needed to say something. She was being weird. She was being rude. She licked her lips; her mouth felt dry.

'Hello,' she said.

'Hello,' Sera said. Her voice was low, and quiet, and slightly rough, and Dana felt as though she might vomit or cry or both, because she knew that voice.

Dana covered her face with her hands.

Sera was in front of her all at once. 'Are you feeling alright? Maybe you should sit.'

Fingertips touched Dana's upper arm. She put down her hands and looked at Sera, who was peering into her face, concerned.

'I'm sorry,' Dana said. 'I'm being so dumb—'

She broke off as Sera reached for her, and Dana reached back. Sera held her, Dana's forehead fitting into the crook between her shoulder and neck. Under Dana's arms she could feel Sera's thick, dark hair, all the way down to her waist, and smell it, too, heady under the sharp sting of sweat that could have belonged to either of them. She could feel Sera's warmth leaking through the clothing that separated them both, and the pump of her heart which meant *alive, alive, alive* and the breath tickling Dana's ear which told her *here, here, here.*

Dana breathed out slowly, deflating, loosening her hold around Sera so she could look at her. Sera let go, but didn't move from where she stood. She was staring at Dana, calculating her, unembarrassed. Sera had never been too shy to stare. Dana remembered then the ill-fitting uniform that she was wearing, and wiped her eyes.

'Sorry about that,' Dana said. She tugged on the hem of her shirt, straightening it. 'It's been a long day.'

Sera smiled, as if something was funny.

'What?' Dana demanded.

'Nothing,' Sera said, still smiling. 'I missed you.'

Dana didn't know how to reply. There were no words that seemed to fit.

'Let's sit,' she said.

Sera sat back down in the armchair and Dana sat in the one opposite her. Sera still sat on the edge of the chair. She was dressed differently than Dana had remembered her— well, differently than she'd expected.

Jake Blake, a retired handyman with a cabin near the Enckles' property, had been the last person to see Sera alive. He had reported that she was wearing a mid-length green skirt, cream cardigan and brown shoes.

'What about her cross necklace? It was silver. Was she wearing that?' Dana had asked him.

'Necklace?' Jake had said. 'How the hell should I know if she was wearing a necklace? Who did you say you were again, kid?'

The jeans Sera wore might once have been black, but were now charcoal at a stretch. Her black polo shirt had lime green buttons, and a logo on the right breast for a bowling alley Dana had never heard of. She wore black boots with double knotted laces. Beside her chair was a backpack with a corduroy jacket neatly folded on top of it. Around one of Sera's wrists was a black elastic band. She wore no other jewellery.

'I never knew you wanted to be a cop,' Sera said.

'Oh,' Dana said. 'Yeah. It just kind of happened, I guess. Four years ago.'

'What did you do before?'

Looked for you, Dana thought. 'Odd jobs, you know. Worked at the cinema, car wash. Nothing exciting.'

'You didn't go to college?' Sera's eyes were as dark as she'd remembered; so black that the distinction between the iris and the pupil was impossible to determine. There were no shadows underneath them like Dana saw under her own green eyes in the mirror, only gentle, thin lines where Sera's infrequent smile caused a crease. The rest of her skin was deeply tanned, almost glowing, as if the sun she'd been in clung to her. If Dana hadn't known that she'd turned twenty-seven that month, she might have thought that Sera was still seventeen.

'No,' Dana said, realising that Sera was waiting for her to answer. 'No, I didn't go to college after all.'

Sera tilted her head, her expression shifting slightly in confusion—or disappointment?

'What about you?' Dana wished she could snatch back her words out of the air, and exchange them for new ones which didn't make her sound like an insensitive asshole. 'I mean—sorry, that's a dumb question, obviously you didn't go to college. Sorry. You probably don't want to even talk about what happened, yet. We can talk about it whenever you're ready. I mean, the sheriff wants me to take your statement, but that can wait until whenever you're ready to talk about it.'

Dana didn't want to rush her; she was probably still processing what she had been through. She would need to give her time.

Sera wasn't looking at Dana anymore, casting her eyes over the room.

'What is that?' Sera asked, her eyes caught on something.

Dana turned to look at whatever had drawn her attention. In a high corner of the room, a small red light blinked.

'Oh,' Dana said. 'It's just a camera.'

'Does that mean that it's recording?' she asked.

'Yeah, but it's just procedure.'

Sera was quiet, and Dana wanted to ask her what she was thinking. Her fingertips hovered over her mouth. Something was scrawled on the back of her hand in thin, grey ink, for a moment reminding Dana of—

'Sera,' Dana leaned forward. 'I don't really know how to say this, but there is something you should know...'

'It's okay,' Sera said. 'I know that Ariel's dead.'

Sera's tone, cool and calm as a weather report, surprised Dana out of her politeness. 'How?'

'I saw it in a paper,' Sera replied.

Oh,' Dana said. Dana looked at Sera, at her brown skin, and white teeth, and shining, clean hair. Sera leaned forward in her chair.

'I actually wanted to ask you a couple of questions. The article didn't go into a lot of detail—'

'Which paper?'

As Sera looked at her, Dana was reminded of when they'd first met. Back then, Dana would look at Sera and struggle to translate her expressions and words into meaning, always falling short of knowing what was on her mind. That had changed, eventually.

'I can't remember which one,' Sera said. 'I was distracted.'

The soles of the black boots she wore were lined with dried mud.

'You were in the graveyard,' Dana said.

She'd thought it wasn't possible, that she'd imagined hearing Sera's voice, that she'd hit her head. Sera's gaze was heavy. The red light of the camera felt like an oppressive weight.

'At Ariel's funeral,' Dana continued. 'You waved at me.'

'Yes.' Her black eyes tracked Dana's facial movements intently, though the rest of her face was still. 'I was at the funeral. I wanted to say goodbye.'

People locked in basements don't catch tans. They don't read the paper; they certainly don't read *The Declaration*, the only publication that had carried the story of Ariel's death. Dana felt as though she were teetering on the threshold of revelation, and she wondered if she'd rather just close her eyes and stay living in this world, but it was too late.

'Sera,' Dana asked. 'Why did you run away?'

Sera didn't reply right away. 'I can't tell you that,' she said.

Her ankle throbbed, and she felt sick. The painkillers Dr Wu had given her had made her sick. Dana looked down at the green carpeted floor, because that was meant to help with nausea.

'You let me think that you were dead, and you won't tell me why?'

There was silence. Dana wondered if Sera was going to answer her at all.

'I'm sorry,' she said. 'I'm sorry, Dana.'

She looked up. Her head swam. Sera was looking at her, but Dana suddenly found she couldn't look back.

Sera ploughed mercilessly into the silence. 'I need you to tell me about Ariel, about what happened to her.'

'What happened to her? She died, Sera. Maybe if you'd been here—'

Dana broke off.

'Maybe what?' Sera said. 'Maybe she wouldn't have killed herself?'

That's not what I meant, was what Dana wanted to say. But she couldn't. They would both know it was a lie.

Dana stood and swayed a little, her ankle tempting to fold underneath her. Sera stood up too, following her with her arms outstretched, as though reaching for someone threatening to jump.

'Can I get someone for you? You've had a long day. You should get some rest. Or sit down. Sit down. I'll get you a drink from the machine. Then, I can call Mr Fisher, he can take you home. Or Gary—can Gary drive now?'

'You know that faking your own death is illegal, right?'

Although she couldn't see her, Dana could feel Sera dropping her arms.

'Am I under arrest, officer?'

Dana shook her head, still facing away from her. 'No. I just want you to tell me what happened.'

Dana put her hand on the door handle and leaned against it. She looked at the wooden door in front of her, not behind her where Sera stood. She was quiet, but so close she could feel the hum of the heat of her skin. Dana took a breath in, and held it.

Sera didn't say anything. Dana let the door swing closed behind her.

♦ ♦ ♦

'Open your eyes,' a voice said.

I don't want to, she tried to tell the voice. No. No, I'm tired.

'Dana, open your eyes,' it commanded. This time, she had to obey.

Awake, she was confused for a moment that she was not in her bed, her bed was not so cold. Lifting her neck, she saw water lapping the bank beside her. She looked down at her body, it was covered in something black, blood? No, mud, blending in with her swimsuit, the patches of skin in between it white in the blue night.

She opened her mouth to speak, and coughed instead.

Her throat was hoarse, but her lips were wet. 'Michael,' she said, 'Where are you?'

'It's alright,' the voice told her; kind, but commanding. Then something else, words she didn't know. 'Go to sleep.'

In the gaps between the trees and her drifting, half opened eyes, she could see flashes of the moon. One arm was taut, pulled above her. Underneath her, the grass moved. The trees disappeared as her head was tucked into the dip of a warm shoulder blade, and was carried down into the bowels of the house. Everything was white, and she was lying on top of concrete.

She could still hear the water, underneath the ground.

'Will she be okay?'

'I think so. Keep holding her head up,' someone else said.

Two small hands laced together to form a basket, cradling the back of Dana's skull. Brown eyes swam in front of her.

'Am I going to die?' Dana slurred.

The girl didn't answer. She opened Dana's mouth and tipped something down her throat, then, pushing the hands that held her head up out of the way, hauled Dana on to her side. An inky splatter hit the floor as Dana retched.

'No,' the girl said.

On the wall behind the girl, something was shimmering gold. Four floating people. No—not, people—

As she pulled Dana's seatbelt over her body, pushing aside the blanket she had been wrapped in to fasten it, Dana's eyes fluttered open. The car was moving, rocking her back to sleep, and Dana fought hard to keep herself awake. It was dark outside, but orange streetlights ghosted over the face of the dark-haired girl driving the car beside Dana. She wore a necklace that matched Michael's. Her face was serious.

'It's okay. Don't be afraid,' she said, eyes not moving from the road. 'I'm taking you home.'

'You're Sera,' Dana accused the driver, slumping on the car door. 'You weren't…at the par-party…'

'No, I was taking care of Ariel. She's too young.'

Dana grinned. 'Me too. I mean, my brother.'

'I see.' Sera's hand brushed Dana's forehead. It was cold, and fleeting.

'You don't like me, do you?'

Sera took her hand away. 'I don't know you.'

'Yeah, you do. You're my age. We've had classes together.'

'When you actually show up, we do.'

Dana laughed, her head hitting the headrest. She tried to extract her hand from the blanket, but it was wrapped too tightly around her body. Her body felt hollow, her mouth tasteless and rough, but if she kept laughing, she could ignore it.

'What are you doing?'

'Why am I in a straitjacket?'

Sera kept her eyes on the road. 'It's a blanket. You were cold.'

'I've never been drunk before.'

'I thought so.'

'Did I do anything stupid?'

'What do you remember?'

'Like, nothing,' Dana said. 'Playing the game in the lake… dancing…Michael…where is Michael?'

Sera didn't answer.

'Where is Michael?'

'You don't remember anything else?'

Dana shook her head. 'No,' she replied, when she realised Sera was not going to look at her.

'He broke up with you. You got upset and drank too much. I said I'd take care of you for him.'

Sera reported the facts the same way anchor-men reported massacres in other countries. A shame, but it had happened so very far away.

Dana's head ached. 'But we weren't even going out, yet. I mean, officially.'

'Oh. Well, it seemed like you were, I guess.'

Dana's face crumpled and, she realised with abject humiliation, she was beginning to cry. Part of her felt like she was watching herself crying from outside the car window. She didn't cry a lot, that part of herself noted. She must have liked him a lot, to cry so much like that.

Sera pulled over and Dana stopped crying, startled. They were on an empty road on the outskirts of town.

'Look at me,' Sera said, fixing her eyes on Dana's. Her voice was low, quiet, but every word sharp and immediate. 'Listen to me. Are you listening?'

Dana nodded. Everything was out of focus, except for Sera's dark brown, almost black, eyes; so dark, she realised now, that it was impossible to differentiate between the pupil and the iris. Under her gaze, Dana felt immobile.

'Everything is fine,' Sera said. 'Everything is the way it's supposed to be. In the morning, you're going to wake up. You won't remember this conversation. You won't remember the basement. You won't remember the lake. And you'll stay away from Michael. Right?'

Dana saw the reflection of herself in Sera's eyes nod. The events of the night, which had been in her hands for examination, began to slip further away.

'What happened?' Dana murmured, slurred. Underneath the blanket, she touched her body. 'Why am I wet?'

'You just went for a swim.' Sera was looking at her. 'Say it.'

Dana's mind softened. That's right, she thought.

'I just went for a swim.'

Sera turned away from her. She started the car. 'You're going to go to sleep now. Right?'

Dana's eyes, heavy with crying, shut before she could be sure if she answered yes or no.

Lazarus is dead

Lord, Martha said, if you had been here, my brother would not have died

Jesus said to her, I am the resurrection I am the life. The one who believes in me will live, even though they die

Do you believe this?

Chapter Seven

Gary opened his eyes at the sound of the front door closing and wondered why the ceiling was so much higher than usual. He'd forgotten: he'd slept on the floor. His bed was above him. A white arm lolled out from underneath the blanket.

He'd forgotten about that, too.

It had stayed in bed all Sunday. It didn't breathe. When it was still, there was almost nothing to differentiate it from a dead body. A real dead body.

Yesterday morning, he'd panicked. Staring at its grey skin and immobile limbs, his breath had started to come quick, but at the same time he felt as if he couldn't breathe. Just when dots began to appear in his vision, its eyes had opened.

It had not looked at him. It had not looked at anything. It had blinked, three times. Then, its eyes had shut.

It hadn't moved again. Gary had watched. The arm, which had escaped the rectangular confines of the mattress and which now protruded into the rest of Gary's bedroom, must have moved while he slept. Maybe it had been dreaming.

Gary held his breath as he got to his feet. He let it go as he shut the door behind him. He didn't want to wake it up.

The light of the TV silhouetted a figure on the couch.

'Dana, is that you?'

On the screen, a woman with chopped blonde hair was holding a container of skin coloured powder. Dipping a brush into the container, she tapped it, and applied the powder to another woman's acne scarred skin. Dana was engrossed. Her unlaced boots were in front of her, as if she'd stepped out of them, one by one, on her way to the couch. The dish of left-over macaroni was on her lap, fork stuck out of it. Beside her on the couch was a mud stained manilla folder.

'Hi. Sorry. Didn't mean to wake you.'

'That's okay,' Gary said. He looked at the clock: it was four AM. 'Where have you been?'

'I had to stay late in work. Because of what happened.'

'Oh,' he blinked. 'What happened?'

'Jerome Smolinski. Sandy Ackermann. Cathy Copeland. Anthony Dorhamer. Ariel Enckles.' Dana looked at him. 'Some freak dug up their graves. Moved the remains. We were out searching for them all day. Didn't dad tell you?'

'Oh, yeah, of course. I forgot. I mean, I just woke up.'

Dana raised her eyebrows. Gary couldn't tell if it was in suspicion, or concern.

'You feeling okay?'

Gary hated when Dana acted parental. He always had.

'Yeah, I'm fine. Just tired. Like I said, I just woke up.'

Dana lifted the remote. The two women were smiling, their skin was the same colour. She changed the channel. 'You should go back to bed. It's late.'

I know, Gary wanted to say. You're the one who woke

me. 'Okay. Night.'

Lying awake on his floor, Gary estimated that an hour passed before he heard Dana's footsteps on the stairs and her bedroom door closing. He felt compelled to lie still, pretending that he was asleep for another forty-five minutes.

The arm did not move again.

By the time his dad left for work at seven AM, he was resolved. He had been stupid, very, very stupid, to think he could hide it. He had to get it out of the house before Dana found it.

He would borrow Brussels and transport the body somewhere else. The woods. Out of town. The next state. Whatever—anywhere that wasn't his bedroom would be an improvement. If he was quick enough, he could be back before Dana woke up, and she would never know a thing.

♦ ♦ ♦

The body had not been unwilling to leave the house, but getting it into the narrow trunk posed some logistical challenges. The problem was that the body seemed to find bending difficult, but it was too long to fit in horizontally. In the end, he was able to get it to lie on its side, positioning its legs so it was in the foetal position. Its eyes were open as he closed the trunk door.

Gary drove more carefully than usual. He'd considered trying to attach the body to his bike, or carry it. He wasn't a great driver: his test had taken him a few tries. Last year, he'd borrowed his dad's car and been pulled over for driving 25 in the 70 zone.

'I'll let you off this time,' Officer Graham had said, his eyes obscured by sunglasses. 'Fisher can keep an eye on you, I'm sure.'

He doubted Dana's influence would cover having a reanimated dead body in the back of her car. Was there a bumper sticker for that? 'Body on Board!'

On the road out of town, Gary took a turn that would take him to the gas station and remembered last January. Someone had climbed in an open window at and massacred that week's egg delivery. Mr Dale had caught the repeat offender on CCTV footage not long after: a racoon, whiskers dripping in yolk. Dirk Dale, Mr Dale's sixteen-year-old nephew, had been caught helping himself to a packet of Camels just a few months ago. He'd denied it, but the video evidence had made the crime undeniable.

His stomach dropped. How could he have been so stupid? In his mind, Gary saw Mr Dale, Lynda and Dirk all standing around the CCTV monitor, mouths open in shock. Should he come clean now? Maybe they would go easy on him, they'd understand it was all a big mistake. He had only turned eighteen a couple of months ago, he might still be considered a minor.

He had to get that tape. He had to get it now.

'Hi, Dirk,' Gary said. Dirk was restocking the magazine rack. He was the only one there.

Gary felt his stomach settle a little. 'How's it going?'

Dirk grunted as he heaved fresh copies of *The Declaration* on to the shelf; actually working for once. *BEAMING BACK TO SCHOOL,* the headline read.

'I forgot something the other night. Just a book I was reading. I'm going to go get it, now.'

Dirk shrugged. 'Whatever.'

Gary could have cried with relief. He hadn't watched it!

Gary ducked behind the counter and went through to the back. Mr Dale wasn't in the stockroom. The door to his office, where the CCTV monitor was kept, was unlocked. Gary pressed the rewind button, just to be sure that it was the right tape. Video-Dirk unloaded the papers, drank a coffee and smoked a cigarette, counted the tills, opened the store, and then there was a long shot of the shut, black interior; they didn't open on Sundays.

Gary ejected the tape, then replaced it with an old one. No one ever checked the footage. No one would notice the difference.

In front of the counter was a smudge of dirt the size of a footprint.

'Hey Dirk,' he said. 'Found my book. Maybe, uh, mop the floor? Mr Dale was getting on my back about that the other day.'

Dirk shrugged. The dirt—the *evidence*—made Gary nervous, but he didn't have time to make sure Dirk did what he said. He hoped he would, for both their sakes; he had it on good authority that Mr Dale was looking to trim staff, and Dirk was first in the firing line.

Walking towards the door, it opened before he could reach it. He recognised the beige uniform before the face, and his heart lurched.

The officer met Gary's eyes in vague recognition. It was Officer Coops: the one that Dana hated but pretended not to. As he walked to the counter, Gary could smell the stale sweat that clung to him.

'Morning,' Coop said to Dirk. He set down a bottle of Dr Pepper, a tube of Berocca and a copy of *Sports Illustrated* on the counter. 'Pump three. You got any aspirin?'

Outside the gas station was a sheriff's department patrol car, long and lean and more than capable of catching Gary if he tried to make a break for it in Brussels. Officer Graham was sitting in the driver's seat, window rolled down. Gary would have to walk past him to get back to the car.

He wanted to run. He couldn't run: guilty people ran, and he hadn't done anything to be guilty about. He had to be confident—you could do anything if you did it with confidence. He would be friendly. But not too friendly, not memorably friendly. He smiled.

'Hi,' Gary said. 'How's it hanging?'

Officer Graham looked at him. Gary swallowed. The officer nodded.

'Hey, kid.'

Gary watched the patrol car and the gas station disappear from the rear-view mirror, exhaling slowly. They had seen him in Dana's car, sure, but that wasn't a crime. He wasn't doing anything wrong. It wasn't his fault that the body had inserted itself into his law-abiding life. In fact, this was even more reason to get rid of it as fast as he could, forget it had ever happened and go back to normal.

It wasn't like he could help it, anyway. It might be walking around, but there was no one inside anymore.

He drove as far as he could in thirty minutes. Didn't want to risk being gone any longer than that. He took Brussels up a dirt road into the woods.

As he parked the car in a small clearing, Gary thought about any possible connection between the body and himself. The clothes, he realised. The pyjamas. He would have to take those home. Burn them. What about DNA? No, that would be fine—the bath would have washed it away.

He popped the trunk. It lay there, just as he'd left it, eyes still open. It did not want to get up.

'Come on,' Gary coaxed.

It did not move.

His arms ached, despite how small it was. It couldn't be more than ninety pounds. Its eyes remained open, reflecting the blue sky breaking through the trees.

He set it down at the base of a beautiful oak tree. He'd leave the pyjamas on, in case it got cold. It could take a while for someone to find it.

That was stupid. He had to take the pyjamas, just in case. He could cover it with dirt. God, it wouldn't care about being naked, why should he?

Gary looked down at it where it lay on the tall grass. The body remained curled, the side of its head flat against the earth, and its eyes looked straight forward. He felt as though he could lift its arm and it would just flop to the ground.

Fanned out against the grass, its not quite red, not quite blonde hair looked like an early autumn leaf. Its skin didn't look grey here, but translucent, almost green, the cartoon pyjamas garish. Gary's eyes filled with hot, tired tears. His chest felt tight, like something was constricting around his heart, his beating heart, because he got to be alive, but she would never be alive, not ever again.

Tears slid down his face. Gary held his head in his hands and let out a sob. It was the only sound in the clearing besides the wind in the trees. He felt like he was hyperventilating.

Holding his hand to his mouth to stop his crying, he looked down at the base of the tree. Her head was in the same place, between two roots, but her eyes were looking up, at Gary.

'Sorry,' Gary said. His voice was hoarse. He wiped his eyes and turned away from it. 'I'm sorry.'

He walked away, unable to stop more tears falling.

'Ga—a—r...'

He turned, heart thudding. Underneath the trunk, it was still looking at him, but it had moved again, mouth open and arm stretched out. Her fingers were still curled inwards, but she was reaching for him. Her torso expanded, and then expelled another garbled sound.

'Ga—a—r—eh...'

He wiped his sweaty hands on his jeans and took a deep breath in. He bent down, to pick her back up again.

◆　◆　◆

Gary went down as many back roads as he could, so the journey home was slow. The body sat in the back seat of the car. Gary had kept telling it to duck its head below the window, but it paid him no attention. Having it in the backseat made him nervous, but the thought of locking it in the trunk again made him feel sick.

The coast was clear; Dana was still sleeping. Gary did not have to carry the body up the stairs. It moved of its own accord, steps slow, but steady. He left it standing up in the centre of the bedroom, positioning Dana's keys on the kitchen table as they had been that morning. When Dana thundered downstairs, hair wet and uniform rumpled, Gary was eating dry cereal in front of the TV by the fistful.

'Tell dad I'll call him later,' she called. 'Have you seen my keys?'

He waited until he heard her car pull out of the driveway.

Upstairs, his bed had been made, pillows plumped. The laptop on his desk was opened. The screen was black. He couldn't remember if he'd left it that way.

It—she—was standing beside his window, eye at the crack between the curtains.

'Be careful!' Gary shut the curtains and pulled her away from the window. 'Someone could see you!'

She didn't look at him. Her lips moved: a single syllable utterance.

'What did you say?' Gary said.

She gazed up at him. Gary thought she looked wounded. She opened her mouth, her gums grey. The sound she made started like an inhale, rising upwards on a curve and spiralling there.

'Hu-h-e-l-l-l.'

'What?' Gary realised his hands were still on her shoulders. He let go.

'Hu-ell?'

It could have been 'hell' or 'help'. It was definitely a question, and not one he knew how to answer.

'You're safe, okay? You're not in hell. I'm sorry for grabbing, that was, um, not cool.' He backed away, sitting on his bed when the back of his knees hit it. The body stayed standing, but he was so much taller that they were almost at eye level. 'It's just that I don't think you would be safe, if they found you.'

The body looked at him. She did not blink. 'Dead.'

'You know that? I mean, I wasn't sure.'

She breathed inwards and expelled the air in a rush that could have been 'yes', or could have been nothing. She lifted an unbent arm and gestured towards the laptop. She put the arm down.

'Oh.' Gary wondered if she had utilised the same step by step guide he had found so helpful. 'Do you remember anything? Do you know how you got this way?'

She considered the question for a moment before shaking her head. No.

'What about those?' Gary gestured in the direction of her

wounded arms, without actually looking at them. 'Do you remember how…how they…' he tailed off.

Gary shook his head, embarrassed. He was being rude.

'What I mean is—' Gary ran his hands through his hair. 'Do you remember anything? From before?'

Her face was blank.

'I can tell you stuff. If you want?'

She breathed in, and for a moment he thought she might speak. Instead, she nodded her head. Yes.

Gary smiled, relieved that he was doing something right. 'So, you're twenty two—no, twenty three. You live here in Lake in the Woods. Lived. Live. You worked at the grocery store.'

The body's face remained still as Gary spoke. She inhaled. She exhaled, 'dead.'

Gary didn't know what to say. 'Yeah. I guess.'

She didn't answer, or look at him. She was silent, answering no more of Gary's questions. He supposed she was as confused as he was, a lost thing that did not belong in his ordinary bedroom. Unwilling to manoeuvre her as he had the night before, he watched her. She did not look of the window again. When she stopped speaking, she stopped breathing.

♦ ♦ ♦

He sat in the kitchen, eyes fixed on the ceiling. The floor of his room creaked through the ceiling as she moved upstairs. Hiding her up in the bedroom would be fine for the moment, but he couldn't do that forever. What if she started to rot? Maybe he should get his own place.

Gary's head ached at the thought. Now was when he should call Dana, or even his dad, or the sheriff. They would know what to do. They would take her away and Dana would work out who had dug her up, and why, and what this had to do with the other graves. But what would happen to her? Gary had seen the movies and their nightmare white rooms full of surgical instruments clouded his mind.

Gary realised then that he still had the tape from the gas station in his pocket. It would be safest to just erase the CCTV footage from the day before and put the tape back, probably.

Their old TV had a VCR slot, but it had been given to Dana when his dad had adapted to DVD. Gary felt uncomfortable sneaking into Dana's room. As a kid he had done it all the time, to steal her cool pirate movies and books, but now he was old enough to buy them himself so he stayed out. Besides, Dana liked her privacy.

It was not tidy. Cups of half-drunk liquid dotted her desk and bedside table, books and papers were piled up beside her bed. Ignoring the underwear that was strewn over the floor, he put the tape in the VCR slot, sitting on her unmade bed with the remote. He rewound until he got to Saturday night. Five PM.

Video-Gary looked up as the door to the store opened and the body walked into Dale's Gas Station. He'd been the first to see her. Except whoever dug her up, that is. Perhaps he would go down in history as the one who discovered the new species, if more had climbed out of the other graves. Or maybe she was unique. He paused the tape.

The poor quality of the footage softened the blow of her unearthliness. When he first saw her, he'd felt like every nerve in his body had been exposed, raw in shock, but on the screen she didn't look strange, just dirty. Almost normal.

He pressed play. In the footage, Gary watched his mouth fall open into an absurd 'o' of recognition.

The CCTV didn't have sound and Gary couldn't remember what he had said at the time, but his lips moved on the tape. She stared at him. She didn't speak, didn't move, and yet, at the time, Gary had felt she was somehow pleading. On the tape, her eyes were blank. After a minute or two of shocked scrambling, he watched them leave the gas station. It had felt much longer when it was happening. Gary rewound it, and watched the exchange two, three more times, before ejecting it from the TV. He should probably destroy the tape now—but there would be time for that later.

Besides, it was an alibi.

Gary's eyes fell on a pile of folders on Dana's desk. They were manilla, like the folder Dana had been brought home last night. He sifted through the pile, in case the mud stained folder was there. After twenty minutes, he wondered if he should give up. There were a lot of them, none of them particularly interesting; he hadn't realised being a sheriff's department officer was as dull as the documents seemed to suggest. Besides, maybe it was too optimistic to think Dana would leave something confidential behind.

Frustrated, he gave up on the folders and pulled open the drawer beside Dana's bed. Inside, was an old high school photo of Sera Enckles, the one Dana had put on the missing person posters. Underneath, something red caught his eye: a photo of Sera and Ariel, together. Ariel looked about thirteen. The two girls were standing by the lake's shore, Sera's long arm draped over her sister's shoulder. Ariel's knees were skinned, but she was beaming with pride at the handmade fishing net she held.

Gary felt breath on the back of his neck and whirled around quickly. She was standing behind him, eyes fixed on the photograph. One hand was outstretched, as though she wanted to touch it.

'Um, that's Ariel. You. I mean—you look like her,' Gary said. Ariel was dead; Ariel was standing in front of him; the two truths couldn't quite co-exist in his head. 'You don't remember?'

'Dead,' she said. She took in a breath. 'H-e-o-ow?'

'How? She killed herself. That's why...' Gary gestured, helpless, towards the cuts on the inside of her arm. 'You know.'

The body turned her hand so the bloodless wound on its forearm faced upwards. The cut had been horizontal, not vertical. Gary was pretty sure he read somewhere that you die slower that way.

'Did it hurt?' he asked.

She was looking at the wound, too.

She nodded. Yes.

'Why did you do it?' he asked. He didn't care if it was rude: he needed to know.

She put her arm down, and turned around. He followed her. She got back into his bed. Her eyes were open, but she didn't blink and she didn't breathe.

Chapter Eight

> Fire is holy, and the wood in Lake in the Woods—the wood still used to build many of the town's homes—burns remarkably well. But what of the unholy? I have wondered at times whether the superstition of ghosts in the lake could have originated in the necessity for water burials: the first grave in the town's limits was not dug until the sixties.
>
> *Lake in the Woods: A Complete History of an American Miracle*, Francis Fisher

'When you love someone, losing them just seems like the worst thing that could happen. Then, when it happens, and for them to choose to leave you—jeez.' He rubbed his eyes. They were wet again, tears clinging to his blond eyelashes. 'Jeez Louise. Sorry. It's been years, but it's still hard to talk about Sandy.'

Stan nodded. 'It's okay, Mr Ackermann. We understand how difficult this must be.'

'Please, call me Dave,' he said. His usually fair skinned

face was red, making his pale blue eyes even bluer.

Sandy Ackermann had been dead for five years. She had hung herself in the woods. Dana had still been working at the car wash then, but she could name at least five people off the top of her head who claimed to have been the one to find her. They all said the branch she'd dropped from had faced the lake, so the water had been the last thing she'd seen.

Dana hadn't known her. From the wedding photograph on the mantel piece, she looked like she'd been sweet and normal and like they would have nothing in common. There had been a note, presumably for her husband. All it said was, 'do not be afraid'.

Dave had looked as if he might be wrapping up crying, but a fresh wave hit him. Dana couldn't remember the last time she saw a man cry and watching the owner of Green's Groceries weep in his living room felt like a dream. A long dream. She didn't need to look at the clock to know they were going to be late to the briefing.

Stan smiled just enough to be friendly without being insensitive. Stan was good at this. Dana hadn't expected him to be.

'Now, I can't imagine what you've been through, and I'm not going to sit here and pretend I can. But it's important to remember when a person takes their life, it's not about how they felt about you. It's about their pain.'

'Yeah,' Dave said. 'Of course, you're right. I don't like to remember her that way, it's just with this whole…' he took a shuddering breath, 'Desecration thing…'

'The sheriff will find the people who did this,' Dana said. It was the first time she had spoken in nearly thirty minutes. 'I promise you that, Mr Ackermann.'

Dave showed them to the door and pressed a Tupperware container of oatmeal and raisin cookies into her hands. The second Mrs Ackermann and their small son had baked them for all the officers, to keep their strength up. He shook Stan's hand with both of his own. 'God bless.'

Dana's ankle throbbed, the pain just barely masked under the pills she'd swallowed dry. Her head was so light, she felt like she was driving drunk. They'd spent the guts of the night before combing the woods, the sheriff certain that the bodies were just around the next corner, just a few minutes more. Nothing.

She hadn't seen Sera in two days.

Stan turned to look at her, the light through the car window highlighting the fingerprint smudge on the inside of his glasses. 'Do you think it could be him?' he said.

She replied with her mouth full of cookie. 'Do I think what could be who?'

'Dave Ackermann. Could he be our guy? Spouses are statistically good suspects, you know.'

'Been watching CSI recently?' she said, crumbs sprinkling onto her shirt.

Stan laughed. It was thin, but still a laugh. 'Okay, Scully, why are you so sure he's not our guy?'

'Besides the crying? He has an alibi—Len's gig, remember—' the box of cookies was in her lap, how unsafe would it be to take just one hand off the wheel for another one? '— and no motive. No motive, no arrest.'

'Looking for a motive is pointless,' Stan said.

He'd reached for the pack of cigarettes in his breast pocket as soon as they'd gotten into the car, but it had been empty. Dana watched him break the empty box down into flat sky-blue card.

'There has to be a reason,' she said. 'It's too much planning for a prank gone wrong, or a crime of passion.'

'But whoever did this isn't thinking straight,' he said, now working on folding the cigarette carton's inner silver wrapper. 'Did they have a reason? Yeah, probably, but I'm not sure it'll be a reason that will make sense to anyone but themselves.' The silver paper was wound tightly now, a knot. 'You don't remember anything else about that night? Even something insignificant could help.'

Dana looked at the road. At first, she'd lied because it made more sense that the truth. Things were different now; no one would call her crazy for saying she saw Sera that night, but she was still covering for her. It wasn't out of friendship. It was clear that Sera didn't consider her a friend, not anymore.

Satisfied, Stan placed the piece of trash on the dashboard. In the sunlight, it shimmered. He turned to Dana, expecting an answer. An answer she wasn't ready to give. She shook her head.

It didn't matter if they were friends or not. Dana knew Sera. Even if she'd been there that night, she couldn't have done this.

♦ ♦ ♦

The daily briefing was already underway. Mel leapt up to pull over two fold-out chairs for them, almost knocking the box of cookies from her hands in the process. The sheriff continued as though he hadn't been interrupted.

'...Our working theory is that the perpetrator transported the bodies to a vehicle in the car park, then they crashed into the gate as they drove off, causing the damage,' he said, nodding at Dana. 'Forensics got back to us—nothing yet. They're running more tests, but it looks like we're going to have to find them either by their vehicle, or through a connection to the missing. It's most likely that we are looking for multiple perpetrators.'

'Uh, sheriff?' Officer Graham asked, raising his hand like a kid in class. 'What's the evidence for that?'

'You ever lifted a body, shit for brains?' Coops butted in. 'People are heavy. We're looking for a big guy, trust me.'

Jerome Smolinski had been buried for over five years: he'd be a skeleton. Dana wondered if one perpetrator would be as impossible as the sheriff seemed to think. But voicing this opinion would mean aligning herself with Jacob over Sheriff Wormwood, so she kept quiet.

Sheriff Wormwood looked to the photographs of the missing on the wall. They were in black and white: Mel had explained mournfully that they were out of colour ink.

'The only connection we have between the missing is that they all lived here, died here, and were buried here. They weren't the only bodies in that graveyard. So why them?'

This, Dana could answer. 'They were all suicides.'

Sheriff Wormwood shook his head. He held up his hand, five fingers spread wide. 'No. Ariel Enckles, Jerome Smolinski and Sandy Ackermann were suicides.' For each name, he put down a finger. He waggled the two left, 'Anthony Dorhamer's crash was an accident, and Cathy Copeland died in her sleep. So—what's the connection?'

Mel tapped his chin with the pen he was taking notes with. Jacob looked deep in thought, brows furrowed. Coops scratched his head. Dana had thought that the question had been rhetorical, and that the sheriff was asking for the sake of gravitas. In the long pause that followed she realised with horror that the question was genuine and a response was expected.

'Sir?' Stan said.

'Go ahead, Officer Wu.'

He cleared his throat. 'I'm not sure about the ethics of breaking the anonymity for someone who's passed, so keep it to yourselves, but Dorhamer was an AA regular. Could it be worth checking out if any of the others had a drinking problem?'

Dana had always assumed that Stan avoided drinking for religious reasons, or something. They all had.

The sheriff nodded, expression muted. 'Worth checking out.'

The day's assignments were given out. Deputy Boldry would co-ordinate further searches—if they haven't dumped the bodies already, the sheriff said, they still might. Coops and Graham would join him. Dana couldn't help but feel a certain buzz of satisfaction that they were the ones who'd spend the day getting muddy and dealing with PTA moms. It was things like that which made her sure that the sheriff liked her better.

Stan and Mel would stay at the station, to go through security cam footage on the road out of town. It didn't capture every car going that way—that would be too easy. They'd make a list of every large vehicle seen on the road the week before, in the hope that whoever they were looking for scoped the graveyard out.

Dana didn't have an assignment. She looked over at Sheriff Wormwood. He beckoned her to follow him.

'Where do you want me, sir?' she asked when he shut his office door behind her.

The sheriff perched on the edge of his desk.

'Morale is low. Until we get somewhere, we need to remind folks what we do for this town. Hilary over at *The Declaration* heard about Sera Enckles.'

No one had spoken to Dana about Sera since that night, and hearing her name made her mouth run dry. She licked her lips. At the corner of her mouth was a thrill of chocolate. 'Oh?'

'She wants to run a story, with a photo of Sera here to go with it. I don't want to spook her. Can you approach her?'

'What about Michael, can't you ask him?'

The sheriff shook his head. 'The mayor doesn't know where she is.'

Dana was confused. 'Well, can't you...tell him?'

Something flashed across the sheriff's face. If Dana didn't know better, she would have said it was embarrassment.

'We don't know where she is, either. After you concluded your interview, Sera walked straight out. I'd gone to get her paperwork ready, the deputy was on a call. The only person in the office was Mel. Apparently, he "didn't think",' he cleared his throat. 'She didn't leave us with any contact details.'

Dana thought that Mel had been more frantic that usual that morning.

'She's not staying at the Enckles' house?' she said.

'Apparently not.'

'What about Joe Enckles? Maybe he's seen her.'

'Haven't been able to get a hold of him. As far as we know, you're the only person who's spoken to her,' he frowned. 'To be honest with you, I thought we'd have a call about a sighting by now. As far as most folks know, she's still dead.'

She knew it wasn't what he'd meant, but the words *she's still dead* hit Dana somewhere vital.

'She's probably left town by now,' Dana said.

'It's a possibility,' the sheriff said, in a way that suggested he didn't think it was at all possible. 'Can you find out?'

Dana didn't want to talk to Sera—she didn't have anything to say that wasn't raw. She didn't want to see her, either, and the feeling was clearly mutual.

'I wish I could help,' she said, 'But I really don't know where she is.'

The sheriff shrugged, unbothered, as if it had just been a passing notion. 'Let me know if that changes.'

◆ ◆ ◆

'That alcoholic thing was smart,' Dana said, squinting her eyes at the screen.

The two TV units that Stan had set up for them filled the office with mechanic heat. Dana was using the newer unit, while he was stuck with the one that had been gathering dust in the evidence locker. She'd offered to swap, but he'd refused. As he rightly argued, they were both shit, so it didn't make much difference.

'Thanks. It's a long shot, but someone had to speak.'

'What, you don't believe your own theory?'

'It was just an idea. Sandra Ackermann taught Sunday School. Didn't exactly strike me as a drinker. Cathy Copeland was a nun at one point, for chrissakes.' Stan's tape had finished. Popping it out, he flipped it to the other side. 'Mel, I've got all the plate numbers from the Wednesday,' he called, waving around a piece of paper.

'Right there, officer!' Mel hissed, one hand over the receiver of the station's phone. 'As I said, Mrs Dorhamer, the sheriff is doing everything he can…'

Cathy Copeland had probably been the only Catholic in Lake in the Woods. There was a rumour that a priest had to be flown in to lay her to rest.

'You know, I hear Catholics drink wine at service, so you never know,' Dana said.

'Yeah, I guess. Oh, come on!' Stan said, whacking the side of his TV as the screen blacked out again. 'Atta girl.

Hey, Dana, think you're over the speed limit here, last Friday. I'll let you off, this once.'

'So generous,' she said. 'You said Sandy volunteered at the church, and, you know, Ariel did, too. Do you think maybe they were all religious, or something?'

'Well, sure, but that's nothing special,' Stan said lightly. 'You're about the only person I know who I don't see on Sundays. Between you and me, you're not missing much.'

Unwillingly, Mrs Trieger popped into Dana's head, wearing her purple *Jesus is the Answer*! sweater. What's the question? Dana wondered. Once, Mrs Trieger caught her staring at it and offered to make her one of her own, so they could match on Sundays. Once, when she was a kid, Mrs Trieger had seen Dana drinking a red can of Coca-Cola and informed her she was going to hell.

'Yeah, I know,' Dana said. 'You go to church on Sunday, everyone does—I get it. But I mean it's not like you're a—' Jesus freak was the term her mom had used. 'Not like you're like, obsessed with God, you know? I mean, what if they weren't regular religious but...next level?'

'Nah,' Stan said. 'Like I said, Copeland was Irish Catholic, so she's out, and then there's Smolinski.'

'What about him?'

'You never heard about him? He used to be the high school janitor. People used to say he sacrificed animals in the school basement, or that he was a devil worshipper. Talk was that he got fired because he got caught with a student—a freshman boy.' Stan shook his pen up and down. The ink had stopped. 'Who knows? People make up all kinds of crap. But if there's a connection between him and Ariel Enckles, beats me what it could be. What was she like anyway? Aside from the preachy stuff.'

'I didn't really know her well,' Dana said. 'Do you want a soda?'

♦ ♦ ♦

Father Enckles was a small man, but he did not use a microphone as Principal Graham did. His voice carried: even when he was silent, the absence of his voice screamed.

'Water is holy,' Father Enckles preached, standing on the school's stage. 'Milk is holy. Coca-Cola...' He held the can aloft, light reflecting off its gleaming red and white shell. 'Is unholy.'

Even though she didn't go to church, Dana had heard the news about Coca-Cola. One Sunday in the height of summer, Father Enckles had declared that the majority of carbonated drinks were unholy. Mrs Trieger had put a sign up on her lawn proclaiming COKE is the DEVILS SPIT. Within a week, all cans had disappeared from the Green's Groceries and the gas station.

A bartering system had already sprouted among the students: Coca-Cola was the most sought-after beverage. It was declared to be the most unholy of them all, perhaps because of its devil red packaging.

'Is Sprite holy?' someone whispered under their breath.

Father Enckles eyes landed on the person. They were in the same row as Dana, near the back.

'Beware non-believers,' Father Enckles said, eyes on the kid. 'Those who laugh at Christ's message. One non-believer is like a lame lamb. It's enough to sicken the entire herd.'

It was all about the herd. He was part of the herd. Principal Graham was part of the herd. Even our police force, he said nodding his head with a smile to Deputy Wormwood, sitting on the principal's left, was part of the herd. And they—the students—were the most important part of the herd, because they would lead it someday.

The cull of the graduated seniors meant there were vacancies: time to step up.

The light of the auditorium bounced off the principal's head as he bowed it down to pray. Dana knew the words of The Lord's Prayer well enough by now to mouth along.

Dana wanted to get through this school year quietly. She wanted to be left alone. The kids in town all knew each other from church. They knew about her.

Summer had been cruel. Autumn would be kinder.

With her eyes closed, lips moving silently, Dana felt the back of her head itch. Someone was looking at her.

Dana risked it and turned her head. Sera Enckles was two rows back, head bent, but eyes open and staring.

♦ ♦ ♦

Dana rolled the can over her forehead. The station's vending machine didn't keep the drinks cold, but the aluminium was still sharp and soothing.

'Anything yet?'

Dana froze. That was Michael's voice.

'We're working some leads,' the sheriff replied. 'Doing what we can with limited resources.'

Michael and Sheriff Wormwood were talking in the empty reception area of the station. The vending machines and payphones where Dana stood were around the corner: they couldn't see her, but she could hear them.

'Still, nothing,' Michael sighed. 'I'm doing my best to keep everyone calm, but it's not easy. How long until we're legally required to hand over to the feds?'

There was a pause. 'Four days. Not including today.'

Dana could picture the look of concern on Michael's face. He could be so convincing. 'Crazy times. How long has it been since we last handed over the reins to the feds? Is it twenty years? More?'

'More,' the sheriff replied steadily. 'Whatever problems have cropped up here, we've always dealt with them. This is no different.'

'Isn't it?' Michael said. 'Don't take this the wrong way, sheriff—you've kept a firm grip on this town, and I say this with the upmost respect—but the council is pretty concerned that nothing's been found. No one can blame you for being in over your head.'

In the sore silence, the only sound was the static hum of

the vending machine beside her.

'Has the council reconsidered my suggestion?'

'Sheriff,' Michael said. Dana could hear the smile in his voice. 'You have to know that dredging the lake is impossible.'

'It would be difficult, but if we ask for assistance from the National Guard—'

'It's impossible,' Michael said, politely. 'But if your team come up with any other suggestions, please let my office know. You know I value your input. Goodness knows,' he said, laughing, 'I couldn't do what you do.'

♦ ♦ ♦

There were four gas stations in town; five if you counted the single gas pump outside of Sloppy Sal's Shop. Dana did. Sal himself was unsure about the blurred black and white print outs Dana showed him.

'Could be,' he said to each one. 'Yeah…could be.'

He pointed at one photo, of a black SUV, telling her that he'd seen a green SUV the same style the month before, but couldn't remember who drove it. 'Nice car, though.'

Stan had taken the lead when they updated Sheriff Wormwood on their progress, while Dana sipped her room temperature Coke and tried not to think about what she'd overheard.

'We're not done yet, sir, but we have spotted a few larger vehicles, as well as some with out-of-state licenses. Mel's sent the information requests through, but there's a couple we can't get anything on,' Stan said.

His eyes narrowed with interest. 'What do you mean, "can't get anything on"? They're unmarked?'

'No, sir. The camera resolution isn't high enough to read all the numbers.'

The sheriff sighed. He looked tired. He looked older.

'Gas stations,' Dana said. 'Some of the stations in town probably have CCTV.'

The sheriff nodded. 'Wu, you stay here, finish those tapes. Fisher, go ask round, take photos of any of the vehicles you've spotted on the footage already with you.'

'Sir,' Mel said. 'What do you want me to print the photos out on? The ink's out and—'

'Figure it out,' the sheriff snapped.

Mel had shut his mouth, flushing.

Only Dale's Gas Station had CCTV. Lynda had said that she'd go and get the tape from the back, but then proceeded to talk at Dana about the missing for fifteen minutes. Dana wasn't sure what Lynda was talking about specifically, as she seemed to deem 'suicide' a word not fit for polite company, and instead of a full stop, she punctuated each phrase with a *they're in my prayers,* moving on from the missing to Dana's poor mother *in my prayers*, to Dana's poor grandparents *in my prayers*, to Gary, to the price of gas, to tourists, and their trailers, which they parked in the woods, maybe college road-trippers, maybe homeless, we don't want that kind of thing here but they're *in my prayers,* and poor Ariel, wasn't it awful?

'Awful,' Dana said. 'Where did you see this trailer?'

Trailer, if you could call it that—more like a rusted tin

can, a UFO, a den of misguidance, sin, and possibly drugs.

Dana hadn't seen anything like that on the footage this morning. Maybe Lynda had just wanted something to say: maybe it was the lead they needed.

'You're in my prayers,' Lynda said, handing over the CCTV tape.

♦ ♦ ♦

Anthony blamed Father Enckles. When he'd confessed to him the problems he was having in the marital bed, he'd told him to imagine that the Lord was with him in his intimate moments.

This had confused him more before Father Enckles had clarified, to avoid sinful thoughts, Anthony may imagine himself in the position of his wife, rather than Christ.

Stan Wu had been more practical. 'Anthony, if you want to have sex with your wife again, it'd help if you didn't have whiskey dick six days out of seven. Maybe start by spending less time at Nyx and more time at home.'

The letters had started soon after that, tucked into his car door like a teddy bear, and the dreams. Jesus's hair in his mouth, he'd rolled on the floor of the church, tongue seized by rapture. Seeking Martha's eyes to say, I will do anything to be good for you.

Anthony knew he was ignorant, but he'd never wanted to be the guy whose wife hated him. He told her he loved her all the time, in the hope that she would say, You too. Even if she didn't mean it. He didn't know if he meant it himself, sometimes. He just needed her to say it. It was like this pressure that built up in his head as if everything—oblivion or recovery—hinged on those words.

'I can help you,' the letters said, writing round and bubbly. Do not be afraid.

♦ ♦ ♦

Bars didn't last long in Lake in the Woods, but Nyx, poised on the outskirts of town, was an exception. The Ackermann's had been running Green's Groceries for decades: in the official story, that was the family business. But everyone knew that they'd made their mom and pop's start-up money from moonshine brewed in the bowels of Nyx's cellar.

With a thriving supermarket to run, the Ackermann's had let Nyx turn feral, but somehow it stayed open. It attracted clientele the other handful of bars didn't. The souvenirs, as well as the bartender's well-polished ghost stories, kept the tourists happy. Its status as a 'tourist place' attracted locals who craved discretion. Dana didn't drink there, but they all did routine sweeps for underage kids who the owner turned a blind eye to. It was on a backroad along the same route as Dale's Gas Station, close enough that the sheriff had already taken statements on principle.

But the silver trailer was new, and the sheriff wouldn't have known to ask about it. If the trailer missed the cameras on the road, one of the staff could have spotted it.

The sign said *closed,* but the door wasn't locked. The music was so loud it was physical, and Dana flinched as she walked in. The tight room smelled intensely sweet and rotten; half-finished glasses sat on empty tables. For a moment she wondered if the bar was open after all, but the usually flickering neon sign behind the bar was dull.

'Hello?' Dana shouted. She couldn't hear herself.

The sticky countertop was covered in glass bottles, chewed straws, crushed cans. Shredded napkins lay in pools of spillage like melting snow. The door at the back of the bar propped open with a stool.

Beyond it, Dana could see the steps leading downwards to the cellar. There was a light on—someone must be down there.

Before Dana decided whether to walk through the door, Shelly Ackermann appeared at the top of the stairs. She was carrying a crate of limes and lemons. When she saw Dana, her eyes widened and her mouth moved, but Dana couldn't hear what she was saying.

'Hi,' Dana shouted pointedly, fingers in her ears.

Shelly hurried. Holding the crate with one arm, she reached underneath the countertop to turn off the music, stumbling. The music stopped, replaced by silence and the fleshy pats of a cascade of sour fruit hitting the floor.

'Sorry,' Dana said, stooping to pick them up.

Shelly was wearing an oversized t-shirt and denim overalls. Her long, dyed black hair was twisted up in a pencil. It looked casual, as if she'd absentmindedly done it, pencil held between her teeth. But Dana knew it was difficult for the pencil not to slip, and it held in place as she stooped to pick up the fallen fruit.

'Thanks,' Shelly said breathily as Dana triumphantly returned the last lime. It was soft, so rotten her fingers almost broke the skin. 'You scared the crap out of me!'

'I knocked. The music's so loud you probably couldn't hear me.'

'Oh,' Shelly said, shaking her head and smiling. 'When we're closed I like to turn it up really loud. Helps get the cleaning done.'

She emphasised the word *closed*. In retaliation, Dana looked around the sticky wreck of the bar.

Shelly's smile did not dim entirely, but it flickered.

'It's moonshine day,' she said. 'I have a lot to do.'

'Moonshine day,' Dana repeated. 'Is that why it smells like that?'

Shelly laughed.

'Smells like what? Shit?' she said. 'Yeah. Not pleasant, but it's part of the process. Here—'

Shelly's eyes darted around the bar, until she found what she was looking for: an unlabelled bottle of clear liquid. She unpeeled a label from a roll and pressed it to the side.

'On the house,' she said, pleased, once she'd finished writing on it.

The bottle sat on the countertop between them, *Dana* and a smiley face written on the label in bleeding Sharpie black.

'I'm on the clock,' Dana said.

Finally, Shelly stopped smiling.

Dana was friendly, but she didn't have friends. If she was a man, no one would think it was odd to be distant. But sometimes being a woman seemed to oblige her to be more open than she wanted to. Some people thought she was sad; Shelly was one of them.

Shelly had viewed her as a kind of charity case for a while. When Dana worked at the car wash, Shelly got her car washed twice a week. When Dana had worked at the movie theatre, Shelly had gone every weekend, spent a long time at the ticket office choosing the title and asking for Dana's opinion.

She'd wore Dana down. If no one else turned up for the screening—because they were boycotting whatever it was, or it was a slow weekday—Dana would close the ticket office and come and sit with Shelly. They'd gone for a beer once or twice.

One night, in the empty screening of *All Dogs Go To Heaven,* Shelly had said, I feel like I can tell you anything. Dana avoided her calls until she got the message.

'Sure, of course. What can I help with?' Shelly said. Still friendly enough, but not as friendly as before. 'Was there a problem with my statement?'

If anything, Shelly's statement had been airtight, with multiple members of the town council confirming that she'd been at Len's gig briefly, before driving back to Nyx and serving behind the bar all night.

'No problem,' Dana said.

'Is this about Sera?' Shelly asked, a crease between her eyebrows.

'What?' Dana blinked. How did Shelly know? 'No. I just wanted to check…did you see any large vehicles you didn't recognise around here over the weekend? Like, a trailer or a…'

Shelly smiled again. 'Oh, I already spoke to the sheriff about all that. And I was detailed, trust me. No one saw anything weird, hippy vans included.'

Shelly pulled the pencil out of her hair. Against the blue eyes and blonde eyelashes—same as David's—her black hair was alien. It should have looked terrible, but Shelly was someone whose moles would always be beauty marks.

It made Dana vaguely ashamed. It had been the kind of week where she hadn't got round to getting the dirt out from underneath her fingernails.

'Was there something else you wanted to talk to me about?' Shelly prompted when Dana didn't say anything.

Dana's ankle twinged.

'Yes,' she said. Then, 'Well no, actually. We're also looking into Anthony Dorhamer's drinking habits. Did he ever come around here?'

Shelly nodded. 'Sure. That guy fell off the wagon so much he may as well have been pushing it.'

'So, he drank here?'

'Yeah, on and off.'

'You didn't try to stop him?'

Shelly shrugged. 'What can you do? It's his life. I mean, it was.' Dana was surprised at her coldness. After a pause, Shelly seemed to remember herself, adding, 'God rest his soul.'

Absently, Shelly was fiddling with something in her pocket. With the bar still between them, Dana couldn't see what it was.

'Did he ever drink with anyone?' Dana asked.

'Anyone he could convince to listen.'

'Anyone you recognised?'

'Sure. Everybody knows everybody round here.'

'Did you ever see him drink with any of the others?'

'The others?' Shelly asked. At the corners of her eyes was a small press of deep purple. She looked tired, Dana thought. Really tired. 'You mean the missing?'

Dana nodded.

Shelly shook her head. 'No. Not that I remember.'

'What about Sandy?' Dana pressed. Sandy Ackermann had been Shelly's sister-in-law. 'Did she ever mention him?'

'Why would she?' Shelly said.

By now, Shelly was holding on to her friendliness by a hair. Fair enough. She was upset about Sandy's body, and it was a stupid question. Dana wasn't sure herself why she'd asked it, except that if she ran out of questions there'd be nothing left to do but finish the conversation and leave.

'I saw Sera Enckles yesterday,' Shelly said. 'That whole thing is pretty messed up, right?'

The CD was still spinning with a silent purr. Dana shook her head slightly and blinked hard and black. With her eyes closed, there was a sudden nothing, as if Dana's brain had turned off and on again.

When she opened them, Shelly was looking at her. There was a complex look on her face, like she hadn't settled on how to feel about something.

'Sorry,' Dana said, a little dizzy. Something of the flat black silence remained on her tongue, like acid. She didn't know what had happened to her. 'I should go.'

Shelly didn't reply immediately.

'Alright,' Shelly said, as if she'd wanted to say something else. 'Just look after yourself, okay?'

'Okay,' Dana agreed.

'Be careful,' Shelly continued.

'I've got to go. Thanks. And sorry. About the fruit, I mean. I guess you can't use it now?'

'Don't worry about it,' Shelly said. 'It was going in the trash, anyway.'

Dana looked at the box of proud technicolor green and yellow. 'Why?'

Shelly pointed to the last lime, the rotten one.

'You have to be very careful with fruit,' she said. 'It's true what they say about bad apples, you know.'

What do they say about bad apples, again? Dana wanted to ask, but she felt that this question was a big, juicy bone.

Shelly wanted Dana to ask, What do they say about bad apples? So she could reply, Why, they ruin the whole barrel and then, as if it were an innocent coincidence, Sera Enckles is a strange one, isn't she?

Dana didn't need to hear it.

'Okay,' she said. 'Thanks again.'

She'd reached the door when Shelly called, 'Dana, wait.'

Dana waited. Shelly didn't rush over this time.

'You forgot this,' Shelly said when she got to her, the bottle of moonshine in her hand. She looked at her; direct and concerned. 'Everything's really fucked right now. I can't imagine what this is like for you. If you need to talk to someone, you can call me.'

Dana already knew she wouldn't. 'That's really nice of you, Shelly, but I'm doing fine. Thanks anyway.'

Shelly didn't say anything. She held out the bottle of moonshine with Dana's name on it.

Dana reached for it so she could leave, pre-emptively embarrassed at her hands smudging dirt on the white label. She stilled.

Shelly's hands were dirty, with black half-moon lines of dirt trapped under her fingernails. Her right hand—the hand she'd written with—was bandaged roughly.

'I'm a good listener,' Shelly said. 'I don't judge.'

Chapter Nine

Gary was slow on the till that morning, every sale taking twice as long to put through. At first glance, the customers seemed normal, but when he turned away and caught them out of the corner of his eye they were smirking or grinning, exposing their teeth. When he looked back, they smiled and told him to have a nice day. He hadn't slept well on the floor and being tired made everything harder, like trying to walk underwater.

After two hours, he asked Lynda if he could stock instead.

'You having trouble on the tills, hon?' she asked. 'I can give you some pointers.'

Gary wondered if Lynda was undermining him on purpose. He smiled and tried to make it convincing. 'Just feel like a change.'

Hidden in the stockroom, he rubbed his eyes with his knuckles and checked his phone for what felt like the hundredth time.

Ariel had not reacted when he had mimed how to use the house phone; he could only hope she had understood. The house should be empty until he got back, but Gary had stressed the importance of staying in his room. He had almost barricaded his bedroom door behind him, before he remembered what Ariel had said about being in hell.

When the clock reached one PM Gary was already out the door, though Dirk hadn't shown up to start the afternoon shift yet. Lynda would get in trouble over it, but he was sure Mr Dale wouldn't mind this once; he'd said he was his best employee, after all.

As he cycled home, the green trees that lined the road merged into one green wall. Trees and trees, and one tree looked so much like the other, that he could let his mind turn directionless and free, forget which way he was going.

A moving thing in his peripheral vision caught his eye. A car had pulled up alongside him, the driver was waving him down. Gary somehow forgot to keep moving his legs and his bike careened off the road; he felt his arm crunch as he hit the concrete hard. He heard footsteps rapidly coming towards him, and he scrambled to get up.

'Gary, are you alright?'

A hand grasped Gary's arm and he turned around, unsure whether to fight them off or run. Awestruck, he did neither, but simply stared at the dark-haired woman who stood in front of him, whose hand, whose warm hand, was too solid to be a dream.

'Sera?'

A smile broke her face open. The ten years since Gary had last seen her were documented in her skin, in the thin lines around her eyes, her cheeks, stripped clean of baby fat, and the scar above her eye, but for all she had changed it was her, smaller than he had remembered her as a child.

'Wow, you're so tall,' she grasped his arm again. 'And bleeding. I'm sorry, this is my fault. I didn't mean to scare you.'

Gary was hypnotized as Sera took his arm and examined the large scrape, blood oozing between her rough fingers. She loaded him into the passenger seat and put his bike in the back. Gary could only sit obediently, eyes alternating between being fixed on her and skittering away, as she told him she was taking him to her place to look at his cut. Sera asked a question and turned to look at Gary when he didn't answer. After that she was quiet.

Sera parked her car by a trailer in a clearing, a few minutes' drive from the main road. The outside of it was silver. Inside, it was green and dank, from the light coming through the small windows. Nothing was new, but everything was clean: the small sink and cooking pot hanging from the hob; the chewed yellow stacks of books, hard single bed at the back, covered in a patchwork throw, handstitched and so worn that the windows of fabric had faded into the same mushy colour.

Sera got Gary to sit down on it, while she boiled water. When the hob was lit, she set the box of matches she had used neatly back down beside it. Out of a large cardboard box full of stacked cans of food and two or three pieces of crockery, she pulled a small first aid kit.

The trailer was compact, but somehow full, strings of plastic beads hanging from hooks, and a star chart on the ceiling:

everything had a place. Gary felt too big, like his presence alone would disturb the balance of its delicate ecosystem.

Sera handed Gary a chipped cup of hot tea while she cleaned his cut with antiseptic. The tea was herbal but soothing sweet: Sera had put in a spoonful of honey. Outside, wind chimes fluttered in the breeze.

'Are you really here?' Gary asked. 'Like, does your heart beat and all?'

As she unravelled the strip of bandage to wrap around his arm, Sera smiled a little, but didn't laugh.

'Heartbeat and all,' she replied.

Gary didn't know what to think. Everyone knew Sera had been dead for years; people just didn't go missing for that long. Was she lying?

Focused on wrapping the bandage around his arm, Sera didn't look at him as she said, 'I thought Dana would have told you.'

She hadn't said it like a question, but it felt like one.

'Dana knows that you're back?' he said, when he couldn't figure out the answer.

'Yes.' Finished with his bandage, Sera nodded to his cup. 'Drink that.'

Gary sipped his tea, watching Sera closely as she made a second cup for herself. It was hard to be sure without a mirror, but Gary was almost certain she was breathing. Besides, her hands hadn't felt cold as they'd put on the bandage. Seeing her dead would have made more sense.

'What happened to you, Sera?'

Sera frowned.

'I came back for the funeral. I'm sticking around until everything is cleared up.'

'What do you mean?'

'Well,' Sera replied. 'Until they recover Ariel's body.'

The tea was no longer sweet. For the first time in days, he hadn't thought about it for a full minute. What would she say, he wondered, if she knew where Ariel was now?

But she wasn't looking for *his* Ariel. The Ariel that was at home behind his locked bedroom door, hopefully sleeping; the Ariel who still didn't respond to her own name, or successfully say words with three syllables or more.

The Ariel that was left.

'I'm sorry,' he said.

Sera spoke without looking at him, her eyes somewhere else. 'Don't apologise. This is nobody's fault but mine.'

'But she was sick,' Gary said. 'Ariel was sick, wasn't she? So, this isn't your fault. It isn't anybody's fault.'

Gary expected her to agree with him: it was the kind of thing he'd heard other people say. Like, there's nothing that anyone could have done, right?

'You don't need to hear this,' Sera said, closing the first aid kit with a snap and standing. 'I'm sorry. I understand if you don't want to speak to me.'

'No! I mean, yes, I do want to speak to you. Obviously. It's good to see you,' Gary said, 'And I'm sorry for your loss. If there's anything I can do, let me know.'

To his surprise, a look of hesitation passed over Sera's

face—he wasn't sure what it was, but it seemed almost like temptation.

'Really,' he said, 'let me know, if there's anything at all.'

Even as he said the words, Gary wasn't sure if he meant them, or they were just ceremonial. Either way, it made him feel like a real adult to offer his help, someone who could be relied on in a difficult time.

Sera smiled again. Gary could tell it was forced, but it wasn't a forced smile like people gave him at work, sharp and stinging. Sera smiled like she was unused to it, and was trying to do it for his sake.

'Let's get you home,' she said.

♦ ♦ ♦

'Shelly went to the funeral?' Stan said. 'That was nice of her,'

Well, Shelly was nice. Had been nice to Dana, specifically, many times. But when Dana closed her eyes, she saw Shelly's hands, covered in dirt, holding a shovel. Nice did not mean good.

She had nothing; Stan's careful expression as she explained her hunch told her that much.

'It means Shelly knew Ariel, or at least had an interest in her. She was Sandy's sister-in-law and Anthony was a regular at Nyx—' Dana remembered the hard blue of Shelly's eyes, the way she'd said *it's his life*. 'And it sounded like there was no love lost there, by the way. That's a connection to three out of the five already.'

Stan's gaze drifted. 'She and Jerome did go to school together. And Nyx is so close to the graveyard...' His eyes were distant, as if he were in the woods himself, imagining it. 'On foot? Twenty—no, fifteen minutes if you ran.' Stan's cigarette bobbed up and down as he nodded. 'Tell him.'

Sheriff Wormwood hadn't been as enthused.

'Circumstantial at best, Officer Fisher,' he said, with the tired air of a parent who did not have time to indulge a child's fancy. 'You're right that Nyx is close. That's why I already asked for an alibi, which multiple people have confirmed, including members of the town council.'

They'd anticipated this.

'She has an alibi for *most* of the night,' Dana said. 'But there's the time on the road from Len's gig back to the bar. We've checked the cameras and they confirm she did leave for the bar at 10:27pm, but there's no video evidence for the time she arrived.'

'The witness statements put her in Nyx around 11pm,' Stan said, taking over smoothly. 'That's at least 30 minutes unaccounted for. The drive takes 10 minutes if the road is quiet, which it was. And—'

The phone on the sheriff's desk rang. The sheriff looked at it, frowning as if it had been rude. He pressed unavailable, before turning back to Stan.

'You're suggesting a woman who weighs 100 pounds soaking wet uncovered and moved five bodies in thirty minutes?'

Dana took this one. 'Sheriff, you mentioned multiple perpetrators,' she said. 'It's possible she just moved the bodies, and someone else uncovered them.'

Shelly's rough hands suggested otherwise, but Dana knew it was a good theory. She raised her eyebrows at Stan.

'Another possibility that we haven't considered, sheriff,' Stan began, 'Was that we don't know that the bodies were moved in one night. Like you said—it's a big job. It would have taken hours. Only Ariel was buried that day, and Ariel's grave was the most thoroughly disturbed. What if the other four had already been moved?'

The clock ticked. Dana considered her breath, as they waited for Sheriff Wormwood to respond.

The sheriff spread his fingers wide and shrugged.

'Why?' he said. 'If that was the case, why would they also be uncovered?'

'That we don't know, sir,' Stan said. 'But if we are looking for multiple perpetrators—which seems a strong possibility—we should consider that they may have had different objectives.'

Different motives. Dana couldn't quite grasp the need for motive, at least not in this investigation. What could anyone gain from this that would make it worth doing?

The sheriff's phone rang. The upside-down letters on the small grey screen read *Mayor's Office*. He pressed unavailable again.

'This is good work,' he said. Dana looked at him, startled. She hadn't expected praise. 'You're right. We should consider Shelly Ackerman as a potential accomplice, if only for Nyx's location.'

Stan nodded. Dana could see the fire in his eyes. Finally, something.

Dana knew she should be excited, too. It was her lead, after all.

'Let's keep an open mind,' the sheriff said. 'It's a lead, but I don't like Shelly for this. Even if she is involved, I don't think she's mastermind material.'

♦ ♦ ♦

Gary didn't know the woman sitting on Mrs Trieger's porch. In front of her was a glass of lemonade, in her hand was a pink baseball cap, *He Saves!* handstitched into it.

Gary walked quicker.

'Gary!' Mrs Trieger yoo-hooed over. 'Come on over here!'

He smiled. He had to. Since his father had converted a few years ago, they'd become better friends with the Triegers, but Gary still felt a little wary of them; Mr Trieger had yelled at him once. Gary had been too young to remember all of the details, but he remembered his own tears and scabby knee, and Dana yelling back.

'Let me do introductions. Gary, this is Martha Dorhamer, a friend of mine from Ladies of the Light,' Mrs Trieger said, gesturing with the sheaf of leaflets in her hand. Martha was reclining on the swing chair, palm trees nestling either side of her flushed face. She older than Gary, but not as old as Mrs Trieger. She wore black.

'Martha, this is Gary, Francis' boy. She was just telling

me all about this, you won't believe it...'

Martha pushed forward her own leaflet. On the front of it was a photograph of Martha with a man. He was tall and strong, but somehow his face was soft; green goopy eyes falling down his cheeks and a weak jaw. They were both smiling and smart.

He was one of the missing, Gary realised. Jerome or...

'That's my husband Anthony,' she said tapping the photograph with a neat nail. 'He was murdered.'

Now Gary remembered him. He was the one who had driven face first into a redwood; rain-soaked flowers and laminated Bible verses still marked the spot on the road. They had done a whole assembly on road safety after it happened, even though everyone had known Anthony Dorhamer was drunk.

Mrs Trieger and Martha were both waiting for his reaction.

'Oh wow,' he said, inadequately. 'I'm sorry.'

'You know, I always liked Sheriff Wormwood fine,' Mrs Trieger continued. 'But I have to say, I couldn't believe it when I read about the evidence that was ignored.'

'It's a cover up, plain and simple,' Martha said, pushing the leaflet into Gary's hand. 'Read this and you'll see. Someone was writing to him. Threatening him, I think.'

'What did they say?' he asked.

Martha raised her eyebrow, pleased to have a receptive audience.

'Over and over, the same four words,' she said. '"Do not be afraid."'

Wow! Gary couldn't help it; his heart was pounding.

'Luke 1:30,' Mrs Trieger said, to no one in particular.

Martha smiled, ignoring her. She put on her black baseball cap and pulled her long, thin ponytail through the gap at the back.

'Read,' she said. 'It's all in there.'

Gary felt pleased, as if he'd been invited to a party at someone's house.

'Oh, Gary, we were just saying that girl who dropped you off looks just the spit of Sera Enckles, bless her soul,' Mrs Trieger said, waggling her eyebrows. 'Is she your girlfriend, or...?'

She tailed off, leaving a gap for his explanation.

'Well,' he started, unsure how to avoid answering.

If Dana didn't want to answer a question, she pretended she hadn't heard it. It was cold, but it worked. But Gary didn't want to be cold. At least, he didn't know how to be.

'The thing is, it is Sera Enckles,' he said.

Something died.

'Oh?' Martha said, face pinched. 'So, after all that, she's fine?'

Gary nodded. It was odd how much easier it had felt to talk about her husband's murder than Sera's survival.

Martha crossed her skinny arms. 'A runaway, then. After all that.'

Mrs Trieger politely said her goodbyes soon after. Her white face wasn't angry, but it concealed something. As he walked away, Gary felt that he had messed something up, but he didn't know how to fix it.

◆ ◆ ◆

Sheriff Wormwood sent Stan and Len Boldry to search Nyx. Why not me? Dana wanted to ask.

'I want you to stay on good terms with her,' the sheriff had said, before she could. 'If she's been coerced into being involved, it's possible she'll reach out to you if things get heated.'

Dana didn't know how to be a shoulder to cry on. Still, she nodded.

Dana stayed in the office, watching the clock, wondering if Stan was finding the bodies at this very moment. No warrant: they'd rely on Shelly being obliging. And if she wasn't, well, that would tell them what they needed to know.

Thinking of the bottle of moonshine in her glove compartment, Dana carefully ignored guilt. After all, if Shelly was involved, she had to be punished. That's the way it was.

The thought left her somehow unsatisfied.

Back to evidence, she thought. Back to things that were certain.

The trailer Lynda had mentioned was on her mind, a silver dollar spiralling in the air. She looked through the notes Stan had left in her absence. There was no mention of a trailer, but on the morning of the funeral he'd noted a vehicle entering the town. Registration unknown, make and model unknown. The time and *Possibly silver?* were the only details recorded.

Dana slipped the tape in and fast forwarded through the

grainy footage. There. A flash of headlights and the body of a long vehicle shining in the sun. She squinted at the passenger seat. Before she could look too closely the tape stuttered, as if a frame was missing. The video-road was empty again.

A glitch.

Dana slid out the hot tape and put in the one from Dale's Gas Station. She approximated the time frames. This time, the early morning road stayed empty. The trailer didn't appear at all.

Running her hands over the black plastic shell, she wondered how to tell if it had been tampered with. One glitch was chance: two was a different story.

Of course, if Stan found the missing in Nyx, it wouldn't matter. But if he didn't, they would have to consider whoever was driving the silver trailer as a suspect.

The driver's face was all dark pixel in the paused tape. Still, Dana hoped Shelly was guilty.

An animal part of Dana's brain snapped to attention, and she turned to look behind her. Michael was standing in the door of the office.

'Whoa,' he said, as if she were a startled horse. 'Melville let me in. Sorry if I scared you.'

He hadn't just arrived. He had been standing there, observing something. They were alone. The list of what he could have been observing was short.

You don't scare me, she thought. She breathed out and let the mask settle. You will never scare me.

'The Sheriff isn't here,' she said. Sheriff Wormwood had

gone to see a man about dredging the lake. 'Can I help you with something?'

He walked further into the office. The young golden Mayor was resplendent in a beige suit, not dissimilar to the colour of Dana's uniform. Her blood ran cold at the thought of Michael as a cop. Michael with a gun.

'You can leave a message with me for him,' Dana said, standing. 'Or Mel at reception.'

Michael didn't move. He just kept standing there, smiling, between Dana and the exit.

'Did you know Sera was alive?' he asked.

Inwardly, she raged. Why did everyone think she wanted to talk about Sera?

'No,' she said. Then, curious, 'Did you?'

She wasn't surprised when he didn't answer.

'Where is Sera, Dana?' he asked.

'I don't know,' she snapped, 'I don't care.'

He lurched towards her. Dana bit down on the urge to scream, as the back of her thighs hit the desk. In his hand, he grasped her upper arm. To an outsider, it might look like a comforting squeeze, but between his fingers the flesh of her arm bulged. His blue eyes were soft. She hated him.

'Dana, you don't need to protect her,' he said.

Up close, his eyes were flecked with navy. He said something; words that she didn't understand, words that were sharp and soft in unexpected places, that slipped through Dana's mind before she could catch a hold of them.

And then, 'Do not be afraid. Tell me where Sera is.'

It was hard to speak. Her voice was hoarse.

'I already said, I don't know,' she said. There was an urge in her to fold and say whatever he wanted to hear, as long as he would let her go. 'If you want to see her so bad, why don't you go out and find her?'

Stepping away, her arm slipped out of his grip, only to reach for her hand instead. He squeezed it with a smile and then let go.

'We both know you can only find Sera if she wants you to,' he said. 'When you do see her, tell her it's not too late to come home.'

He walked away, not looking behind him as he left.

♦ ♦ ♦

It was almost midnight when Gary heard voices from downstairs. Ariel was lying on the bed in her sleeping-not-sleeping state, so he closed the door behind him and tiptoed down the stairs.

Hovering by the kitchen door, he peered in the crack to see Dana leaning against the counter, a bowl in one hand, a fork in the other. She knew Sera was alive. She had done for a couple of days, but she had carried on as if nothing had changed, as if this news didn't affect anyone else.

Dana kept everything to herself, like she didn't trust anyone. Gary just didn't get that.

'I can't say I understand,' she said, spooning out a second helping of the potato salad Mrs Trieger had left. Gary didn't really understand why she'd bothered, but he had to admit it was pretty good. 'With all the volunteers, we've covered a lot of ground, but found no trace of the victims. Why not dredge it?'

Dad frowned. 'You know the lake is steeped in history. The pilgrims who founded the town thought it was a miracle. This situation is bad enough without desecrating our heritage.'

Dana speared a potato with her fork, rolling her eyes. Gary watched for signs in Dana that something had changed, the world had shifted, but there were none. '"Our heritage"? Dad, you were born in Poland.'

His dad frowned. 'That doesn't matter—'

Numb from holding himself still, Gary wavered on his feet and knocked into the door. Dana started, hand jumping to her belt. Even after she registered that it was just him, her eyes were wide in prey mode.

'Oh, Gary,' she said, after she'd let out a long breath. 'Sorry, hope I didn't wake you. You okay?'

'I'm fine,' he said. 'How come you called them victims?'

They both looked at him.

'Come again?' Dana asked.

'Well, they weren't murdered, right?' he said. 'I thought they were the missing?'

Dana swallowed. 'So, what, you're saying it doesn't matter what someone does to them?'

'No. Of course not. But they're not really victims, right?' he pressed. 'Unless they were murdered?'

Dana opened her mouth to speak, but his dad interjected

before she could. 'Remember that their families certainly are victims, Gary.'

'I didn't say they weren't!' he said. 'But I was just curious about why you called them victims, not *the missing*.'

Gary had read over the leaflet in detail. Martha's argument that Anthony was murdered was persuasive. In the months leading up to his death, there had been late night phone calls, hours where he couldn't say where he'd been. It had made him wonder if she was right, if Sheriff Wormwood was hiding something about Ariel and the others.

Dana rinsed her empty bowl in the sink, facing away from them.

'It's not that deep, Gary,' she said. 'I just don't like that word.'

'Because of Sera?' Gary said. 'But she's not "missing", anymore. Right?'

The water kept running from the tap, but Dana didn't move. Her back was rigid. Gary felt a swooping sense of satisfaction; nobody ever expected him to know anything.

Dana turned with the bowl still in her hand, dripping on to the floor, and his satisfaction was replaced with fear.

'What did you say?' she asked. Her voice was low and crawling, like thunder.

Maybe she hadn't heard him right? Maybe she would believe him if he said he said nothing.

'What's this about Sera?' His dad looked from him to Dana and back to him. 'Has there been a development?'

Neither of them spoke. Dana was still staring at him.

Gary swallowed. He was anxious, but he wouldn't feel guilty—Dana had no reason to be mad. If she had just told them, this wouldn't be happening.

'Someone say something!' their dad said.

'I saw Sera today,' Gary said. 'She's alive.'

His dad's face creased in confusion, looking back and forth between them both. 'Gary, that's not funny.'

'It's not a joke,' Gary said. His voice cracked like an actor about to corpse. 'She's alive—I saw her. So did Dana.'

His dad looked to Dana to deny it. Leaning against the counter she was small, her uniform huge.

'But why did you not tell us?' he demanded when she didn't. Confusion made his dad angry. He didn't like to not understand things. 'Dana, why did you keep this secret? Imagine if someone had asked me about it—how embarrassed I would have been not to hear it from my own daughter?'

'I'm sorry that I embarrass you, Dad,' she said.

'Don't put words in my mouth,' he said.

Gary wondered if he could leave.

'It's police business,' she said, finally. 'I couldn't tell you. Gary,' she turned to him, ignoring her father. 'Where did you see her?' Dana paused. 'And what was she driving?'

◆ ◆ ◆

Ariel was on the bed. Her back was against the wall and her legs were crossed. On her lap was a celebrity gossip magazine Gary had brought home from work. The same page had been opened for twenty-five minutes. She would look at the page in front of her, but she wasn't interested enough to turn to the next one and Gary couldn't be bothered to get up and do it again.

He'd thought she was getting better—more alive, more like a person—but now he wasn't so sure. He'd found some of his mom's old clothes for her to wear and the neckline of her dress was low enough that he could see the beginning of her autopsy stitches.

At first, dressing and undressing in front of Ariel had been strange. He'd been worried that it wasn't respectful. He'd wondered if he should change in the bathroom instead, but he didn't want his dad to notice anything different. Usually, Ariel did not even seem to notice, but when he turned around with his pyjamas on, her eyes were on his jeans, crumpled on the floor and the leaflet that had fallen out of the pocket.

He picked it up and held it out to her. Her eyes were greedy on the faces as she took it.

'It's Anthony,' he said, pointing to the man. 'Anthony Dorhamer.'

Her fingers loosened on the paper like a mouth opening in shock. One hand crept to the other and then held her wrist; holding, he realised, her self-inflicted wounds. The careful wounds, the beautiful ones.

He felt as though he'd done something bad to her. Reaching behind him for his desk drawer, he stuffed the leaflet inside.

He turned back to her. She looked frightened.

Dana told him once that they didn't do autopsies for every death. They did it when people died unexpectedly.

Was Ariel a victim?

'Ariel, did you hurt yourself?' he asked. 'Or did someone hurt you?'

Ariel stared at him. Then, she nodded; once up, once down. Gary knew he should be scared. If Ariel had been murdered, and whoever murdered her was still out there, they might come after her. They might hurt her. If Gary were smart, he should get away from Ariel. He should tell someone.

Gary sat down on the bed beside her. Her eyes were still on him, and he moved slowly. He reached for her hand. He held it. It was cold. He held it tighter.

'Ariel,' he said. 'I won't let anything happen to you, I promise. I'm going to keep you safe. I'm going to figure out who hurt you.'

Chapter Ten

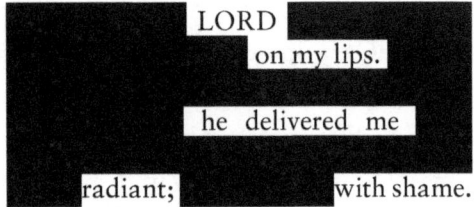

Psalm 34

The silver trailer was larger than it looked on the traffic cam footage; Dana was surprised that Sera had been able to drive it up the narrow dirt path. In front of the trailer was a foldable deck chair, an upturned crate and a small campfire with a large pot heating over it. Her car—the Dodge Dynasty LE that Stan had been trying to identify from the footage for days now—was parked nearby. Everything there could be discarded or packed away in under ten minutes.

The door opened and slammed closed in the wind. Sera. In her arms was a small pile of wet clothing, which she began to hang on a line stung between two trees. The dark clothes were stark against the green, like hunted birds.

The wind didn't cover the sound of Dana's footsteps through the tall grass. Sera looked over at her, but didn't stop what she was doing.

'Gary told you where I was,' Sera said, instead of hello. She looked irritated, but Dana didn't know if it was at seeing her or because of her hair, loose over her shoulders, blowing into her face.

'I wasn't trying to stalk your brother, Dana,' Sera said, swiftly undercutting the protective little speech Dana had been practicing all morning. 'He fell off his bike and hurt himself on the road. What was I supposed to do?'

'Why aren't you staying at the house?' Dana replied.

'Because they would be about as happy to see me as you are,' Sera flapped out a pair of jeans with a snap.

The comparison annoyed Dana, but she couldn't figure out a way to dispute it without either confirming or denying that she had been happy to see Sera. This was complicated by the fact that she didn't know which would be the truth, and she also didn't know which would make her more uncomfortable.

'There are procedures you have to go through to get your identity legally reinstated. It's our duty to do them,' Dana said.

'Don't worry about it,' Sera said. She hung up the last piece of clothing; a t-shirt that, damp, had turned murky grey. 'To be honest, being dead has it's perks.'

Sera crouched down to stoke the fire, the flame wavering in the breeze. The clear water inside the pot was beginning to steam.

'What are you doing?' Dana asked, almost involuntarily. 'Are you cooking or something?'

Sera looked down at the pot, and then back at Dana. 'No. I was heating water to wash with.'

Dana grimaced. 'Have you heard of showers? The Jesus-Loves-You Motel has plenty.'

'I have everything I need here,' she said gesturing back at the trailer.

Dana's eyes lingered on it. She knew she should search it, or at least take a look around. No warrant needed if Sera said it was okay.

But if she didn't? *That means she's got something to hide.* Her own words, said about Shelly. It had seemed okay to say when it had been about Shelly.

Sera glanced behind her again, and then back at Dana.

'Do you want to come in?' she said, the possibility of something bright in the corner of her mouth.

And if she found something?

'No,' Dana said, sharp and stupid.

Whatever might have been possible was gone. Sera stood.

'Well then, what do you want?' she said, wiping her hands on her jeans.

'I came to ask you a favour,' Dana said, launching into the sales pitch she'd practiced in her rearview mirror. 'The community's morale is low and it's getting in the way of our work. The sheriff thinks that we need something to lift everyone's spirits. The editor of *The Declaration* heard about you—heard that you're back, I mean. She wants to do a story, take a photo of you and the sheriff together.' Dana paused. 'It would be for the good of the town.'

Sera's eyebrows drew together in vague disapproval. 'If you're resorting to distraction, you must be desperate. You really don't have any leads, do you?' she asked.

The sheriff had called Dana late, on her home phone. She'd been awake, considering whether it was worth knocking on Gary's sullen locked door. He had simply said, Shelly's clear.

Stan had called her immediately after. It had sounded as if he was driving. There was a shovel, Stan said. It was dusty. Nothing else? Nothing else relevant.

When Dana pressed him, he only added, She's got some weird hobbies.

Dana did not let her resolve falter. 'Sometimes people need some good news.'

Sera shook her head. 'I'd like to help you, but I don't think that this would be a good idea.'

'It's not to help me, it would be to help the town.'

Sera didn't smile, but somehow she looked amused. 'That's even less tempting.'

'Look,' Dana snapped, 'One of the only good men in this town could lose his job, and you might have the power to do something about it. I know it won't be easy, but if you can help, you should.'

In her anger she'd stepped much closer than she'd intended to Sera; too close. She couldn't get angry, not in her uniform.

Dana stepped back so quickly that it shot a sudden spike of pain through her ankle.

'Do you want to sit down?' Sera said. She sounded concerned, and Dana hated her for it.

'No,' Dana said, pinching her eyes closed to try and stop the dizzy colours spiralling behind them. 'Thanks.'

Sera took the pot off the fire and set it on the crate. 'If I do this for you, can you do something for me?'

'Depends.'

'I want to go home,' Sera said. 'To get some of my things. For old times sake. If I help you, will you let me in?'

Sera had been an unsentimental teenager, but grief and time changed a person. Logically, there was no reason why Dana should be suspicious of her request. 'Why can't your mom?'

'She's not my mom,' Sera said.

'Well, what about Michael,' Dana said. She could feel Michael's hand gripping her arm. She wanted to tell Sera about it. But there was no reason to. 'Or your cousin, Joe. You could ask him.' Sera had always seemed closer to her grown-up cousin than her two siblings.

'I'm asking you.' Her gaze was steady. A hair was caught in the corner of her mouth. She looked so much more real than she had in the station.

'I can't guarantee anything,' Dana said. 'But if you do the article, I'll try. Deal?'

Sera considered it for a moment. 'I'll do a photo. No questions.'

Dana nodded. A compromise, but good enough.

◆ ◆ ◆

When he came to school with his acoustic guitar, the Youth Pastor often told the students that god was a friend. The best friend they'd ever have, in fact. When he said this, Mrs Enckles nodded along, eyes sleepy and lips thin. In her muted long skirts and jumpers, she was nothing like any of her bright children. But, when the Youth Pastor left, she reminded them that god's friendship came with certain expectations.

When Dana thought of god, she thought of someone with large, obnoxious teeth, bleached white, no eyes. As for friendship, she didn't think of it much. Like god, it was something that other people did.

It became clear over time that Sera considered Dana an inconvenience, and an inconvenience who couldn't understand religion or maths.

As she crossed another answer out, Sera sighed heavily. God, how Dana had come to hate that sigh. Sera's black eyes flickered over the rest of Dana's answers, already hunting her next mistake.

The library was quiet, like always. Dana and Sera met three days a week, for an hour, after school. Sera had been tutoring her for around a month, with little to no perceivable improvement in Dana's ability to do sums or quote the Bible. Sera had never alluded to their previous meeting. Neither had Dana. In fact, Sera barely spoke. After she'd finished marking her work, Sera would go through it, methodically detailing each of Dana's mistakes. Then would teach her something else, give her more homework and say *goodbye* so formally that Dana half expected her to hold out a hand to shake.

Don't worry, Dana thought as Sera put a big red cross through an entire paragraph, I don't want to be your friend, either, so there's no need to work so hard at being a bitch.

♦ ♦ ♦

Dana kept her eyes on the road, so she couldn't really see or hear Sera sitting beside her, but every couple of minutes she couldn't help but glance over, as if to check Sera was still there.

'Look, before we get to the station, I just need to check a couple of details with you about your vehicle. It's just routine stuff we're asking everyone with bigger cars, but if you'd prefer to do it more officially, that's fine too.'

'About my car?' Sera said, surprised. 'Okay.'

She had arrived into town on the day of Ariel's funeral, in the early hours of the morning. She had been driving her Dodge Dynasty, pulling her trailer behind her. She did stop for gas at Dale's Gas Station, confirming Lynda's statement, and had been served by a moody teenage boy. Dirk, Dana assumed. Yes, she was sure it had been Dale's Gas Station, yes, definitely that date.

Dana pushed away the thought that she and Sera had been in the same place on the same day. If the bodies hadn't been uncovered, would she ever have known?

'Is there anything else you want to tell me?' she asked instead, unsure how to phrase what she really wanted to know.

Sera waited.

'Shelly Ackermann said she spoke to you the other day,' Dana continued. 'What did you two talk about?'

Sera kept staring out the window at the rush of trees zipping by.

'Nothing interesting,' she replied.

Dana's eyes ticked over to Sera, and then away.

'She doesn't like you very much,' Dana prodded.

'Well,' Sera said. 'Who does?'

There, Dana had to admit she had a point.

'I'm assuming these vehicles won't be registered to you,' she said.

Sera didn't look at her. 'I didn't steal them.'

Her tone was neutral, but somehow Dana felt reproached. 'I didn't say you did,' she said.

Sera glanced over at her, and then away.

'Sorry,' she said. She was wearing the same expression of barely hidden distrust as when she'd realised Dana had been driving a patrol vehicle rather than Brussels. 'Cops make me nervous.'

♦ ♦ ♦

It had been Mrs Trieger who'd organised it, but all the Ladies of the Lord had pooled their funds. It hadn't been cheap, she'd admitted to Sandy, but then what miracle was?

Sandy had smiled closed mouthed at the sudden obligation. If this didn't work, if her stupid body still couldn't get pregnant after they'd gone to all this trouble, she would just feel beyond guilty.

The Faith Healer was handsome, but not too handsome, like an actor in an infomercial. His broad hands covered the span of her naked stomach, while the Ladies of the Light stood around him in a circle holding hands.

'Say it with me, now!' he said. Leaning over Sandy, his voice was too loud. She could feel spit land on her cheek. 'God is good! God is good!'

'God is good,' they cried. Sandy screwed her eyes closed. 'God is good!

'Say it with me, now!' he said. 'Be gone, demons! God is good!'

'Be gone, demons!' Mrs Trieger's voice rose above the others. 'God is good, God is so good!'

Afterwards, they drank homemade lemonade, and the Faith Healer left with a *Lake in the Woods is EDEN!!!* sweatshirt, which he promised to mention on his radio show.

Dave knew all about the surprise, and he kissed her eagerly that night, and the next, his body like a golden bear.

If Sandy pushed herself to wonder who was the happier one in their marriage, she would have to admit that it was Dave. She tried not to hate him for this. Ultimately, he was just better at being happy; it wasn't his fault that had never come easily to her.

She lay in bed six months after she had been healed, another pregnancy test lax in her hand. Sandy didn't get it. Her body was certifiably holy. She hadn't drunk Coca-Cola in years.

The phone rang.

'Hi Sandy,' Shelly said. 'Still not pregnant?'

Sandy wasn't surprised she already knew. Shelly had a touch of something about her; she knew how to decode dreams. She had told Sandy months ago that something was coming.

A baby? Sandy had asked.

Something much bigger, Shelly replied.

'Still not pregnant,' Sandy confirmed.

'Great,' Shelly said. 'Let's have a girl's night. You bring the nail polish, I'll bring the moonshine and margarita mix.'

Sandy knew she should object, but Dave liked when she spent time with his sister. That's why she was doing it, she thought. For Dave.

'Okay,' Sandy said. 'Not too late. Yours or mine?'

'Come to the bar,' Shelly said. 'There's someone I want you to meet.'

♦ ♦ ♦

Dana pulled the files out of the drawer, her eyes flicking over the five faces. Sandra laughing on her wedding day, arm and arm with David. Anthony red faced and happy. Cathy holding hands with a small child. Jerome glowering. Ariel. When Dana thought of Ariel, it wasn't Ariel from her memory that she saw now, it was the girl in this high school photo.

Hilary had asked if they had any fresh photographs of the missing she could use in *The Declaration*. Dana had volunteered to double check, though she knew they didn't. It was weird acting professionally around Sera; she'd felt faintly embarrassed calling Sheriff Wormwood *sir*.

They only had one photograph of Jerome. His face was blunt, baggy black shirt and hair wet with gel, glowering at the camera from a patio swing chair, patterned with palm trees. He didn't much look like a devil worshiper. He just looked like some guy who used shower gel to wash his hair. A whole life and all that was left behind was a single unflattering photograph.

Back in the sheriff's office, Hilary had finished her debate with the photographer over the best lighting for the photo. Hilary had won, probably because she was *The Declaration*'s most senior member of staff—not to mention, the only one who got paid. The sheriff and Sera were behind his desk, hands clasped in a frozen handshake. The staging made it look as though Sera had won a prize, but both their faces were solemn.

'Why don't we try a smile?' Hilary said, beaming herself. 'And maybe something less formal? Sheriff, put your arm around her, go on!'

The sheriff and Sera regarded one another with mutual trepidation.

'You want us to…hug?' Sera asked.

'I don't think that's professional,' the sheriff said.

Their compromise, standing side by side, reminded Dana of a line-up: though Sera was slighter, she and the sheriff were not so different in height. Sera blinked under the flash of the camera.

'Oh, doesn't she look gorgeous?' Hilary said.

No one answered her. The photographer moved in closer. He'd be able to capture every eyelash sweeping across her cheek.

'Officer Fisher, why don't we get one with you?'

Hilary, Sheriff Wormwood, the photographer and Sera were all staring at her.

'Uh, no. Thank you.'

'But you were the one who found her, weren't you?' Her pen was poised. 'In the graveyard on Saturday?'

Dana looked at the sheriff. He had been clear that Dana's role in discovering the empty graves was to remain in the station. As far as everyone else knew, an anonymous phone call had tipped them off. Almost imperceptibly, he shook his head; he hadn't told her. Someone had blabbed.

Hilary was waiting for an answer.

'No,' Dana said.

Saying as little as possible seemed safest. It took a moment for Hilary to realise that Dana was finished speaking.

'Oh, my mistake, officer,' Hilary said. She looked at the sheriff, wide eyed. 'Where was Miss Enckles found?'

The sheriff didn't reply. He looked at Sera. Hilary was looking at her, too. Sera's face was bland and bored, as though all of this cop talk was going over her head.

'There's some things we don't know yet, Hil,' the sheriff said, when it was clear Sera was not going to speak.

'The people need answers, sheriff. About something.'

Sheriff Wormwood smiled tightly. 'Couldn't agree more,

Hilary. Why don't we go across to Cooper's and talk about it over a coffee?'

'Sorry,' Dana said to Sera once they'd left a few poses later. 'I told her no questions, and I didn't expect she'd need an hour-long photoshoot.'

Sera's face didn't change. 'I guess the camera loves me.'

Despite their saccharine rewrites after she'd disappeared, most people had thought that Sera was nice, quiet, smart: all codewords for boring. Only Dana had known what they hadn't—Sera was funny, if you listened.

She pushed the memories away. More what ifs.

'There's a couple of forms you need to fill out, and then I can let you go. We should have done it the other day, but we can do it now.'

'Forms?'

'Well, like I said, you don't have a legal identity right now. You need to get that reinstated. It's an administrative nightmare, but you might as well do it. Next time you, I don't know, want to vote, or get pulled over, might be handy to have an ID.'

'Who's going to pull me over? I'm pretty sure every cop knows who I am. If they don't, they will soon, now that I'm front page news.'

'Well,' Dana said, not looking at her. 'I mean, when you leave again.'

♦ ♦ ♦

'Why don't you like to be around other people?' Sera asked.

Dana almost laughed. Only Sera could ask *how come you don't have any friends?* in a way that seemed so polite and reasonable.

The truth was, Dana had realised by now that there was something sick inside her which other people could see and sense and knew to avoid, save themselves catching it.

Michael had been the exception. Maybe he'd wanted to save her. Or maybe he hadn't known who she really was until he'd touched her and come away with his hands soiled.

But Dana didn't say this to Sera. She didn't know how to, it wasn't something that she had the words to even think.

'Other people are boring,' she smirked, letting her gaze linger on Sera significantly as if to say, *including you*.

Sera didn't blink. 'Must be lonely,' she said. It wasn't said sympathetically, but like a clinical, potentially relevant, piece of data.

'As if you have any friends,' Dana snapped, surprised into being a teenage valley girl in a badly written movie.

Sera turned back to the page, her face blank. 'I have my family.'

Dana's cheeks flushed. Crazy mother, townie father. 'Lucky you,' she muttered.

Sera looked up at her. Her face wore an expression Dana didn't recognise. 'I'm sorry,' she said. 'That was rude.'

Dana felt hot and unsteady. The school counsellor had told her the five stages of grief were like stops on a journey, and some people spend longer at one stop than the others. *Anger isn't a bad thing, if you channel it.*

'What happened at your house that night?' Dana said. 'I don't remember.'

Sera's answer was studied. 'Michael broke up with you. You were drunk. I drove you home.'

'He was drunk too, though,' Dana said. 'Wasn't he?'

'No,' Sera said. 'Michael doesn't pollute his body.'

Dana had thought the same thing. Michael couldn't have been drunk, he wouldn't do that. But the taste of flat beer on her tongue, and his hands in her hair persisted. Dana tried to keep it hidden, but the memory just wouldn't die.

'Does your mom know you had that party?' she asked.

'Of course,' Sera said, turning the page. Dana couldn't put her finger on it, but something told her Sera was lying.

'Does she know you tutor me?' Dana asked. Sera stopped, hand in her text book. 'Does Michael?'

Her silence was her answer.

'Why do you bother?' Dana said. 'I'm not getting smarter. If I keep going this way, I'll flunk out by January. I know you volunteered.'

Sera smiled at her. Her smiles were bland, as if the intention was not to indicate happiness, but to appear unthreatening.

'I want to be your friend,' she said.

It was like being hot and cold all at once, the humiliation. How unfair it was, all these lies. She had never liked Sera, but she'd never thought of her as cruel before.

♦ ♦ ♦

Through the one-way window that connected the office to reception, Dana watched the back of Sera's head, bent over the form she was filling out. The sheriff had offered her his desk, but she'd insisted on sitting in the waiting area on the uncomfortable plastic seats. The form would take a couple of weeks to process, and then there were other legal hoops to jump through. All in all, the process of returning Sera legally from the dead could take months. Sera could be here for months.

Dana turned to the computer. She'd resent the information request with the plate numbers from the Dodge Dynasty and the trailer's updated description while Hilary had been getting set up. They probably hadn't processed yet, but when they did, she wanted to be the first to know.

Just because Sera wouldn't tell her where she'd been, didn't mean she couldn't find out.

There were two messages already. The Dodge's last registration was listed as ten years ago, Colorado Springs. There was no information about it being sold, so little to suggest how it came into Sera's hands. Dana took down the address and contact details of its last registered owner, anyway.

The other message was from a police department in Texas. A trailer matching that description and VIN had been reported as stolen six years ago, from a coastal town full of retirees and palm trees. The officer was looking for it in connection with a more recent cold case, a breaking and entering. Matching prints had been found at both scenes.

Shit.

She clicked on reply. Her hand hovered over the keyboard. She should pass whatever she knew on to them. Maybe she could learn more about Sera in the process.

She had to. It was her duty.

There was a raised voice in reception. The sheriff was back. He was standing in front of Sera, who had stood up too, but still had her back turned, so Dana couldn't see her face.

Dana let go of her gun. She didn't remember reaching for it. Her heart was still pounding. She had to pull herself together.

'What's going on?' she said, walking in between the two of them. Sera's face was calm, but her body was tense, her eyes focused on the sheriff as though he was a threat. The sheriff's mouth was in a tight line.

'Everything is under control, officer. Why don't you get Miss Enckles a glass of water?'

'I don't want a glass of water,' Sera said, 'I want you to respect my legal right to silence.'

Sheriff Wormwood spread his hands, as if to show they were empty. 'I sincerely apologise. I was just making small talk.'

'Like hell,' Sera said.

'I apologise. Perhaps you'd be more comfortable answering questions from Officer Fisher?'

Sera turned to Dana. 'If you brought me here to question me, just say so.'

Dana thought of the message she'd just read, the unanswered questions, her voice that night in the graveyard, her muddy shoes. She could no longer ignore the fact that by not at least considering the possibility that Sera was a suspect, she was not doing her job.

'No, I didn't,' Dana said, much more certain than she felt. 'I can drive you back now. The paperwork can wait.'

The sheriff opened his mouth to say something, but Sera replied before he could.

'I'll finish this, then let's go.'

Sheriff Wormwood's eyes flicked back and forth between the two of them. Dana kept her face business-like, trying to tell him somehow, *I'm on your side.*

He left them in reception, silent except for the humming of the vending machine.

♦ ♦ ♦

Once they were near the entrance to the clearing, Dana pulled over to the side of the road. Sera unbuckled her seatbelt but didn't get out. Sera had thanked her at the station. Dana hadn't replied: she wasn't sure she wanted to be thanked. They'd both been silent since. Dana couldn't think of a single thing to say. It was surreal to think that they'd been best friends. That once, she'd known Sera's face as well as her own, and liked hers better.

'Something's bothering you,' Sera said. It wasn't a question. 'What are you thinking about?'

Reality had turned out better than her dreams. Sera wasn't dead, she wasn't hurt. She remembered Dana. She was here.

'Palm trees,' Dana replied, hands loose on the steering wheel.

Sera sighed. The familiar sigh.

Why wasn't it enough?

'When will you let me know about that favour?' she asked when it became clear Dana did not intend to elaborate.

Getting access to the Enckles' house seemed less likely than ever now, but Dana had promised.

'Soon,' Dana said. 'What did the sheriff ask you?'

Sera frowned. 'He can tell you himself. Nothing important.'

'You seemed pretty riled up.'

Sera looked at her hands. 'I just have to be careful.'

'Why? The sheriff is a good guy. He just wants to help you.'

Sera made a face that was both familiar and annoying.

'What?' Dana said.

'I forgot how small town you can be,' Sera said.

Dana stared. She realised then why Sera's eye rolling had seemed so familiar. It was the same face she'd made whenever Dana got the answer to some "easy" maths question wrong.

'What's that supposed to mean?'

Sera sighed. 'Just because someone is in a position of authority, doesn't mean you can trust them. Cops mess up people's lives all the time.'

Dana's cheeks felt hot. Sera was talking to her like a

child and didn't expect to be challenged about it. Things had changed.

'I don't trust the sheriff because he's a cop, I trust him because he's a good person. I'm not an idiot, Sera, but cops here aren't like big city cops. The sheriff is just trying to do what he can do to solve this case just like me, because, in case you forgot, I am a cop,' she said, 'And all I want to do is help. So yeah maybe I am *small town*. Unlike you, I haven't travelled. Maybe I should put my loved ones through hell so I can get a little life experience, too.'

Dana closed her eyes. She took a deep breath, hands clenching on the steering wheel. She had to stop losing her temper like this.

When she opened her eyes, Sera's face was still. Dana wished she could be that unaffected, wished that she could feel less.

'It doesn't matter. I looked up your vehicles. One of them was reported stolen, a department in Texas got in touch with us about it. I'm not going to tell the sheriff. I don't even know if I'm going to follow it up, yet.'

'Then why are you telling me about it?' Sera said.

Dana wanted to scream. Around Sera, she was an exposed nerve.

'Because you lied, Sera! I asked you if there was anything else I should know, and you lied to me. I'm beginning to understand why the sheriff is asking you questions.'

'You haven't been honest with him yourself,' Sera said.

The tables had been turned: Dana felt like she was the one being interrogated.

'No, I haven't been,' she said. 'Do you want me to change that?'

'No. At this point, it would jeopardise us both.' Sera said. She returned to her clasped hands. 'You didn't have to lie for me. I wouldn't have asked you to.'

Dana knew she should feel more conflicted, but her doubts earlier had been just that—doubts. If Dana told the sheriff that Sera had been there that night, he might do something he'd regret.

'Yeah, well,' Dana said. 'It's done.'

What she meant was, if your hands are bloody, so are mine. It wasn't always true. Dana had always liked herself the most when it was.

Sera smiled and hid it quickly.

'Don't leave, once this is over,' Dana said, the words tumbling out before she could stop herself. 'It's not too late to come home.'

Everything in Sera's body tightened, as if she'd been shot, or struck by lightning. Her fingers clumsily scrambled for the door handle, a blind spider trapped in a jar. The expression on her face stayed the same.

'What are you—,' Dana said, grasping Sera's forearm, *don't go*. 'What's wrong, Sera?'

Underneath her fingertips, she felt Sera's pulse pounding.

'I didn't dig up those graves, but the sheriff is right,' she said, pulling her stuttering arm out of Dana's hand.

'What do you mean, the sheriff is right?' Dana said, unbuttoning her seatbelt to follow. Out of the car, Sera turned back to look at her, cold.

'Just stay away, Dana,' she said. 'Stay away from us.'

♦ ♦ ♦

On the desk in front of Stan were manilla folders from the traffic violation records, stacked thick like pancakes. Before he'd even opened his mouth, she knew that his interviews hadn't turned up any leads.

'Didn't you already go through those?'

He shrugged, hair greasy, eyes hopeless, 'Could have missed something. Me and Deputy Boldry are going to comb through them one last time.' He tried to give her a smile. 'The sheriff sent everyone home for the night. You should head home, get some rest.'

So should he. But what was one more sleepless night?

Sheriff Wormwood was still in his office. His hands were laced together, and he was staring down at the flyer Martha Dorhamer had been handing out. "*What ELSE are they hiding?*" the garish red letters screamed, hovering over a picture of Anthony, and the one of Sera that had been on the missing person posters.

'We'll get there, sir,' she said, awkwardly. 'Something will turn up.'

He folded up the flyer and put it in his desk drawer without comment: Dana wondered if she had overstepped the line. 'What can I do for you, officer?'

Dana thought of the voice that night, the silver trailer, of the message from Texas, of Sera, of Sera, always of Sera. 'I just wanted to ask what you said to Sera earlier.'

He looked at her. 'I asked her if she was hiding something.'

Dana blinked. Of course, Sera was hiding something. That was just the way she was.

'Sheriff, I know the timing is odd, and Sera is—' Dana paused, '—difficult, but I really don't think she's involved in this. We should refocus our efforts to other suspects. I think it still may be too early to rule out Shelly Ackerman completely.'

'Shelly has an alibi and we've searched her premises. At this point to continue to consider her a suspect based on a pair of dirty hands would be not only illogical, but wrong,' he replied sharply. 'I never said Sera was a suspect.'

'I know that, sir,' Dana said. 'I just needed to say it.'

The sheriff leaned back in his chair. He crossed his arms, and considered her.

'I also told her that this situation was more dangerous than people realised, and that I think she knows that,' he said. 'I wasn't just saying that because I love the sound of my own voice. You know better than anyone what some people in this town are capable of.'

At once, Dana felt hyper-aware of the room she was standing in—the windowless air, the florescent light, the sharp sting of her own tired body—and as if she was somewhere else entirely, déjà vu of a dream. But she didn't know better, she didn't know what he was talking about.

'You mean the Enckles?' Sheriff Wormwood nodded. 'Sera's not like them. She never has been. She's a good person.'

His eyes were almost soft. It took her a moment to realise it was pity.

'People change,' he said. 'You don't know where she's been. I hope she's not involved in all this, but we can't just hope when it comes to police work. We have to know.' He stood and put on his wide brimmed hat. 'At the risk of sounding like a sanctimonious old man, let me give you some advice—there's usually more than one version of the truth. The trick is working out how to not pick the one that suits you.'

Dana didn't want to get it. 'What do you mean?'

There was a breath of mint, as the sheriff unwrapped a flat stick of gum. 'I mean, if you really think Sera isn't involved, find me some evidence about whoever is.'

♦ ♦ ♦

It was nearly midnight when she got through to someone at the phone company.

She had been surprised to discover that you didn't need a Judge's Order to access call records. Nyx was a business, so they were considered public information. Fucked up—that would be what Sera would think.

Maybe so, Dana thought, but it was convenient.

Request done, she put down the phone. Stan, asleep and drooling on traffic violations, twitched. She held her breath. A moment passed, and he didn't open his eyes.

He was still looking into vehicles. She hadn't mentioned the silver trailer. Sometimes, she convinced herself that she hadn't brought it up because it was a dead end, and just not worth mentioning. Other times, she knew that wasn't the reason.

She opened the drawer and took out the photo of Jerome. Something was tugging at her. Palm trees. Where had she seen those palm trees before?

The realisation hit her all at once. She'd seen that swing chair a thousand times, sat on it even, sipping lemonade on the Trieger's front porch.

Chapter Eleven

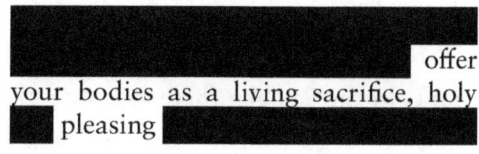 offer
your bodies as a living sacrifice, holy
▇ pleasing ▇▇▇

Romans 12

Solving a murder was not as easy as Gary had anticipated. A day of hard investigation had yielded little result.

He had started by collating all the information he could about Ariel's life, Ariel's family and Ariel's death. He'd arranged articles from *The Declaration* and notes on his wall with blu-tack. Ariel had watched him from the bed, immobile.

'Tell me what happened that night,' he'd asked. 'Talk to me, Ariel.'

She'd taken a breath in to speak; Ariel still only breathed when she had something to say.

'D-e-e-ad.'

He would have to solve this on his own.

During his four-hour shift at the gas station that evening,

he bought some coloured string, putting it through the till as he watched the clock. His intention was to connect relevant bits of information with the string: red would be for clues, blue for possible leads, green for things he didn't understand. Gary had considered the colour code system carefully, but as he cycled home, sailing through the night, he wondered if he should have bought gold stars instead.

That was the night Ariel learned to talk. The house was dark. In the kitchen there was one plate, a fork, a knife and an empty glass on the drying rack. Dinner for one. Dana hadn't been home, then.

When he walked upstairs, his dad opened his bedroom door, in his pyjamas. They'd shrunk in the wash, the leg ending just above his ankle, thin and shot through with blue veins. His dad had bad circulation: seeing his feet exposed gave Gary a pang of something between embarrassment and shame.

'Dad, it's late,' Gary said, 'you didn't have to wait up for me.'

'I wasn't,' his dad said. 'I can't sleep, as you've left your music on. I could have turned it off, if you hadn't locked your door.'

Gary tried not to let his panic show. Now he was listening, he could hear a faint noise coming his bedroom, though he wasn't sure it was music.

'Sorry, dad,' he said. 'I'll turn it off now, okay?'

'Good,' he said. Gary expected him to retreat back into his bedroom, satisfied. He didn't. 'Have you heard from your sister today?'

Gary felt guilty. Dana had left for work early the last two mornings. He hadn't seen her since they'd argued in the kitchen, hadn't heard from her except a missed call on his phone yesterday.

'No. I guess she's busy.'

His dad's mouth went into a firm, unhappy line. He nodded, and closed his bedroom door.

'Goodnight,' Gary said, under his breath.

Ariel was standing in the middle of his bedroom, looking at the wall.

'Ow 'or...ay ing dom om. Ay illbe un...'

Gary didn't want to stop her, but he didn't want to attract any more of his dad's attention. He shushed her until she whispered. When he lay down on the floor to sleep, he could still see her mouth moving above him, but she made no sound.

When he woke, her mouth still moved. He waited until he heard his dad leave for work, and then began to encourage Ariel to talk more and louder.

'Come on, Ariel,' he said, flapping his arms like wings, almost shouting himself. 'You can do it!'

'*Ay* ingdom come...

Thy ill be...'

It wasn't noise, but the words ran together, no barriers between them. This was real improvement. Once he'd realised what she was trying to say, he'd spoke the words along with her, although he only vaguely knew them himself.

'Thy kingdom come.

Thy will be done...'

The noises became words, though still stiff in their lack of inflection.

'As it is. In heaven.'

♦ ♦ ♦

Shelly, Jesus whispered in her ear, Are you ready to receive revelation?

She woke in a daze, bed wet beneath her. Jesus came to her in a thirteen-year-old dream; handsome face slack, hands bloody, his sweet-smelling hair still caught in her mouth and leaving the taste of chocolate. It was as if the atoms which formed her body had been rearranged and turned her to gold.

In service, legs swinging, she waited for Father Enckles to notice this change, to say in from of the whole town, this girl, my God, look at this girl.

'Who is ready to be saved?' he thundered, huge.

Me, she thought. Me, me, me.

He never called on her, and Jesus didn't come back. She waited for him. She waited for Joe Enckles to kiss her, and when he did, she waited to love him. She waited for her turn to play Mary in the Passion Play, she waited on Michael as he carried the polystyrene cross across the square. You should be in movies, he said. She waited for him to touch her bare knee under the table, waited for them to be alone together again. She waited for her father to die, waited to inherit the grocery store, waited for her brother David to pull himself together. When she reached for Joe's belt he said, I'm waiting and Shelly thought, Yeah, me too.

Something miraculous was bound to happen to her. It just hadn't happened yet.

It wasn't until the night of the Enckles' party that she realised what she'd been waiting for, and she couldn't help but feel cheated.

'Joe,' she asked, head in his lap the next morning, 'Am I a bad person?'

Early morning, when it was still half night, she'd crawled into his bed wearing nothing but a wet bikini and mud; her lips dry, mouth still tasting of shocky vomit.

Shelly hadn't touched it. She'd seen CSI. Never touch the body. She'd just looked for long enough to be sure. Open eyes and open mouth. As if it wasn't obvious.

She had never been in Joe's bedroom before. It was neater than she expected, and as clean as a guest room. It could have been anyone's room. Michael's was identical. Handing the contraband moonshine to Michael, he'd given her a wink, as if they were co-conspirators.

Why Dana Fisher? Why had Dana Fisher been chosen, not her?

His fingers, which had been stroking her hair as if she were a small, frightened animal, stopped at her question.

'No,' he said, reflexively, and then, 'Why do you ask?'

Shelly wanted to say, I'm not sure Jesus wants me anymore, and I don't know why.

'I don't know,' she said. Not knowing how to describe

dead eyes in a still warm face, or an alien abduction. It had all unfolded like the movies. Shelly loved the movies. She, too, wanted to be touched by an angel. 'I just feel like I did something bad.'

Joe's hand touched her cheek. She expected him to make a joke. He was always smiling. That's what she liked about him. That's what she hated about him too.

'Did something happen last night?' he asked, his face was serious and older. People were different in their own homes.

Shelly considered telling him the truth. But she knew what it was not to be believed.

His head snapped up then, at the sound of a car was pulling into the drive-away. His aunt and uncle weren't supposed to be home for hours, why were they so early?

'Sera,' Joe muttered. 'Stay here,' he said to her, all business. 'Don't come out. When you hear the windchimes, run out the front door.'

Shelly knew how to hide. She pulled on Joe's big dry boy's clothes and crouched by the door, eye to the crack. When the windchimes called from the back door, she crept down the stairs, bundled up bikini in her arms, and stole a pair of shoes.

She should have started running. Instead, she crouched by the side of the white wood house and watched through the window until the coast was clear. Then, she went back inside.

Shelly pressed her eye to the crack of the basement door. Five members of the family stood in a semi-circle. Michael was standing in the middle, facing them. He was naked.

Father Enckles was speaking, but she couldn't hear what

he was saying, couldn't see any of their faces except Michael's. It was blank.

Father Enckles pointed. Sera removed herself from the line and walked towards Michael, dull hair heavy, rope in her hands. She tied his hands behind his bare back.

Joes' fingers twitched. Shelly wished, very badly, that she could see the expression on his face.

Someone had taken the tarp cover off the devil's pulpit. It was a pool of water Joe's dad had built in the basement: 5 feet wide and miles deep. For baptisms and stuff, Joe had told her. You know.

Michael was walking towards it. Sera walked behind him. Surely not, Shelly thought. No.

Yes. She pushed him in. After a moment, his head re-emerged. He was treading water, she realised. His father spoke again, but she couldn't hear him. They all turned around to go back upstairs, except for Sera and Michael.

Shelly tore her eye away and ran.

As she cut across the grass towards the woods, she looked back. There was a flash of colour from an upstairs window, like a brightly scaled fish in a dirty river. Ariel was looking down on Shelly, hand pressed against the glass, reaching.

◆ ◆ ◆

Gary sat opposite her at the kitchen table, the recorder whirring as its tape span. He held a mug of coffee between his hands. Ariel looked at it. After her initial experimentation with eating, she appeared mildly disgusted by the appearance of food, but was interested in liquids. Gary paused the tape and made a second coffee. Ariel didn't drink it, just held the cup between her hands.

'So, I figured since you can't remember anything, I'd go from what I know about you and we can see if anything jogs your memory. These,' Gary had laid out photographs on the table, and he gestured to them now. 'Are all the main people I know about from your life. I'm not saying any of them killed you or anything, but got to start somewhere.'

He took her silence as acceptance.

Gary held up a photo of a smiling, middle aged couple. They were wearing almost identical sweatshirts.

'These are your parents. Pamela and Joshua Enckles. Joshua is dead now. He used to be the preacher. Pamela is a stay-at-home mom, I think. I guess she's an old lady now,' Gary looked at them, unsure of what to say. 'Your dad kind of has your eyes.'

Ariel spared them a glance and tapped her left index finger.

Gary picked up the next photo.

'This is your brother, and that's your cousin. So that's Michael—he's the mayor—and that one's Joe.'

Michael's photo had been easy to find online, but the only photo he'd even been able to find of Joe was a crowd shot from a school play, his face blurred and barely visible.

Gary looked at Ariel as she reached out to touch each photo individually. He repeated their names, slowly, as she tapped each one.

'Joe...Michael. Anything coming back to you?'

Ariel's eyes flicked disinterestedly over the boy's handsome face. Gary put it down and ploughed on to his next photographs. Ariel jerked her head from side to side.

'Alright,' he pushed them aside. 'This is your older sister, Sera. She disappeared ten years ago. Nobody knew where she was. I guess they thought she was dead, but she's back now.' He wasn't sure how to describe his encounter with Sera. Ariel didn't need to know everything. 'She seemed sad when I saw her.'

Ariel regarded Sera's high school photo. She was smiling with her mouth closed. Now he was looking at them side by side, Gary realised how little alike the two sisters were. Sera wasn't pale or pink like Ariel used to be. Her skin was warm, her hair thick and dark, eyes black. Even Ariel's eyelashes had been pale.

Ariel had stopped looking at the photo of Sera. She was looking at him, now, as if to say, What's next?

As if he were cutting a deck of cards, Gary spread the next four photos on the table with a flourish. The missing.

'Where is Dana?' Ariel asked.

'What?' Gary startled. He wasn't sure he'd ever heard Ariel speak so clearly. 'She's at the station, I guess.'

'There's no...photo. Was she a...main person in. My life?'

He wasn't sure what to say.

'How do you know that? I thought you couldn't remember anything.'

Ariel's eyes bored into him, alien and remote.

'There is a photo of me. Of us. Together.'

Gary thought he had misheard Ariel for a moment.

'Why did you go into Dana's room?'

Ariel's right shoulder switched in an approximate attempt at a shrug.

He gestured to the flush of photographs. 'What about these people, do you remember them? Sandra Ackermann. Jerome Smolinski. Cathy Copeland. Anthony Dorhamer. They're like you,' Gary laughed, nervously, 'Well sort of like you. They're missing.' The thought struck him suddenly. How had it never occurred to him before? 'Maybe they've come back, too!'

Nothing changed—her eyes didn't flicker, her breath didn't sharpen or shallow, her hands didn't clench. But yet, something invisible that had been there a just a moment ago was gone.

'No,' was all she said. 'No.'

Gary stopped recording after that.

He could get no response from Ariel for the rest of the day about the photos, or the crime scene, or why someone might have wanted to kill her. He turned to his wall and got out his string, and stood there with it mute in his hands, like a cat who didn't know how to play.

His dad got home at five PM that evening. It was Gary's turn to make dinner. Potatoes. Single melted cheese slices. Dana didn't come home. She didn't reply to Gary's text, either.

When Gary headed back upstairs to check on Ariel, she was lying in the same position as he'd left her in, eyes open.

She was sad, he realised.

He got it. Sometimes, he just wanted to crawl into bed and sleep for a year. Not like he wanted to die, but it was nice to think of taking a break from things. Go somewhere where you could just forget it all. Be someone else. Sleep was good for that. He wasn't sure Ariel could sleep, though; just live half-awake.

He sat on the bed beside her.

'Ariel, I know this must be hard but...the man—or woman—' Gary wasn't sexist, 'Who killed you, they might have done it to the others.' The missing. 'They could do it again. People could be in danger. Can you tell me anything else about what happened to them?'

There was no response. Gary shifted on the bed, yearning his body towards Ariel's face.

Gary took her silence as an answer.

She moved her mouth. He could smell her breath, a whisper of salt.

'What did you say?' he asked.

It wasn't until he put his ear by her mouth that he heard her.

'Because she's like me,' Ariel was murmuring, as if she were talking in her sleep, 'She's like me.'

Chapter Twelve

> I met my wife when I was working a two-week supply job. Neither of us belonged to the city, and we were both alone. Those were my drifting years. I was not a drifter by choice, but circumstance. My family had immigrated when I was a child, we had no roots. Rebekah was more than a wife, more than the mother of my children: she became home.
>
> *Lake in the Woods: A Complete History of an American Miracle*, Francis Fisher

To get up the steps that led into the church, Dana had to manoeuvre around the stacks of bouquets, her feet scattering the silver tealight shells like empty beer cans. When she got to the door, a flyer had caught on the sole of her boot like toilet paper; *"What ELSE are they HIDING?"*

Though she saw the church every day at work, she hadn't been inside since she was a small child. It reminded her of school; white walls, rows of wooden pews facing towards the boxy pulpit. Handsome faces we carved into its white wood.

Not Jesus: no beards, and they weren't mournful enough. Dana's biblical knowledge pretty much ran dry after that, but she guessed by the halos encircling their heads that they were meant to be angels.

The pews were empty, except for one bent and dull blonde head.

'Hi, Mrs Trieger,' Dana said. 'I hope I'm not disturbing you.'

Mrs Trieger looked up. She was tired and pale, but when she saw it was Dana, she smiled.

'Hello, dear,' she said, with a serenity that set Dana's teeth on edge. 'Come for some peace at last?'

Dana slid into the pew. 'I haven't come to pray, if that's what you mean.'

Despite the early morning light streaming through the high windows, the room was cold, the seat hard.

'You don't have to pray,' Mrs Trieger said, still smiling. 'I don't always pray. Sometimes I just come here to have some time with my thoughts. God is a good listener, even if you don't have anything to say.' She pointed at the baby blue sweatshirt she wore today. *GOD PROVIDES.*

Dana didn't know how to respond to that without being rude. She took the photo of Jerome out from her pocket. 'I wanted to talk to you about this.'

Initially, Dana had considered the possibility that it was a coincidence, but when she'd compared the chair on the porch to the one in the photograph that morning, she'd found a small stitch on the headrest matching one faintly visible beside Jerome's head. Still, the chair could be second hand. There could be any number of explanations as to why the last known photograph taken of Jerome had put him on her neighbour's porch; they didn't necessarily know each other at all, or well.

But when Mrs Trieger looked at the picture, her placid smile froze in place.

'What did Phil tell you?' Mrs Trieger said. She looked away, and then back again.

'I haven't spoken to him.' Dana said, the *yet* unsaid. 'How did you know Jerome Smolinski?'

Mrs Trieger looked down at her lap, her hands smoothing her skirt, over and over. The more anxious Mrs Trieger appeared, the more anticipation Dana felt.

'Will it help you recover his body?' Mrs Trieger said the words so quietly, her lips barely moved. 'If I answer your questions?'

Dana's heart thrilled, but she tried not to let it show.

'Yes, but I can't guarantee that what you say can stay confidential.'

Mrs Trieger looked at the wooden faces carved into the pulpit, as if they would open their mouths and tell her what to do. Dana wanted to shake the secrets out of her, but she knew she had to wait.

She nodded as though she'd reached her decision. She turned back to Dana.

'Jerome was my son,' she began.

Lena had been young when she got pregnant. Too young,

and too unmarried. Her parents had been disappointed, of course: she'd never find a husband, now. She dropped out of school and stayed at home all day doing housework with her mother, who couldn't bear to look at her without being moved to tears. Dana had to understand, things were different then.

Lena never wanted to have a baby so young, she wanted to get back to her life, she wasn't ready. So, her family spoke to Father Enckles and asked him to adopt the baby.

Why Father Enckles?

That's what you did in times like that.

But why would he adopt him?

Because he loved children.

Father Enckles knew a mother who couldn't have children, a great sorrow. When the baby boy was born, he was given to his new family and took their name.

'Things were different then,' she repeated. 'The law wasn't so strict about that kind of thing.'

Dana thought that wasn't entirely true, but she said nothing.

With the knowledge that he'd been adopted, Lena went back to school. She forgot. She met Phil. They fell in love, got married and tried for a baby. And then tried again. And again. Mysterious ways.

It was a sign. Jerome was a teenager by then, and not the cute puppy his family had adopted any more. He wouldn't go to church, he wouldn't go to school, he stayed out all night and came home high. He bit, and Father Enckles thought he could do with good influences.

'I don't blame his parents. He was difficult. He had mood swings, like a red mist descending on him. It reminded me of my father. Sometimes I wonder…' she shook her head. 'But he could be sweet, when he wanted to be.'

They weren't family, Mrs Trieger stressed, not really. Jerome didn't like Phil very much, but still, they would have him over for dinner every couple of months, and they gave him money. Just at Christmas, at first, but Jerome wasn't at school anymore and couldn't hold down a job, or a place to live; he slept on couches and, when he couldn't do that, slept in a tent in the woods.

'Who did he stay with?' Dana asked.

'His friends. If you can call them that,' Mrs Trieger said. 'They came and went so quickly, that I can't remember them now. Jerome didn't make things easy for people who wanted to help him.'

Dana wondered why Mrs Trieger hadn't taken Jerome in—their house was more than big enough—but found she didn't want to hear the answer.

'I want you to know that all of this is in service of the investigation, not my own curiosity,' Dana said. 'Before Jerome died, did he mention anything that seemed at all strange, or unusual?'

She had purposefully avoided specifying how Jerome had died, but Mrs Trieger still looked around the empty church, as if someone would overhear. Suicide was such a dirty word, even unsaid it was violent.

'Not that I remember, but we weren't seeing much of each

other at the time. He had the job at the school,' Mrs Trieger explained. 'He always came around more when he was hard up, so I didn't see as much of him when he was working. I thought, maybe, he was settling down. I wish I'd known…' her hands were shaking again, fingers twisting in her lap, 'I knew he had…darkness. But I never thought he could do something like that.'

Mrs Trieger's sobs were small. Dana patted her on the arm. There. There. She didn't know what else to do but wait for her tears to stop. While Mrs Trieger cried, Dana tried not to think about it too hard. She found she could keep going if she did it half-awake and drifting.

After a few minutes, when Mrs Trieger's breathing had evened out and she had dried her cheeks with the tissue Dana had given her, she asked her final question.

'One last thing—I was told that Jerome was involved with a—another man.' Dana had almost said boy, but she corrected herself quickly, already on thin ice. 'Do you know anything about that?'

Mrs Trieger tensed. Much more, Dana noted, than she had before.

'What does that have to do with—?' Mrs Trieger started. 'I mean, what are you asking, exactly, dear?'

The embarrassment spread from Mrs Trieger to Dana, but she plowed ahead regardless. 'Well, did he mention anyone special in his life?'

Mrs Trieger nodded again, her voice pressed flat, as if saying it quietly would make it less true. 'There was someone.

A man.' After a moment, she added, reluctantly, 'He wanted us to meet.'

Someone serious, then, and decidedly less seedy. A boyfriend. This was it. Dana was so close. She tried to keep her voice even. 'And did you?'

Mrs Trieger took a deep breath, as if she was going to say something, but nothing came. Her hands were clasped so tight that her knuckles were white.

'Mrs Trieger?'

Her face was like a birds', fine bones trembling inside, an earthquake making its way to the surface.

'Well I,' she looked up at the ceiling again. A tear slid down her face, dripping off her chin. 'When he told me he was—the way he was, I asked him to stop coming to the house.' Her voice cracked. 'It was the last time I saw him. A few months later he did that to himself.'

Dana did not comfort her.

After a silent moment, Mrs Trieger wiped her face and began to babble.

'I tell myself I couldn't have changed it. Not through praying or pleading. He was always meant to be unholy. It's all in the blood,' Mrs Trieger looked at her, as if it had been Dana who berated him. 'It wasn't his fault.'

'How do you know he was unholy?' Dana asked her. Can you smell it on someone? She wondered. Is it in the way they walk?

'Father Enckles told me,' Mrs Trieger said. 'I begged him to adopt him, but he wouldn't. He wasn't right. My boy couldn't help it. It was my fault, for conceiving him sinfully, out of the light of the LORD.'

'What about Ariel?' Dana said, pressing a fingernail into Mrs Trieger's wound. 'She's unholy now too, isn't she? In hell, just like Jerome. And she was conceived in the light.'

Mrs Trieger's eyes narrowed, guilt becoming cruelty.

'Not from what I heard,' she said. 'Don't you know, dear? They say they're all adopted, charity cases that Joshua took in from godless homes. Save the Mayor, of course.'

'Sera and Ariel are adopted?' Dana asked. 'Who says?'

Dana knew she should be surprised, but she felt only dull recognition; as if she'd already known this fact, but had somehow forgotten.

'Why everyone,' Mrs Trieger said, eyes shining with vindication. 'You'd know all about it if you came to Ladies of the Light's Thursday meetings, dear.'

Dana stood up and straightened her trousers. Time to go.

'Jerome was fired from the school,' Dana said. 'Not long after he told you he was gay. Correct?'

Mrs Trieger stared up at her.

'I don't know anything about that, dear,' she said.

But Dana could see it. Mrs Trieger twisting the curled telephone wire around her fingers, hissing an anonymous tip from a concerned parent down the receiver to Principal Graham.

'Yes you do,' Dana said.

♦ ♦ ♦

Ariel was the first one to catch a bite and it happened quick. A demure tug on her line as if the fish had wanted her to know it was ready; then it was there, flopping around on the bank of the lake. The three of them stood over it. First, they'd been excited, but now they were struck dumb.

'What do we do with it now, Dana?' Sera asked.

Dana had assured Sera that she knew how to fish—her name was Fisher, after all—but she'd done so on the assumption that they weren't actually going to catch anything.

'Kill it, obviously,' she replied. She picked up a rock and handed it to Ariel. 'Here. Use this.'

The rock was much larger in Ariel's hands than it had been in her own. Ariel looked at the rock, and then back down at the fish. Dana wondered if she was going to cry. If it was Gary, he probably would have cried.

Sera was frowning. Dana prepared herself for a lecture. *Ariel's just a kid. This is disgusting.*

'Are you sure that's how you're meant to do it?' Sera said. 'I think we should break its neck. Faster.'

She spoke with authority but made no move to touch the fish. It was still making slippery movements on the grass, though with less gusto. If the hook hadn't already killed it, it would be dead soon enough. Dana wasn't sure at all about the rock. It might crush the guts. She didn't know much about fishing, but she knew that would be bad.

Ariel moved, rock still in her hand. She bent down and

put it back on top of the grass where it had come from. She placed it gently, as though she didn't want to disturb the fish, nearly still now. She wrapped one hand around it's body. A thin line of blood ran from between her fingers, down the outside of her hand; on the back of it she'd written CALL HELEN. Dana shivered. Fish had cold blood. Dana used to think that girls together had to do certain pink and glittering things. It was nice to be with other girls who were a little alien, who weren't afraid to get dirt underneath their fingernails.

Ariel threw the fish back in the water. It sailed in the air, still and lifeless like a skipping stone, before it hit the surface with a *pat*. Dana thought it was dead. But as it sank beneath the water, it sprang to life, wriggling with vigour and diving deeper. Ariel watched with a smile. Beside her, Sera frowned.

'I don't want to fish anymore,' Ariel said. 'I'm thinking of becoming vegetarian.'

◆ ◆ ◆

Dana climbed into the deep end. There was a drop from the bottom of the steps to the floor, at least five feet. As she landed, she hissed in pain: her ankle was still tender.

Teenagers always needed to scream, and it was only down here that the lunchtime carnage in the hallways drifted away. She'd come to Lake in the Woods High School for the students records from 2004 and 1997; the year Jerome had worked at the school and the year he graduated.

If what Stan had said about Jerome having a relationship with a freshman was true, his name was on one of those lists. But if it had been a lie Mrs Trieger told in petty cruelty, Dana might never find the guy.

The tiles were white and blue—the shade of blue that was reserved for swimming pools. Up close, it wasn't clean. There were pockets of dirt in the corners, empty beer cans, cigarette butts and smeared ash. It was probably a good place not to get caught.

She'd thought that she'd solved something, but she wasn't sure what exactly. If the missing had all been adopted, sure, that was a connection, but how likely was that? How many out-of-wedlock babies could one town hold?

What she'd taken for a beer can was spray paint; Dana nudged it with her foot, and it rattled away. The tiles had been scrubbed enough to remove the message, but not enough to get rid of the grey stain it had left behind.

Could the secret adoption of Jerome link him to the other missing? She knew from Sandra Ackermann's medical records that she had lost several pregnancies before her doctor advised her to stop trying. Theoretically, she and David could have been considering adoption before she'd killed herself.

Dana had checked Ariel's medical file on the drive over. She didn't know what she was looking for—didn't know what an adoption would look like on paper, much less a secret one.

There was nothing, and Mrs Trieger had offered no proof. Yet, the more Dana thought about it, the truer it seemed. Put

Sera beside the Pamela and Joshua Enckles, and it was almost obvious.

'I told you to stay out of there!'

The janitor appeared, looking over the edge of the pool down at her. Frank. He'd worked there before she was a student, and he'd been an old man then.

'Hi, Frank.' As she looked up at him, she had the feeling that she was underneath invisible water. 'Just me. Mind if I ask you a few questions?'

♦ ♦ ♦

Being friends with Sera was a delicate balancing act and questions were often the tipping point. The wrong question made Sera's eyes go blank and her answers vague: she'd make an excuse to leave, and they might not see each other for a couple of days. Dana had learned through trial and error which subjects could be pursued and which were to be avoided at all costs, but she wasn't sure yet which category her current avenue of thought belonged to.

'Come on, it's not a big deal.' She grinned. 'I'll tell you mine if you tell me yours.'

Sera rolled her eyes. They were sitting on the shore, the fishing lines abandoned and limp in the water. Dana had finished her first can of Coca Cola and was halfway through her second: Ariel hadn't wanted hers, or the candy Dana had bought.

I can't, she'd said. It isn't holy.

'Please tell me what I have done to lead you to believe that I care?' Sera held her own warm can loosely in her lap. 'I only ask so I can make sure to never do it again.'

Dana wiped the sugar from her mouth. She'd been melting a marshmallow on her tongue, feeling it liquify.

'Yeah right. I know you really want to know, so here goes. Billy Madden's birthday party. We were nine, maybe? Someone suggested spin the bottle. It was...' she thought back to his lukewarm paddling pool, the damp press of intimate flesh and the paper plate of folded white fondant which made her sick after. '...wet. And that's about all I can say for it. He was very into tongue.'

Sera wrinkled her nose in disgust, looking out at the water where Ariel was swimming. Her legs, exposed under her summer dress hiked up at her hips, had already gone light brown. The sun suited her.

'It sounds like he was too...into it.'

'Yeah,' Dana laughed, delighted. 'Way too into it.'

'Do you like it?' Sera asked.

Sera was still looking out at the water. Ariel was further away now. Dana could hear her splashing, but she'd swam too far out now to be seen. 'What?'

'I mean when you're doing that. Do you like it?'

The bag of candy was empty. Dana ran her finger along the plastic seem at the bottom, catching stray sugar underneath her nail. 'I guess? It depends. Some guys really don't know how to do it, so mostly it's just gross.'

'Did you—did my brother...is that what you did?'

Dana's insides felt cold, like she'd swallowed an ice cube and it was stuck in her throat. Every time she thought she'd forgotten, something came out of nowhere to remind her.

'Did your brother what?' Dana lolled her own tongue out of the side of her mouth and waggled it. Sera frowned. Dana grinned. 'That's pretty twisted, Sera, he's your brother you know.'

'No,' Sera snapped. 'I mean, did you and my brother kiss? Or more?'

Dana expected Sera to be blushing. She wasn't.

'I don't want to talk about it,' she said. She wished she'd never brought the whole thing up. Only, a couple of weeks ago she'd seen some freshman making out, hands wandering, heavy petting, all of it. Sera had been across the hallway, watching the two with the strangest expression on her face. She looked curious, but disgusted, like it was a nature documentary or two cows in a field. She hadn't known that Dana could see her.

Sera took a large sip of Coke and turned to look at her.

'I didn't mean to make you uncomfortable,' she said.

'I'm not uncomfortable,' Dana said. 'You've never done it, have you? Kissed anyone, I mean.'

Dana only caught the tail end of Sera's expression.

'No.' Sera's voice was still. 'No. I've never kissed anyone.'

Sera said the word gingerly, as though she knew what it meant, but was uncertain how it was pronounced. Dana's gleeful thrill at getting one over her turned into sick regret. She wanted to snatch the words back from the air.

'Well, like, don't worry about it,' she said. 'It's fine. I mean it's not mandatory. It's not like there's an age limit on when to have your first kiss, and mine was gross anyway, so like, nothing to be jealous of or whatever. I bet you'll kiss tons of people whenever you go to college.'

She should wait for the right person. She was too good to waste her first kiss.

Sera looked out over the water. 'I'm not allowed to do that.'

'Do what? Go to college, or use tongue?'

Sera turned to look at her. She wasn't teasing now. 'I'm not allowed to touch anyone like that. None of us are.'

It took her a moment to realise that Sera didn't mean the two of them *us*. She meant the *us* that included Sera, her parents, Ariel, Joe and Michael. The *us* that would never include her.

'Oh, of course. You're waiting for marriage.' Dana laughed, fingering the hem of her denim cut-offs. 'No wonder you think I'm disgusting.'

'Not until marriage,' she said finally. 'I mean, not ever. We can't do it ever.'

Dana squinted at her, confused. 'What do you mean?'

They'd talked about something else then. Dana knew that for sure. But she couldn't remember what. When she tried to remember, it was all black, until,

'Stay here,' Sera said. 'I'll be right back.'

Ariel swam back. The orange sun was setting behind her, and she became a shadow. When it got shallow enough to walk, Ariel strode onto shore, dripping and freckled, and Dana felt overwhelmed by the Enckles all of a sudden.

'Hey Dana,' she said, grinning. There was something in her hand. It was an animal. It was a fish. Or, sometimes, Dana thought it might have been a bird. Whatever it was, it was still moving. 'Come here for a second.'

♦ ♦ ♦

He kept his head down, got the work done, was the most positive thing Frank had to say.

'What about when he left?' Dana pressed.

According to his employment records, Jerome had quit after only four months. No one in the school office had even remembered him.

They were in the maintenance supply closet, Frank sitting on an upturned metal bucket. There was a shovel leaning on the side of the wall.

'It seemed pretty sudden,' Dana continued. 'Did anything prompt it?'

The creases of Frank's face gave him a permanently cross look: she tried not to take it personally.

'Smolinski didn't quit. They told him not to come back. My bet is some teacher complained about him sleeping here.'

'He slept in the school? Why?'

'How should I know? Like I said, he kept his head down. Wasn't exactly what you'd call a conversationalist.'

Frank agreed to show her where Jerome had lived. It was

in the basement, near enough to the pool to get a shower in the morning, far enough that Frank would be the only person to come across him by accident. He pointed to a narrow space, just about wide enough for two people to squeeze into. Not a room as much as a burrow, dark and safe.

Dana filled in the blanks herself. Rent for a single person was expensive in Lake in the Woods. She knew: she'd looked. The woods were too cold to camp in winter and, from the sounds of it, Jerome didn't have a home to go to for Christmas.

There was nothing left of Jerome's home except for spots of hardened blu-tac and markings on the walls. She brushed her fingers over them. The graffiti had been scraped on with a small, sharp object. Most were just rows of lines, like a prisoner counting down the days. There were mindless patterns, a penis and one elaborate tree, the roots gouged deeply into the brick. It was smooth under her fingertips, the edges softened with time. Song lyrics. Do not be afraid.

Near the bottom, where she imagined Jerome might have slept, she found a 'J' with a heart carved around it like a protective moat. She pulled away her hand with surprise. Jerome had not created these carvings: his lover had.

Dana stayed there for fifteen minutes, but there was nothing else to find. Frank had been ordered to clear the place when he'd 'quit'.

He hadn't thrown out everything, though. Jerome's things were in a cardboard box at the back of his closet, covered in dust. It was hers: no one else had come for it.

'Did he say where he was going to go?' Dana said. 'He was fired in January, right? It would have been too cold to camp.'

'No. I loaned him twenty bucks. You don't get severance pay when you quit.' Dana wondered if his frown lines deepened, or if it was in her imagination. 'Never did get that money back.'

Dana collected the records from the administrator and left. As she pulled away from the school's parking lot with the feeling of cutting class early, the screen of her phone flashed. Stan.

'What's up?'

'"What's up?"' Stan said. 'Where have you been? Did you forget about the briefing?'

She'd lost track of the time. 'Shit. Is he mad?'

'No,' Stan said, 'Because I covered for you. Told him your ankle was worse and you had to see my dad. Where are you? We still need to locate these vehicles.'

'I know, I know,' she said. 'Look, can you cover for me for another couple of hours?'

There was a pause. 'Why?'

'It's hard to explain. Can you just cover me for little bit longer? It's important.'

Stan didn't answer right away. 'Are you alright?' he said.

'Can you cover me, yes or no?' Dana said.

The silence afterwards stung.

'Sure,' Stan said slowly. 'As long as you can give me a good reason. Not now, but soon.'

Dana wondered if she should apologise.

'Thanks, Stan. Oh, and I'm waiting for a fax. Can you check if it's come through?'

There was another stilted pause. 'What's it about?'

'Well, it probably won't go anywhere,' she said, 'But it's public information, so I figured we might as well check Nyx's phone records.'

She tried not to worry about how long the silence stretched on for.

'Dana,' Stan said. 'Does the sheriff know you requested those records?'

'No,' she said. 'I'll tell him if it goes anywhere.'

'Okay. I think you should tell him either way.' He paused, as if he was thinking about what he was going to say next. 'We could really use you here, you know.'

Dana didn't know what to say. Stan sighed, the phone crackling with the hushed electric. 'Be careful,' he said, then hung up before she could say goodbye.

Shoving her phone into the glove compartment, Dana tried not to think too hard about how many people had told her to be careful recently. The box Frank had given her was on the passenger seat.

Frank had been hiding something. Could be information. Or it could just be regret that he hadn't done more to help Jerome. The way he'd brought up the money reeked of defensiveness. It sounded to her like Jerome had asked to stay with him, Frank had said no but had given him the cash out of guilt.

Maybe he'd been disgusted to find out about Jerome's sexuality when he'd cleaned out his squat. Inside the box, she found pictures of pretty-faced men, carefully cut out from the kind of magazines which came with a free lip gloss. Frank could have been worried that Jerome had been making a pass at him.

There wasn't much else in the box. An insulin pen, stiff with age. No doubt paying for the privilege of diabetes had been a financial strain. Hand knitted socks with holes in the toes. A broken compass. A slim, hardback book of Greek mythology, with a goat headed god on the cover. Maybe this was how the devil worshipping rumour started; she'd certainly found nothing to suggest any truth behind it. Other pictures, these from travel magazines. Snowy mountains and sunsets that said there is another possible world.

At the bottom of the box were clothes. A pair of jeans, a boiler suit to match the one Frank wore. Inside the pocket was a card with a hanged man on it, and a swiss army knife. She ran her thumb along its edge, thinking.

Nothing in the box told her who his lover was. Frank had been genuinely bewildered when she'd asked if Jerome was friendly with the students; maybe the whole thing was a ghost chase. Someone had stumbled into his nest, seen the pictures on the wall, and the rumour mill had started. But what about Mrs Trieger? He'd told her about someone: it had cost him too much to be a lie.

What about Frank? He'd kept ahold of Jerome's things for a long time, that alone was enough to make him a candidate.

Though, if the men in the pictures were anything to go by, he was too old and hairy to be his type.

She laughed. It was pathetic: she was trying to think as if she was him. As if a box of scraps was enough to reconstruct a whole life.

She pushed her thumb into the knife edge. Her flesh bounced back whole. It was completely blunt.

She'd assumed that the 'J' on the wall had been for Jerome, that his lover had carved it. But what if Jerome had carved it himself?

Dana pulled out the list of the 1997 graduating class. She'd check the 2004 records too, but she had a hunch she wouldn't need to.

There had been one other boy in the class that year with a name beginning with 'J': Joe Enckles.

♦ ♦ ♦

It felt so bold, to be walking across the white porch of the Enckles' house in her bare and dirty feet. Sera didn't want them to stay for long, or even go inside.

'Just going to get you cleaned up,' she said, more than once, until it sounded like, and then leave.

Dana sat on the white wood steps, and Sera brought towels to clean the blood from her hands and the mud from her feet.

'I've never killed anything before,' she confessed. Sera sat at the step below her, examining a splinter in the heel of

Dana's foot. Sharp tweezers were in one hand, and Dana's ankle in the other.

Sera toggled her foot slightly as she replied, 'I know.' Finding the tip of the splinter with the tweezers, she warned, 'This will hurt.'

Dana hissed as Sera began to pull it out. It didn't hurt that much, but the feeling was strange and unfamiliar, like touching the roof of your mouth with your tongue. Dana wanted to pull away, but she kept her foot still.

Finally, Sera held the shard of wood up to her face, pinched between the tweezers, examining it. It was about the size of a matchstick, and sodden with blood. Her foot still held up by the ankle, Dana's back was braced against the step. In the steady twilight, crickets chirped. Sera was a star, Dana thought. A cold star.

Sera's eyes flickered back to Dana, surprise passing over her face like the fluttering wings of a rare bird. As if she'd forgotten herself, forgotten that anyone was watching.

Gently, Sera lowered her foot back flat on the white wood step, but she didn't take her hand away.

'I'm sorry you got hurt,' Sera said. 'I shouldn't have left you.'

'It's alright,' Dana said. Sera's fingers, curled around Dana's ankle, were warm and dry, like the towel she'd used to dry Dana's feet with. Her words came out clumsily, as if they didn't fully belong to her. 'It wasn't your fault.'

In the dark, the whites of Sera's eyes reflected the light from the house, a lure in the water. There was something wrong, something she didn't want to say. Dana wanted to pull it into reality, examine it, so she could work out how to fix it.

A car turned the corner, the winding dark driveway. Sera let go of Dana's ankle. She stood up, bolt straight.

Mrs Enckles got out of one side of the people carrier, ashy bob as neat as ever. A man who must have been Sera's father got out of the driver's seat. Father Enckles. A small man. He didn't look like Sera, or Ariel, though she could see Michael in his smile: all tooth.

Sera introduced them. Car trouble, Dana had pulled over for help. A bandage.

Mr Enckles praised Sera for helping out her classmate. Dana smiled and thanked them all for their hospitality, as if Sera's mom and dad had been there to help, as if they'd invited her to stay for dinner.

Dana looked behind her as she walked back to Brussels, but the family were already inside. On the porch was a smudge of blood where her foot had been.

♦ ♦ ♦

Martha Dorhamer was at the front of the crowd, a copy of this morning's issue of *The Declaration* clutched in her hand. Dana could almost taste the metallic tang of panic on the air.

Coops was by the door of the station. Mel, behind him, looked as if he wasn't sure what side he should be standing on. Coops' arms were spread wide, and he was wearing what he probably thought was a congenial smile. If he was trying to placate the crowd, it wasn't working. A sandy head caught her eye: David Ackermann was towards the back of the group. She wondered if she should step in; she wasn't any good at that stuff, but if they'd sent Coops and Mel out they must be ready to try anything. Martha thrust a copy of the paper in Mel's chest, and Dana caught sight of the headline.

FAKE DEATH SHOCKER: ENCKLES' SISTER QUESTIONED

The office was empty, and the sheriff's door was shut. Dana closed the door to the evidence locker behind her and went out again through the fire exit. Stan was there. When he saw Dana, he straightened up.

'There you are,' she said, as if she'd been looking for him instead of leaving.

'The sheriff wants to talk to you,' he said. He'd smoked down to the filter.

It had taken her much longer than she'd expected. If Stan hadn't been able to cover for her, she'd understand.

'What did you tell him?'

He dropped the butt and crushed it under his boot. 'That you were with me, trying to find the right tape from Lynda. The one you had was from the wrong week.'

She'd forgotten about that. It seemed so unimportant now. 'Thanks. What the hell did Hilary write?'

Backwards, Stan kicked the fire door and went back inside. Dana followed him.

'See for yourself,' he said, handing her *The Declaration*.

It was one of the photographs of Sera standing beside the sheriff, stoic. Dana skimmed the article. *Person of interest. Statement taken. Whereabouts unexplained.* Finally, the money shot: *refusal to co-operate.*

'How did she know that we interviewed Sera that day?' she said. It had been reframed and distorted, but there was no denying that they had questioned Sera, or that, so far, she was the only person who had been questioned officially. 'I doubt the sheriff would have told her.'

'I don't know, but I haven't seen Jacob around today,' Stan said, glancing at the sheriff's closed door. 'He's been in there with Len and the Mayor for an hour. They're planning on holding some memorial service tonight, cool things down. Radio announcement any minute now. Where have you been, Dana?'

She'd been planning to tell Stan the truth, so she hadn't given herself time to think of a lie.

'Just a personal thing. It doesn't matter.'

Stan's forehead creased. He took off his glasses to polish them quickly with his shirt. He looked exhausted, she realised.

'Look, Dana, I know you and Sera were friends. But I hope we're friends, too,' he said, voice hushed, glasses back on and smudged.

Dana didn't know what he was talking about. 'She's got nothing to do with it.'

She hadn't meant to be so sharp. Stan didn't seem ruffled, but his hand went to the pack of cigarettes in his breast pocket.

'You can't save people. Not from themselves. Not unless

they want you to,' he said. 'Know what I mean?'

Dana didn't, and she didn't want to. 'Sure,' she said. 'I get you.'

After a respectful pause, she opted enough time had passed to change the topic. 'And the phone records?'

His mouth firmed. He was angry, she realised with surprise. Stan didn't get angry.

'I called them and cancelled the request,' he said. 'Dana, that was bordering on misuse of power. We searched her premises. She has an alibi. Maybe Shelly's a little odd, but she doesn't deserve to have her privacy invaded for no good reason.'

'I thought you were my friend,' Dana said.

'I am your friend,' he said. 'That's why I did it.'

Dana found herself sick of Stan, sick of other people deciding what she was allowed to know.

Chapter Thirteen

▓▓▓▓▓▓▓▓ I speak in the tongues of men and of angels, ▓▓▓▓▓▓▓▓ understand all mysteries ▓▓▓▓▓▓▓▓ but I am nothing.

The white walls were not as high, the floor perhaps not as polished, but otherwise the house was just as Dana remembered.

'Is it still classed as breaking and entering if we have a key?' Sera asked, standing close enough that her arm brushed Dana's, 'Or is it just entering?'

'We're not breaking and entering,' Dana said, walking deeper into the hallway.

By the door was a shoe rack, on the table above it was a stack of mail, a paper. Dana flipped through them. She wanted to look serious, as though she were looking for clues that would be unnoticed by the civilian's eye. The door to the living room was open. Dana caught a glimpse of the family portrait and the piano; keys uneven, it smiled at her crookedly.

'Not breaking and entering, then is it trespassing on a crime scene?' Sera said, still standing by the door.

'This isn't a crime scene,' Dana said, omitting that it was just trespassing.

Dana hadn't told the sheriff or Stan where she was going. It was better to ask for forgiveness than permission, after all. Ideally, they wouldn't find out and she wouldn't have to ask for either.

She checked her watch. The memorial service would be starting now. They had an hour and a half, if they were lucky.

'You asked me to take you here,' Dana reminded her, when she didn't move from the door.

Sera didn't reply. She was looking at the shoes.

Dana stuck out her hand. Sera blinked. Her hand was a gift she didn't know what to do with.

'Come on, then,' Dana said, waggling her fingers, 'Aren't you going to give me the tour?'

◆ ◆ ◆

Dana could have kept driving when she saw Ariel hitching by the side of the hot summer road—someone else would have surely picked her up, hair a flare in all the green—and part of her wished she had.

The first thing Ariel did when she got into Brussels was change the station, and in the time it took to drive her home, she'd asked Dana more questions than she'd ever been asked in her entire life. How's your summer going? Do you miss school? fired out with the same cheerful fourteen-year-old intensity as What happened to your mom and Do you miss Sera?

Sera rarely asked Dana questions. She made observations, presenting them to be confirmed or denied.

Ariel had insisted Dana stay for a glass of orange juice, to repay her for the ride. The orange juice was in a white jug in the refrigerator: it seemed everything had its place.

Ariel took two glasses from their position in the cupboard and poured, but took her time handing it over. On her hand was faded ink, something she hadn't wanted to forget.

Dana thought she seemed the type to forget things.

Sat on the counter with her freckled legs crossed, Ariel kept the questions up. Do you ever have dreams that feel real? Pouring out another glass of OJ, Do you believe in God and do you believe in other worlds?

The sun began to set. Dana should leave.

When she opened her mouth to say goodbye, Ariel said, 'Sera should be home soon, if you want to say hi.'

Dana had not seen Sera since school broke for summer three weeks ago. They had been standing outside of the library.

Sera had said, 'Goodbye.'

Since the day they went fishing, something had changed. Their friendship did not exist outside of semesters, the time they spent together revolving entirely around rides home from the library or sitting together at lunch. They never planned to do anything; hanging out was mutually accidental.

Sera had been silent, waiting for Dana to reply. Dana hadn't known what to think or what Sera wanted her to say.

'Yeah,' she'd replied. It haunted her still.

Ariel smacked herself on the head with the back of her hand. *MILK MILK MILK* .

'I forgot! I was meant to tidy up the basement,' she hopped down from the counter, 'Can you help me? I don't want to get into trouble.'

♦ ♦ ♦

Dana touched the hem of a shirt between her fingers. The basket of folded laundry was the only clean thing in the kitchen. The sink was full of dirty dishes; in the fruit bowl, the apples were soft, skin clammy.

'Look at this place,' Sera said, nose wrinkled. Something smelt sweet, like rotting onions. 'You still think Ariel killed herself?'

Dana turned away from the laundry, looking at the calendar on the wall. It was open to August, a month behind.

She'd read the autopsy report. Ariel had cut her arm open and bled to death in a locked bathroom. Suicide was difficult to come to terms with. It was possible that Sera's conspiracy theory—that Ariel was murdered—was nothing more than a coping mechanism.

That didn't mean the Enckles were good people. There were links between at least four of the five missing and Joe Enckles. And Dana didn't know if the secret adoptions were criminal or not, but it was unusual. Just because Ariel wasn't murdered, didn't mean the Enckles weren't involved in the grave robberies.

'All this tells me is that Joe and Michael don't know how to do their dishes,' Dana said. 'There's no evidence that it wasn't suicide, Sera. If you really think that one of your family members murdering her is more likely, then there's a lot you're not telling me.'

There was a wooden bang. Turning, she saw that Sera had opened one of the kitchen cupboards, her head stuck inside.

'What are you doing?' Dana asked.

Sera looked at Dana, as if surprised she had asked.

'I'm hungry,' she said, flatly. Pulling out a box of crackers, she offered them to Dana. 'Want one?'

Dana opened the fridge, wincing at the contents. The vegetables in the crisper had wilted into dark green mush. There was an almost full carton of sour milk, a packet of bacon and Clingfilm covered sympathy casseroles. There was a warmth at Dana's side then, as Sera came and stood behind her, peering into the fridge over her shoulder.

'I'm not *that* hungry.'

'Yeah, me neither,' Dana said, closing the door, the light it bathed them in going out.

Sera opened a drawer. There was metallic clattering as she began to search through it.

'What are you looking for?' Dana said.

Sera ignored her.

Was she protecting someone? Joe? Love made people do unexpected things; so did fear.

'If you tell me, I can help you find it. We don't have a lot of time.'

'I'm looking for evidence of what they did to Ariel,' Sera closed the drawer with a slam and opened the next one; dead batteries, sewing kits, thumb tacks. 'Since my word isn't enough.'

Dana couldn't help it. She laughed.

Sera stared at her, 'What?'

'I'm sorry,' Dana said, still laughing. 'You seriously expect me to take you at your word?'

Sera pressed her lips together: *yes*.

'Sera, you've given me no reason to trust you,' Dana said, flatly. 'I barely understand why you came back, and I still don't know why you left. So far, you've told me your family is "dangerous", but not how or why. Super useful,' she laughed again, mostly because she could. 'Do you know how frustrating it is to spend hours of legwork finding out something you could have just told me?'

Dana felt vindicated as Sera dropped the bowl she was looking inside; finally, she had managed to get her attention.

'I'm looking for a silver key,' she said. 'It opens the basement.'

Dana waited for her to continue.

'Okay,' she said. 'Why? What's in the basement?'

The tap was dripping. For a moment, Dana could have sworn Sera looked disappointed.

'My dad—' Sera stopped. 'Joshua used to keep stuff down there.'

'Stuff?' Dana said. 'What kind of stuff?'

Sera crouched on the floor, opening the cupboard under the sink.

'Are you kidding me?' Dana said to her back. 'I'm risking my job to be here, and I don't even know what we are looking for!'

Dana rolled her eyes, then sighed in a way that conveyed to Sera that she was rolling her eyes. Crossing her arms, she walked towards the kitchen window. It looked out towards the lake. The surface was smooth as glass.

She pressed her eyes shut; she could hear the water from here.

'Not by blood.'

'What?'

Black spots danced as Dana opened her eyes. Sera had straightened.

'You said I thought that a family member murdered her. As you've discovered, we aren't family, not by blood.' Dana nodded. Sera closed the cupboard door. 'Let's look upstairs.'

♦ ♦ ♦

Dana's house wasn't big enough for a basement. She'd been to a birthday party when she was seven, and there had been an air hockey table in the basement, along with a washer-dryer. The basement in Ariel's house didn't have an air hockey table or a washer-dryer. Just some rolled up mats, a sheet of tarp covering half of the floor and four angels painted on to the wall, all white, with gold hair and blue eyes.

This seemed odd, but then Dana didn't know what was expected. However, even without a basis for comparison, the swords hanging on the wall of the Enckles' basement were a surprise.

'This one's mine,' Ariel said. The blade was silver, with a gold handle. It was bright, the lightest of the four. Ariel weaved it through the air, one-handed, her left hand held out behind her for balance.

Ariel kept moving. It was more intentional than a dance. As she moved through a sequence, the sword began to whistle, Ariel's body melting into the air, leaving only the impression of small, quick bones, the dark birthmark on her back rippling.

One of the painted angels held a sword, Dana realised. It was stabbing the angel opposite it, but neither of them looked sad. They just had relaxed, open-mouthed expressions, eyes looking upwards, like kids did when they were making fun of each other with sex noises.

Jesus people were so weird.

Ariel held the sword in a final lunge, pushing her whole body forward. Then, after a beat, it was over. She turned to Dana, grinning.

'That was cool,' Dana said, lamely. 'Is it for school or something?'

'Thank you, thank you,' Ariel said, putting her scrunchie wrapped hand over her heart, as if to say it had been touched. 'You want to try?'

Before Dana could figure out if she did or not, Ariel had thrust the sword into her hand. She was holding it. Dana's arm, unprepared for the weight, began to sink; she looked at Ariel with new respect.

'Is this real?'

She'd thought it was a toy. Dana held it up in front of her eyes, to see her squinting face in its reflection.

'Of course, it's real,' Ariel said.

'I mean, is it sharp?' Dana asked. On the blade was an inscribed message. *Made in China.*

'Silly,' she said, freckles folding into her smile. Ariel lifted another sword—this one duller and longer—down from the wall, repeating the movements she'd made with it. Her eyes were a funny shade of blue. Funny strange. 'Come on, follow me.'

'No, thank you,' Dana said, putting down the sword. 'I should go home. What did you need help moving?'

Ariel stared at her for so long that Dana wondered if she'd accidentally been rude.

Ariel still held her sword. Dana could hear water running.

'Help me move this, please,' she said, pointing at the sheet of tarp.

Her voice was almost cold. Dana did as she asked, pulling off the sheet together.

Underneath it was a rough hole in the ground, hewn with stone, about the size of Brussels. It was full of water, so black that Dana couldn't see the bottom.

Instinctively, she moved away from the edge.

'What's this?' Dana asked.

Ariel smiled. 'It's the devil's pulpit. No one knows how far down it goes.'

Dana didn't know how to react. This, by any stretch of the imagination, was not a normal basement item.

'What's it for?'

'Baptisms and stuff,' Ariel replied, as if she was half listening.

'Isn't it dangerous?' Dana said, before she hissed in pain.

Something had bitten into her arm. Looking down, she realised that Ariel had pushed the edge of her sword into her skin.

Ariel had cut her.

Dana looked up at her, too confused to be angry. Ariel looked almost as scared as she was. The blood was dripping on to her white sport socks.

'Sorry,' she said. 'Sorry. I just wanted to see what would happen.'

♦ ♦ ♦

Sera led the way, and the floorboards of the staircase sang. They passed Sera's old bedroom without stopping. Involuntarily, Dana wondered which would be worse; if it had been gutted entirely or if it hadn't been changed at all.

Dana followed her through the corridor. There were black and careless stains on the cream carpet. With a jolt, she realised that they were footprints. They might have been left by the paramedics, Sheriff Wormwood, Stan.

The door to the bathroom hung weakly open, the handle and hinges broken, the sides of the frame splintered.

'Don't you want to search the bedrooms first?' Dana said.

Sera shook her head. 'Michael, Joe and my mom will have their keys on them, but Ariel probably hid hers somewhere.'

She tugged the switch. The light flickered on, and the fan began to hum.

The bathroom wasn't as large as the house warranted; tub, toilet and sink pushed close together. The hand towel was green, matching the spearmint toothpaste that cheerfully sat on the sink with the brush holders. There was no shower curtain. No bathmat.

Sera's breath hitched. Following her gaze, Dana saw what she had seen. Around the plughole, some residue was caught, as if the tub hadn't been rinsed thoroughly enough after a red bath.

'Where you there?' she asked.

Dana knew what she meant.

'No,' Dana replied. 'The sheriff said it wasn't appropriate.'

Necessary had been the word he had used. It wasn't necessary for her to be involved. As if sometimes pain was necessary, and sometimes it wasn't.

Sera was looking through the medicine cabinet. It was half-hearted.

'What did she use?' she asked.

'A kitchen knife,' Dana said. 'Most commercially bought knives aren't sharp enough to cut that deeply, so she probably sharpened it with something.' Hot water sped up the process, though the bathwater had been cold when they found her. 'It's unlikely that she experienced much pain.'

Dana knew there was no way of knowing that. She suspected Sera knew it, too. A pointless thing to say.

'Was the knife here when she was found?' Sera asked.

Ariel hadn't turned up for her morning shift and hadn't answered her phone, so David Ackermann had called her next of kin, her brother. Was everything alright?

The bathroom door had been locked from the inside, but the tap was still running. Michael called the sheriff's department at 6:35am. By the time Sheriff Wormwood arrived at 6:53am, Michael and Joe had already broken down the door. Dr Wu arrived at 7:10am with Stan. An ambulance had arrived by 7:47am.

They declared Ariel officially dead at 7:59am, but time of death was assumed to have occurred hours earlier. The ambulance escorted her to the hospital, where an autopsy was performed at the request of the sheriff's department. Approximate time of death, 1:15am. Statements were taken from all but Mrs Enckles, who was resting at the recommendation of Dr Wu.

There was no note. Had there been a knife?

'I'm not sure,' Dana said. Then more certain, 'No. No knife.'

Sera nodded, as if she had expected as much.

'What is it?' Dana said.

Sera shook her head. 'She didn't use a kitchen knife.'

'How do you know?'

'People don't change,' Sera said. 'Remember what she was like?'

She wasn't looking at the cabinet anymore, but intently at Dana. The bathroom was small, the sound of the fan deafening. Now they were facing each other, Dana was close enough to see the fine lines under Sera's eye. They weren't crow's feet yet, but they would be someday. She had done a lot of living lately.

'Are you alright?' Dana asked. A stupid question. The only one that mattered.

'No,' Sera said. 'Not really.'

Dana opened her mouth to say something—what, she wasn't sure—when Sera's hand came up to cover her mouth. Mouth still open, she breathed against Sera's palm, like the wet steam of a cup of coffee. Her tongue, instinctively, brushed the rough skin of Sera's palm. Salt, for a second. Red, she flicked her eyes up to meet Sera's.

'Someone's here,' she whispered.

♦ ♦ ♦

They sprang apart as the door to the gym swung open. It took Dana a second to recognise Michael. It was because he wasn't in his uniform, she realised. How weird to see him in the school, but not in uniform.

'Sera, did you forget that I said I'd pick you up from school today?' he said, smiling soft.

'No, Michael. I didn't forget.' Without looking, Dana

could sense the tension that was in Sera's body. 'I was just coming.'

The smell of chlorine always made Dana feel embarrassed—it was the association of accidental nudity happening at any moment in the changing rooms—now it made her feel sick.

Michael kept smiling at his sister. They all had this talent, the Enckles, for blandness. When Michael smiled, it could mean anything.

'It's the last day of school,' he said at last. 'Don't you think it's time to leave childish things behind?'

Sera was bland, too, but in a different way. Her expressionless face could have any number of emotions tucked away behind it. But it was her hands that gave her away, so that's what Dana watched. They were by her hips, fingers outstretched and flat. She was afraid.

'Leave her alone,' Dana said. 'You can't bully her anymore.'

Michael raised his eyebrows.

'Oh, that's right,' he said, laughing. 'I forgot about your little witch hunt. All the way to the Town Council. Very ambitious, Dana.' Bland, bland, bland: he was such a nothing man. 'Don't worry, dad didn't take it personally. We had a good laugh about that last family night, didn't we, Sera?'

Dana looked at Sera from the corner of her eye. Dana didn't realise she knew. It seemed like too much effort to work up the courage just to say she failed.

Sera was rigid, lightning about to strike.

'Stop it, Michael,' she said.

Michael stepped close to Dana and reached out to touch her. Dana's stomach flooded with something cold, like a cracked egg. He brushed a strand of hair out of her face, fingertips jostling her earrings as he tucked it behind her earlobe. Dana wanted to stop him. She wanted it to be over.

He put his hand by his side and smiled, like a child kissing a woman he didn't know, not knowing it was wrong.

Dana's legs were shaking.

Sera stepped between them, pushing Michael back with both hands.

'Leave her alone, I said!' Sera shouted.

Michael stumbled, clean white sneakers sliding a little on the wet chemical tiles. He looked at Sera surprised. Sera was electric, her hands fists.

'Dana,' Michael said, angry. 'Jump in the pool.'

She jumped. Afterwards, she remembered being pushed in, but at the time, there was just the water breaking over her skin.

♦ ♦ ♦

Now that she was listening, Dana could hear it, too. A floorboard creaking. And then again.

Someone was coming up the stairs.

Sera's hand was still cupped over her mouth, so Dana moved her eyes from side to side frantically. What do we do?

She looked towards the bathroom window. They could fit

through it. There was a ledge around the front porch, but the bathroom looked out towards the back of the house.

The stairs were round the corner from the corridor—it was possible whoever it was hadn't seen them yet—but they would soon, and there was no other way out without passing them.

Another creak. There was no choice; they had to jump.

'It's too high,' Sera whispered rapidly. 'Even if you don't break your leg, you'll make too much noise. When I let go, wait five seconds, then go into the nearest bedroom and shut the door.' Dana shook her head. Sera ignored her, clamping her hand more firmly over her mouth. 'I'll go out and get him away from the stairs—you run.'

Abruptly, Sera let Dana go, turned around and strode down the corridor, calling, 'Honey, I'm home!'

There was no time to think of a better plan, so Dana did exactly what Sera had told her. Shutting the bedroom door behind her, she pressed her ear to the crack. Please don't be Michael, please don't be Michael, please don't be Michael—

'Mom?' Sera's voice was still close enough to hear. 'Why... are you here alone?'

There was no answer. In the silence, Dana held her breath so she wouldn't sneeze—the room was full of dust.

'What are you doing here?' Mrs Enckles replied, politely. Same classroom voice. 'Are you the cleaner?'

Sera didn't reply immediately. Dana didn't blame her. Was this a trick?

'No, mom—it's me.' Sera said. 'It's Sera.'

'Sera...' Mrs Enckles replied. Dana re-adjusted; her voice was becoming fainter. 'I'm sorry. I don't think we've met?'

'I'm your daughter,' Sera said, insistent. Dana cringed. Gift horse, mouth.

Mrs Enckles' thin voice became much louder. 'My daughter is in hell,' she said. 'Did Raphael make me forget again?'

Suddenly, the direction of the footsteps changed. 'If you made me forget again, you're in big trouble!' Dana scrambled—they were getting closer.

The door swung open. Mrs Enckles' breathing was harsh and heavy.

Dana, crouched under the single bed, held herself very still. Mercifully, the floorboards she lay on weren't coated in dust.

'There's no one here, Pamela,' Sera said. 'She's gone.'

'She made me forget again, didn't she?' Mrs Enckles said to Sera's wrapped-up empty room. 'Always was a bad girl.'

Dana waited for what felt like hours under the bed. After twenty minutes, Sera returned. Dana saw her black boots first, and then heard her second.

'She's asleep,' she whispered. 'Let's go.'

When they reached the hallway, Dana stopped Sera with a hand on her arm before she could open the front door.

'It was in the floorboards under your bed,' Dana whispered, the silver key glinting in her hand. 'Let's go look—'

Sera opened the door. 'No,' she said.

Dana stared at her. 'But this could be our only chance.'

Sera grabbed her hand. 'Let's go,' she said, again. They ran.

By the time they reached Brussels, hidden in the trees, Dana was thoroughly pissed.

'Well, I hope my job was worth it,' she said, still catching her breath, 'Because that was a waste of time.'

'She won't remember,' Sera promised, frustratingly unaffected by the run. 'We can go back later.'

Dana gaped. 'Go *back?*' she said. 'We already got caught once, and you want to go back?' She wanted to scream, she wanted to take Sera by the shoulders and shake the truth out of her. 'What exactly is in that basement?'

Sera's face was grim and exhausted. 'You need to see it.'

'Okay, so you already know what's down there,' Dana said. 'Why don't you cut the crap and just tell me?'

Sera shook her head. 'You won't believe me. Come on,' she moved towards the car. 'Let's go.'

Dana stood still. It felt like the forest was screaming around her.

'...Dana?' Sera said. 'Are you alright?'

'Losing you hurt more than losing my mom,' Dana said. 'I know it's wrong, but it's true.'

Sera didn't say anything. Dana wished she would. Wished she would shout. Wished she would leave. Wished, for one secret moment, that she had stayed dead.

'I hate that you can make me feel like I'm not enough,' Dana said. Her eyes were hot. Her own words left her exposed, but she didn't have it in her to regret them. 'Why don't you trust me?'

Sera stared at the ground. She was crying, too, but

she wasn't wiping her tears away. They did not make her ashamed.

She said, 'I do.'

'Then tell me why you left,' Dana said. 'Whatever it is, I will believe you.' She took in a breath. 'I promise.'

Sera looked up at her. 'Alright,' she said. 'What do you know about angels?'

Chapter Fourteen

> At first I thought that angels, named angels, were to be found only in the Bible. I soon learned that, on the contrary, the Bible was the last place to look for them.
>
> *A Dictionary of Angels (Including the Fallen Angels),* Gustav Davidson

'There's always four,' was how she started. 'In a family. There's always a Michael, a Gabriel, an Azazel,' she swallowed, 'And a Raphael. We're God's First Children. His most holy children.'

Sera's story was drawn out slowly, as if each word was buried so deep inside that they could not be extracted without taking chunks of her with them. She didn't remember the orphanage or her dead birth parents, *part of God's will.* But she remembered Pamela telling her in Enochian to use the big girl toilet. She remembered being trained by Father Enckles, practicing with a child-sized sword, treading ice cold water for hours; exercises for her body and her mind to prepare her for carrying out God's will. Remembered punishments, only drinking water and eating boiled eggs.

She looked at Dana when she was finished.

Dana didn't know what reaction to have. Angels belonged on Christmas Cards. Even for super Christians, this seemed too much.

'So,' she said, trying to be as matter of fact as possible. 'Your family believe that they are angels?'

Sera sighed. Her explanation had been methodical and precise, clearly Dana hadn't been listening.

'No. We're inheritors of the divine body. The descendants of angelic beings and humans interbreeding.'

Breeding. Something about that word sat with Dana strangely; the way it made sex sound necessary.

'I thought you guys weren't related?'

'We're not. Though I guess we must all be distant relations, because we all share the same ancestors. Pamela and Joshua found us.' Sera's mouth twisted, as though she'd swallowed a pill dry. Some words wore thin with repetition, but hers were heavy. 'They saved us.'

Pamela and Joshua had recruited children to indoctrinate. No wonder Sera ran.

'How did they find you?' Dana asked.

Sera tapped her shoulder. 'Birthmark. There are other ways, too.'

Dana could almost hear Sheriff Wormwood's voice. *There's usually two versions of the truth.* Dana remembered seeing a birthmark on Michael's shoulder for sure. Maybe Ariel's too? Though she could be confusing it with a freckle. But Sera?

She thought of Sera's bare back, and her mind turned blank and black. Though she must have, surely, at some point seen her skin.

Sera turned in her car seat so her back was facing Dana and used the tip of her fingers to push down her T-shirt. Over her left shoulder blade was a birthmark like an indigo ink spill, or a deep bruise.

When Dana touched it, she expected it to feel rough. It was just warm skin. It could be a tattoo, she reasoned.

Sera pulled the T-shirt up and turned around again, her hair falling over her shoulder.

'What are the other ways?' Dana asked.

'Well,' Sera said, reluctantly. 'There's our powers.'

'Powers,' Dana said. 'What kind of powers?'

Sera shifted, as if she was embarrassed. Was this a joke? Dana wondered. A really weird joke?

'It's hard to explain,' Sera seemed to be searching for the right words. 'You know how Jesus was God, but also human?'

Sera used Christs' name as if she knew him personally.

'You're saying you're Jesus Christ?' This was becoming too *Jerry Springer* for Dana. 'Walk on water, heal the sick?'

'Don't be stupid,' Sera snapped. 'We can do things that other people can't, but we're not messiahs, just messengers. We carry out his will. Guide humanity.'

'So, when you say messengers,' Dana said, slowly, 'you mean, delivering messages from god?'

'Yes, exactly,' Sera said, as if Dana was finally grasping it.

'Joshua was in charge, so he passed the messages on to us. I guess Michael does it now.'

Oh god, Dana thought. She believes this shit.

'Okay,' Dana said, trying to put that thought aside to focus on the problem in front of them. 'What do you think your family have to do with the bodies?'

Sera ran her hand through her hair. 'I don't know, but I know that Ariel wouldn't have killed herself. You don't understand,' she said, before Dana could speak, 'We were taught that we're vessels of god, that our bodies are like…religious objects. Ariel was devoted. The rest of us were nothing in comparison to her. She couldn't have killed herself. If she's dead, it must be because she broke a rule. A big one. Usually, they would have found another way to punish her.'

Dana went cold. Did Sera break a rule?

'Do you have proof?'

'No,' Sera said. 'But with what we can do, there might not be any.'

This was all so vague: Dana needed specifics.

'What can you do?' Dana asked. 'Your powers. What are they exactly?'

Sera didn't reply. Stan had agreed to cover her for an hour or so, and it had been well over two. Dana couldn't afford to go back to silence. 'Sera, spit it out,' she said.

'This isn't easy,' Sera said, her words like a whip: Dana tried not to flinch and waited.

Sera sighed. 'I was never able to do much. Dad used to say there was too much human in me.' She closed her eyes for a moment and then continued. 'We can do different things. Our powers are meant to balance each other out, so no one has an advantage.' She started counting on her fingers. 'Joe is our Gabriel, the angel of revelation, a messenger. He knows when people are lying. His powers counter mine,' she said it almost in a rush, 'Concealment. Ariel is Azazel. Her main responsibility was to carry on the divine body,' at Dana's confused expression, she added. 'Bear children, I mean. I'm surprised she never...' she shook her head. 'Anyway, Michael is our Michael, he's the warrior.'

Dana blinked. She felt like she should take notes. 'Sera, break this down. What do you mean powers?'

Sera grimaced. 'I never completed my training. But our bodies are strong. We can fight. We can perform miracles, reorder reality to our will. Probably most real saints have had a strong angelic bloodline.' She paused. 'I think Michael can read minds, make people do things.'

'Read minds?' Dana said. 'Sera, this is...'

Crazy. It was crazy.

'You don't believe me,' Sera said, voice hovering on the edge of something like anger.

Dana chose her words carefully.

'I believe that you believe what you're saying,' she said. 'I believe that your family are dangerous.'

'But you don't believe me,' Sera said.

Her cell phone rang. She jumped. It felt like an intruder in this strange world inhabited only by the two of them.

It was Stan.

'Get over here, Fisher,' he said without preamble. 'The Mayor's making an announcement.'

♦ ♦ ♦

Dana felt sorry for the school kids singing *Tears in Heaven* at the front of the church, leather shoes polished, top buttons done; it was hot. The lucky sitting members of the congregation shifted in their pews, sweat trickling down their backs, empty cups of flat dime-store pop in their hands. Father Thomas was still putting out plastic fold-out chairs.

Dana crept down the side to where she could see Stan's glasses glinting. Martha Dorhamer was front and centre, with the council members. David Ackermann was in the front row too, his wife jostling their small son in her arms. Michael Enckles smiled at the baby, and then smiled at the singing children.

Michael can read minds. Impossible, of course, but Sera believed it and that scared Dana. *He can make people do things.*

Sera had made her promise not to repeat what she'd said to the sheriff. Dana had said she wouldn't and meant it. She would be as likely to tell the sheriff that the bodies were abducted by UFOs.

A hand brushed the back of her arm, barely there.

'Dana,' Gary whispered. 'Hi.'

'Hi, yourself,' she replied, looking up at him. He needed to wash his hair, and the sleeves of his hoodie were stretched over his hands.

It felt like she hadn't seen him in days. Impulsively, wanted to hug him. But she didn't.

'Did I miss much?' she whispered. The person next to her looked over her shoulder; *keep it down.*

'Mr Ackermann made a speech, there was a few prayers,' Gary said, 'There are sandwiches in the hall, but I wouldn't recommend them. Do you know what the announcement is?'

Dana nodded. The sheriff arrived just as she was wondering where he was. Making his way to the front of the church, he stopped to exchange a few hushed words with Martha.

'I think they're bringing in state police,' she said.

'Oh. If it helps them find out what happened to Ariel, that's good, right?' Gary asked, unsure.

Dana watched the sheriff shake her hand. She would never have guessed he was speaking to the woman who'd spent the past week shouting obscenities down the phone at him.

'Right. I'll see you at home, okay?'

'Oh,' Gary said. 'Okay.'

The song came to a merciful end, Dana hoping the applause would cover her as she made her way towards the front. Standing to the side with Stan and Len, the sheriff was easy to spot; he'd kept his wide-brimmed hat on. The kids exited the makeshift stage to crowd around the side. They looked thirsty.

Michael stood, and Dana half-expected him to stand in the pulpit.

'Thank you to our school choir for that rendition of the great Eric Clapton's *Tears in Heaven*. It was Sandy

Ackermann's favourite song. And thanks to you for sticking with us on this hot night.' There was a smattering of laughter as Michael fanned himself. 'David, I hope there's still some of that lemonade you brought left!'

If he can read my mind, Dana thought, he already knows what Sera told me.

Michael looked into the crowd, smile fading.

'You were running a good race. Who cut in on you to keep you from obeying the truth?' The words shivered in the air. The laughter cooled off. 'A week has passed and we are no closer to recovering the bodies of Sandra Ackermann, Anthony Dorhamer, Jerome Smolinski, Cathy Copeland and Ariel Enckles,' his eyes were bright, 'Ariel. My sister. Our sister.'

If you can read my mind, Dana thought, go fuck yourself.

'It's been a week. At this point we are required to hand over the case to state authorities. But this isn't for the state to deal with, is it?' He looked around the crowd, meeting the eyes of one person, and then another. 'If you want my opinion, this is a family matter. Because each and every person sitting here tonight is family, one way or the other.'

In the crowd, some people nodded, Mrs Trieger among them. Dana looked at Stan, hoping to find an ally in disdain. His glasses reflected the light; she couldn't see his eyes.

Michael smiled. 'After speaking with our state liaison, a compromise has been reached. I'm happy to announce that we have been granted an additional three days to handle things ourselves. If we all pitch in, I see no reason to have to involve external authorities at all.'

Someone whooped. There was applause in earnest.

Dana couldn't see the sheriff's face, but Deputy Boldry's face was pinched, he was sweating.

'Of course,' Michael said, his smile turning serious. 'Compromises are difficult. To demonstrate our reignited commitment to apprehending the perpetrator of this heinous crime, the Town Council has called for an emergency re-election in the sheriff's department. Alvin Wormwood will be stepping down from the role.'

Was Deputy Boldry sheriff now? Was that why he looked so anxious?

'Al has been an inspiration for us all. He leaves big shoes to fill. Together, we've come to the hard decision that, as your most senior elected official, I should assume the responsibilities of sheriff.'

Dana's stomach dropped.

There was no whispering, or outcries at the news. Still, Michael waited a moment before continuing.

'You know me as your mayor. I've spoken to you tonight as a grieving brother. Now, I speak as your sheriff. I vow to do whatever is necessary to bring justice to our town.'

Mary fell at his feet

Jesus,
she said, if you had been here, my brother
would not have died

Chapter Fifteen

The deck chair was gone and the laundry line bare, embers hissing through the wet earth that had been kicked over where a fire had been lit. The sunset was like honey, thick and heavy. Somewhere, thunder waited.

The Airstream door was open, and Dana didn't knock. Sera looked up from the bed where she sat.

'What's wrong?' she asked. She held chewed pen in one hand and scrap of paper in the other, using a Bible to lean on.

'Michael's the sheriff,' Dana said. She held out a copy of *The Declaration*. 'Look at this.'

Sera didn't take it. After a moment, Dana used it to fan herself. The Airstream trapped light like a tin can and her sweaty-sticky skin was hot.

'I called you,' she added, when Sera didn't reply.

'I know,' Sera said. To which part, Dana wasn't sure. 'Joe told me.'

'You saw Joe?'

'Yeah,' Sera said. Standing up, she put down the pen and the Bible too, with dull thud. 'That's why I missed the meeting. I've got to hit the road before morning.'

'He gave you a lead?' Dana said. 'That's great! We can take my car—it'll be faster.'

She was still holding the paper, her sweat turning the pages translucent and making the thin ink bleed.

'No,' Sera said. 'I don't have a lead. What I meant is, I have to get out of here.'

Sera didn't get flustered, or stammer or say *um*, but there was something in the chipped way she spoke that was awkward.

'Get out?' Dana said. 'To go where?'

The sunlight was hitting Sera through the narrow doorway; she was burning amber.

'Where I go is irrelevant,' she said. 'What matters is that I'm not here.'

Before she went to sleep, Dana would often climb down half-conscious staircases. By the time she put her foot down on the last one, she would be expecting stone but just find air and jolt awake in dark surprise.

'You're running away,' she said. 'You said your family are dangerous, that Michael killed Ariel, and maybe killed the other four, too. Now he's sheriff. He's never been more powerful. And you've decided now is the time to take a road trip?'

Sera shook her head. 'He's not interested in killing anyone right now, Dana. What he wants is to keep the government out and keep his backwater kingdom intact. To do that, what he needs is a sacrificial lamb and, frankly, I am not interested in being his Iphigenia.'

Dana rolled her eyes. Even when the room was a piece of shit trailer, Sera still had to be the smartest person in it.

'You're leaving because he wants to blame you for the grave robberies?' Dana said. 'But you didn't do it.'

'And so...?'

'So,' Dana said, 'How's he going to find evidence?'

Sera didn't laugh, but she looked as if she was thinking about it.

'Dana, it's easily done. Michael is good at getting what he wants, he always has been. Even if he wasn't, you know what he is now.'

Her unsaid words were so dark with significance that Dana felt a wave of second-hand embarrassment.

'An angel?' Dana clarified, with as straight a face as she could muster.

The expression on Sera's face was muted as ever, but she was holding her body tense.

'You don't believe me,' she said.

Dana wasn't good at pretending. *I believe that you believe it,* she should say. Or even, *I want to believe.*

'No, I don't,' she said. 'I'm sorry.'

Sera's eyes shuttered blank like an no vacancy sign.

'I have to load up,' she said, pushing past Dana, out the open doorway into almost-red almost-night. Dana watched her. The sweat on her skin had cooled, and now her uniform stuck to it like a fly to paper. With her back to her, Sera busied herself as though there were still things to pack, but the camp was already gone, the embers now cold. All that was left to do was get in the car and drive.

'You have to be gone before morning?' Dana said.

Sera turned back to face her, becoming a shadow with the light behind her.

'Yeah,' she answered.

'One for the road?' Dana said. 'I know you're driving, but just one? For old times' sake?'

As soon as she'd finished speaking, Dana tried to work out how she could pass it off as a kind of joke. Sera didn't even answer, just walked over to her car and opened the door.

This couldn't be how it ended. But maybe it would be easiest this way: no goodbyes, no promises—

Sera closed the door and turned. In her hand she held a half full bottle of green-tinged moonshine.

♦ ♦ ♦

Gary had never been to Nyx, though he'd heard some kids he went to school with boast about drinking there. Not that he wanted to drink. I mean, he might. That's what detectives on TV did when the going got rough, after all.

To his disappointment, the interior was not as illicit as he'd imagined. Nothing was new but everything was clean, ashtrays and bowls of fresh nuts on the booth tables, a pool table no one was using. Dreamy country music drifted towards him—a woman singing about a broken heart, a guitar—and on the TV, hitched high above the bar, a college football game played out in silence.

Only two things stood out to Gary. One was the sign behind the bar. It was flashing neon: a jug of blue water being poured one moment, the next a red light shaped like a wine glass. Clever.

The second was the fact that it was busy, and yet he couldn't see anyone he knew.

Gary opted to take a quiet seat at the bar, a bit away from the beer-soaked crowd. When the pretty bartender approached, he sat up a little straighter in his stool.

'What can I get you, honey?' she asked. She was smiling, but her eyes weren't. Gary wondered if she'd been the one to come up with the neon sign.

'Um, Martini,' he said, with what he hoped was a playful grin, 'On the rocks. Shaken not stirred.'

Her smile stayed in place, red and shiny, but her eyes became, if possible, slightly more dead. 'We don't do Martinis.'

'Oh, I know,' Gary said. He didn't know what he was doing here. 'I was joking!'

'In fact,' she continued as if he hadn't spoken, frozen blue eyes narrowing, 'I'm not sure there's anything on the menu that caters to a young man with such sophisticated tastes.'

'Come on, Shelly, just give the kid a beer,' a man a couple of stools down called. 'I think we both know you're not going to get a visit from the cops tonight.'

In his peripheral vision, Gary thought he saw Shelly rolling her eyes, but he was too busy staring at the man who had spoken to be sure. His stiff shirt was unbuttoned, tie loose enough that the silver cross necklace he wore was visible. In front of him was a paper napkin, torn to shreds, and an empty glass.

He was smiling at Gary.

'Pardon?' Gary said.

'Is beer good?' Joe Enckles repeated. 'Or are you really set on that Martini?'

'No, no, beer sounds awesome,' Gary said, 'I mean, it sounds good. How much do I owe you?'

Joe flapped his hand, as if to wave the question away. He had a tattoo on one of his fingers: two black dots, so small they could have been mistaken for freckles if the ink hadn't bled.

Shelly put a glass of beer on a coaster in front of Gary. He drank it manfully. It tasted like shit.

'First time?' Joe asked, eyes dancing. One was green, one was brown. Gary wondered if he was about to be made fun of.

'No, I've drank alcohol before.'

'Glad to hear it,' Joe said with a wink. Gary wasn't sure he'd ever been winked at before. 'But I meant first time here.'

'Oh! Yeah,' Gary scratched his head. 'How could you tell?'

Joe laughed. He had very white teeth. 'You've got that look.' He caught Gary eyeing his drink. It looked like Coke with a squeeze of lime, but something translucent crawled around the ice, not quite mixing. 'Do you want to try this?'

Gary raised his eyebrows. Was he serious? Joe pushed the glass towards him and nodded.

'Go ahead.'

Gary didn't know much about Joe Enckles, and for a moment he wondered if this was the scenario all those *don't-*

accept-candy-from-strangers stories had prepared him for. On one hand, he was Michael Enckles' shadowy right hand. The only reason Gary had not to like Michael was that Dana didn't, but that was enough.

On the other hand, Joe had been Ariel's cousin, too.

Maybe this was the lead Gary had been waiting for.

He took a sip. It was sour with lime and raw with alcohol.

'What do you think?'

'I like it,' Gary said, truthfully.

Joe laughed with delight.

'Did you hear that, Shelly?' he called, patting Gary on the back. 'This is a man who can hold his liquor!'

Shelly, who was uncapping a significantly less fun beer for the man at the end of the bar, rolled her eyes.

'Yeah,' she said. Someone was shouting at her from across the room. *Sweetheart, what's with the music? Did someone die?* 'That's what they all say.'

Ariel had been different since he'd shown her the photographs of the other four missing people. Something had changed—if he hadn't known any better, he'd think she was rattled. He couldn't face another night in his room, investigating murder. It was all too real now.

She changed the music—still country, but now up-tempo and crass—but this, too, was met with groans from the peanut gallery.

'What the hell is this? Madonna?'

'This shit is what happens when you let chicks pick the music,' the first man laughed. His smile, both stupid and confident, was quickly wiped away as Shelly aimed the soft drink tap between his eyes and released: direct hit.

Gary stared, as startled as if he'd been hit himself. Coke dripped down the man's nose, on to his shirt, into his open mouth. Joe covered his mouth, laughing, eyes wet with silent tears.

'If you don't like it,' she said, holding the hose like a pistol, 'You know where the door is.'

The man left, still dripping, the words *stupid bitch* under his breath.

Shelly kept her eyes on him and her finger on the juice gun until the bar door swung behind him. Only then did she put it down.

'Another round, boys?' Shelly asked, not looking at them.

Gary felt oddly flattered to be included as one of the boys.

'You want one?' Joe asked, holding up the empty glass they'd both drank from.

Gary had so many questions about Ariel. What was she like as a kid? What were her parents like? Did she have secrets? He didn't know what information he needed to solve Ariel's murder—so he wanted to know everything.

But he had to gain Joe's trust before he risked getting personal. A sure-fire way to achieve that would be to keep him here and keep him drinking.

'Do they do tequila shots here?' Gary replied.

♦ ♦ ♦

'You know,' Sera said, 'Technically, there haven't been any grave robberies?'

Dana turned to look at her, the bottle loose in her hand. 'How's that?'

Sera looked back at Dana soberly, despite the fingers of moonshine she'd burnt through.

'A cemetery is a burial place,' she explained. Despite her heavy boots, she picked her feet carefully on the forest floor. The way deer did. 'But a graveyard is a burial place attached to a church or a place of worship. So, technically, Ariel wasn't buried in a grave. So, technically, there haven't been any grave robberies.'

'So, technically, what was she buried in?'

Dana had led the way. She knew the woods better than Sera, always had. There was the sound of water not too far away. Sera stood by a redwood tree, weeping sap, running her fingers down the bark. Dana took another swig that she really didn't need, burned, and then held out the bottle for Sera.

'Just a hole,' Sera said, peeling the dry wood away in dead strips. 'Have we been here before?'

'No,' Dana said, relieved at the change of topic. 'To be honest, we're a little lost.'

'I thought it looked familiar,' Sera said, finally taking the bottle. 'Guess one tree is like another.'

Sera rarely said things so banal and meaningless. She was comfortable in silence and didn't care if you weren't.

'Pretty sure I dug a hole there a couple of days ago,' Dana

said. 'Stan thought we found something, but it was just animal bones.'

Sera drank. She didn't flinch as the moonshine hit her tongue. When she was finished, she held out the bottle back to Dana. Dana took it and drank, hoping that Sera would say something.

By the time she grimaced and wiped her mouth, Sera still hadn't spoken.

Dana didn't know what to say. Her legs felt wavy; she sat down on a log. The wood rasped against her skin, no moisture left after a too dry summer. She used to lie awake at night thinking of all the things she would say to Sera if she could. If she had five minutes, thirty seconds, ten seconds, what would she tell her? What did she need her to know?

'Tell me about your life,' Dana said. 'Out there.'

Sera sat beside her on the log. Dana passed her the bottle. Sera took a sip. Under the trees and the dark sky she was green and blue, like someone underwater.

'Well?' Dana said. 'It's been ten years. You must have stories. Come on, give me something to work with here.'

Sera looked down at the bottle in her hands. Small creatures moved in the trees.

Dana's cheeks were hot. She wanted to take it back, say forget it. But she also wanted to know Sera. So, she waited.

'It's not that I don't want to tell you,' Sera said eventually, 'I used to write you letters.'

Dana's heart stuttered. 'What did you write about? In the letters.'

Sera shrugged. 'Stupid stuff,' she said. 'Stories I heard in bars. Books I found in the trash. The shitty Spanish I managed to learn. People I met,' she turned to Dana, not smiling, but softening. 'There are so many people out there, Dana. For a while, I was sure that I'd never be able to hide. I only travelled at night. I hid my face. But the first day I was in a city—a real city—I realised just how small this place is. I walked down one street and passed more people than I'd seen in my whole life,' she grinned at her, the white points of her teeth glinting, 'And none of them knew who I was!'

Sera looked at her, eyes bright. Abruptly, Dana realised how close they were sitting, how she was staring. She took the bottle of moonshine, the alcohol smudging on her lips, turning them numb. Around Sera, she felt hypnotised.

'Why didn't you send them?' she asked, wiping her mouth.

'I wanted you to remember me like I was,' Sera said.

I never wanted to remember you, Dana thought.

'I didn't want you to know the bad things about me,' Sera continued, when she didn't speak.

'The last ten years can't have been all bad things,' Dana said.

'I am the bad thing,' she said. 'You don't remember that.'

Her voice was uneven; maybe she was drunker than Dana realised. She didn't know how to comfort. 'Sera, I don't believe any of that—sin, hell, god, secret languages, *angels*, whatever. It's all bullshit, it's just other people in costumes. You never used to believe in any of that, either!'

'I don't believe in it as in I *agree* with it,' she said. 'I don't believe in it. Some of it's just made up, like Enochian was just made up by English colonisers,' Sera looked at the ground. 'But we can do things. That's real, unfortunately. I believe it in like I believe in gravity.'

Sera fell quiet, as if she was burying inside.

'So, what can you do?' Dana stood up. 'You have powers? You can walk on water? What?' Dana gesticulated, forgetting the bottle in her hand, leaving the air smelling of spirits.

Sera watched her.

'Okay, let's pretend magic—or whatever—is on trial,' Dana sat back down and crossed her legs. 'I'm the prosecution.' She prodded Sera's chest with her finger, 'You're the defence. I charge you with bullshit. Angels aren't real, neither is magic. Would the defence like to submit any evidence to this court?'

Sera rolled her eyes. 'As if the justice system is interested in the truth—'

Dana held up her hand. 'Am I to understand the defence has no evidence? Alright then, I'll submit the charge—'

'Hang on, hang on,' Sera said, standing. Dana tried to contain her smirk.

Before Dana could ask what she was doing, Sera had taken her hands, and pulled her to her feet. She didn't let go, clasping Dana's still hand with her warm, thin fingers in the space between their bodies. Her face was so close that she counted the cracks on her chapped lips.

'I can't do much,' Sera said. 'I used to try, but I'm not like Ariel and Michael. I can't do big stuff. The only thing I can do is make things disappear.'

Dana blinked. Was this still a game?

'What?' she said. 'What do you—'

'Quiet,' Sera said, closing her eyes. 'I need to concentrate.'

Dana spluttered a little more, but stopped when Sera squeezed her fingers tight. Her eyes were closed, her face still. Dana had a dream once that she held Sera's hand in hers, her thumb rubbing repetitively over and over her knuckles.

No, it hadn't been a dream, had it? They had been in a dark corner of school. It had been one of those days where Sera needed to retreat deep inside herself, so holding hands had been the easiest way to say, I'm listening, I'm here with you.

Memories were pressing in on her. She was cornered by them. Soon, there would be no other option but to let them in.

Sera's eyes were still closed, but her face wasn't slack, she was intent. Her breathing was the only sound, except for the trees in the wind. Dana readjusted their hands so they were holding. Sera smiled, like a child sleeping and Dana leaned in, and she hit the forest floor, the one arm trapped under her body the only thing that had saved her nose. Her tongue flailed like a fish out of water, sudden and sore.

She sat up. 'Sera?' she tried to say.

Like a drowning person trying to shout for help, blood and saliva filled her mouth like water. Her mouth was all hot teeth and blood: she'd bitten her tongue.

The bottle of moonshine lay on its side, spilling into the night. Dana was alone.

♦ ♦ ♦

Gary was going to vomit. He wasn't sure exactly how many shooters they had done—he'd lost count around number three, along with his ability to taste anything—and he hadn't even gotten any information yet from Joe. Joe, who was currently raising his hand and looking around for Shelly in a way that meant another round was imminent.

This had to be stopped.

'So, Joe,' Gary said. They had introduced themselves—Joe shaking the offered hand with gravitas and a hidden smile—but it was the first time Gary had said his name, and it sat oddly in his mouth. Joe was too ordinary a name for him. 'How come you're buying me all these drinks? Are you celebrating?'

Shelly nowhere to be seen, Joe put his hand down to return his full attention to Gary.

'Have I got something to celebrate?'

He was smiling, but it was a smile that was parked at a crossroads, undecided which way it would go. At the nearest table, overflowing with beer pitchers and baseball caps, loud, uneven singing had broken out.

'No...I mean, maybe—' Gary stammered.

Joe put a hand on his forearm as if to say, Stop, please. 'How come you're drinking all these drinks with me?' he asked.

There were shards of tangy lime flesh between Gary's teeth: he ran his tongue over them, not sure what to say.

'Let me guess,' Joe said, taking his hand away, looking around for Shelly again, 'Girl problems?'

Gary blinked. 'No,' he replied, scandalised.

'Oh,' Joe said. 'Boy problems?'

While he tried to figure out how to say *No* in a way that would communicate he was not gay, but being gay was fine, good, even, but really, he wasn't gay, Shelly returned, zipping behind the bar, a tray laden with empty glasses on one arm.

'Not right now, Joe,' she said. Before he had even drawn breath, she'd rushed off again with a crash of dumped glass and bounce of ponytail.

When Joe saw Gary's face, he laughed.

'I'm just messing with you,' he said, taking off his suit jacket. Standing on the rung of his stool, he reached over the counter to grab at plastic cups. Under the neon light, his white shirt turned blue, turned red. Water, wine.

Joe turned round with two cups, handing one to Gary.

Gary sipped it. Water.

Joe sipped his own, smiling. Probably not water.

'Those kids over there look about your age,' Joe said, nodding his head at the drunken choir. 'Seems unlikely that you don't know their names, that they don't know yours. I'd bet you've had classes with them. Probably played together as kids. And yet, the whole time you've been here, they've ignored you, you've ignored them.'

Gary had gone to school with some of them, but he wasn't sure what Joe was getting at.

'I wasn't bullied,' he said.

'No,' Joe said, 'You kept yourself to yourself. Nobody hated you. They liked you—when you were useful—but that's all. Maybe that was fine, or maybe you just were used to it. Either way, something is eating you. Something you can't tell anyone about.' Joe shrugged. His dark eye held the light's reflection like faint stars. 'Why else would you be getting drunk with a stranger? So, go on, tell me—what's eating you?'

His heart thudded: cheeks still hot from the rush of tequila. Ariel was at home in his room, hidden. Safe. Joe couldn't know.

What if he told him? People would come and take Ariel away.

Would that be so bad?

'Nothing's eating me,' he shook his head, and shot Joe a grin. 'I'm fine.'

Joe was looking at him, jaw propped up on his palm. The more he drank, the softer his face became; now it looked like it could slide down his hand like an egg yolk and pool on the counter.

Gary felt his cell phone buzz in his pocket, and then again, and again. He ignored it.

◆　◆　◆

At first, Dana had been pissed enough to yell like a cop. *Sera, where are you? Sera, can you hear me?* Her cell phone, and the small blue rectangle of light it would have given her, had been left in Brussels. In the dark, she fell, scraping the palm of her right hand. It wasn't deep, but the fall startling tears into her eyes, *Sera, this isn't funny anymore.* Her tongue began to throb. Alone in the dark, again. *Come back.* Sera gone, again. She began to shake. *Please, come back.*

Like a lost bear, she stumbled on to a campsite—if it could be called that. A sleeping bag was stashed underneath a low hanging tree, as if the branches might provide shelter to the cold night, and ashes, where a fire had once burned.

Dana wiped her cheeks; she felt jolted back sharply into reality. The sleeping bag had a soft plasticy sheen. It looked new. She put her hurt hand inside it. Still warm. Leaning a hand on the tree to pull herself upright, her fingertips landed on something strange, a gash as if the bark had been wounded. Following it like thread, she realised it was in the shape of a heart.

Something shifted in the trees.

'Hello?' Dana put her hand to the gun on her belt. 'Sera, is that you?'

By her feet, the ashes became embers.

Between the trees, stood a man. In the dark, she could only make out his boyish broad shoulders, his hair glistening wet with gel, his eyes reflecting the burning fire.

♦ ♦ ♦

'Tell me, Gary,' Joe said. 'What do you want from your life?'

He handed Gary his cup. Through the thin plastic, Gary could feel the ice-cold liquid moving inside.

Gary took a greedy sip: not water. 'My life?'

'Yeah, man,' Joe said, 'Your life! What's the plan? Get married? Kids?' When Gary didn't answer, Joe continued, 'Get out of Lake in the Woods, see the world?'

'I...' Gary blinked rapidly.

He wanted to be assistant manager. He was good at computers. At least, he liked the idea of being good at computers. He was harbouring an undead entity in his bedroom. Somehow, none of this seemed relevant.

'I guess I never really thought about it.' Remembering then that he was supposed to be gleaning information from Joe, he asked, 'What about you?'

'Me?' Joe asked. For the first time, Gary felt like he'd caught him off guard.

'Yeah, you,' Gary said, wishing he had the personality to pull off a wink. 'Is your life going according to plan?'

Joe whistled lowly, standing. Gary's heart sank. Had he offended him? No, he was still smiling. But then, he was always smiling, wasn't he?

Joe lifted the hatch at the side of the bar and went behind, pulling two fresh glasses out from under the counter.

'Is my life going according to plan,' he repeated, cutting up a lime roughly, running it around the edge of the glasses. 'Over the course of this evening, I like to think you've come to see me as a sort of paternal figure. A big brother, if you like.' Ice hit the bottom of each glass like a bell. 'And so, I was planning to gift you some sage words of wisdom. But the truth is, I don't think I thought about it before, either.'

He splashed each glass with Coke. 'I never had to plan,' he pushed one glass towards Gary, and held the other up in a toast, 'Because I've been following God's plan.'

Joe clinked his glass against Gary's.

'Amen!'

As he drained his glass, some of it leaked out of the corner of his mouth and ran down his throat, splashing on his white shirt like river water.

A glass smashed; Gary jumped, his drink splashing over his hand. The man at the end of the bar had fallen off his stool, and lay on the floor amongst the shards of a broken bottle.

It wasn't until Gary got closer that he realised he knew him.

'Well, lookee who it is,' Stan Wu slurred. His glasses were lopsided on his face. 'Is your big sis here, huh?'

'Officer Wu?' Gary's hands, reaching out to help him up, hovered uncertainly. Stan was like a crab on his back, trying to right himself with spikey and uncoordinated movements. 'Are you alright?'

'Oh, give me a break,' Shelly said, summoned by the sound of broken glass. She pulled Stan to his feet, his eyes dazed. 'He's fine. Just drunk. I'm going to sit him outside and call someone to pick him up.'

'Can I help?' Gary asked, because he felt he ought to.

'No,' Shelly slung Stan's arm around her shoulder. 'You'll just get in the way.'

Joe wasn't behind the bar, but nice leather jacket held

his empty seat. Bathroom, Gary thought. A cigarette. He sat back down with his still untouched drink, to wait for him to come back.

♦ ♦ ♦

Shelly took Dana through the back door into the office and sat her down at a chair in front of the desk, as if she were here for a job interview.

It wasn't much: a clean ash tray, a lampshade, the body of which was a pin-up girl in a sailor hat, cardboard boxes on the floor as if Shelly was unpacking. She was probably still putting the place back together after being searched.

'You're welcome to sit in the bar,' Shelly said, sitting on the desk in front of her. The bottle she held in her hand glugged as she poured moonshine into two glasses pinched between her fingers. 'But honestly, I wouldn't recommend it. It's full to the brim of people determined to behave especially foolishly.'

The woods hadn't been empty, either. Between the trees, Dana had seen lit tips of cigarettes, heard the whisper of low talk, laughter, the sound of shook-up spray paint like firecrackers. In the parking lot, kids she recognised from their driver's licenses sat in the open trunks of cars, crushed cans at their feet, weed perfuming the air. She should have probably done something about it.

Shelly held out a crystal glass to Dana, the kind old men drank scotch from. The liquid inside it was clear, but slightly green.

'No,' Dana said. 'Thank you.'

Shelly shrugged and drank it herself in one clean mouthful. Dana shivered; her head was still reeling.

'Can I use your phone?' she asked.

'My service is down. Sorry,' Shelly grimaced, 'It's that storm that's brewing. Probably hit a wire a hundred miles away and now we're cut off.'

'That's all we need,' Dana said.

'Yeah, tell me about it.' Shelly's eyebrows furrowed. 'I take it you're not exactly thrilled about your new boss, either?'

Dana shook her head. She couldn't think about Michael right now: she had to find Sera. She had questions to ask, that felt inappropriate now they were back inside and surrounded with reality. 'I don't want to talk about it. Look, do you think you can give me a ride? Or even just a flashlight, I'll walk back to my car.'

'Honey,' Shelly shook her head. 'The way you were just standing there—I'm still not sure you don't need a doctor. What happened? Did you get lost or something?'

Dana hadn't been lost. She'd followed him, all the way to the parking lot. Every time she'd slowed—on the verge of remembering something she had to do—he had stopped to wait for her.

All four of them had.

Dana didn't know how he'd been there and, instinctively, she'd been certain that his intention was kill her. But once they'd reached Nyx they'd just slipped past Shelly and Stan, inside the bar, like the four of them were co-workers going for a post-shift drink.

'I can't let you go back out there alone,' Shelly continued.

'I'm not alone,' Dana said.

'You mean Sera?' Shelly said. 'I don't see her.'

Dana didn't reply.

'I heard she's skipping town,' Shelly said. 'Maybe she thought it'd be easier to just slip away.'

Annoyed, Dana wanted to argue that Sera wouldn't leave without saying goodbye, but, historically, this was untrue.

Shelly finished the second glass of moonshine and stood.

'We should clean that before it gets infected,' Shelly said, gesturing at Dana's hand. 'The first aid kit is in the basement.'

The basement was half-kitchen half-storage unit, walls lined with endless bottles of vodka and huge wooden barrels. Moonshine. There was a stove, large, well-worn copper basin, pipes connecting them, a process Dana couldn't make sense of. The air tasted sweet, and Dana could see the breath in front of her face. Summer was just coming to an end: Dana hadn't been cold like this since February.

Dana ran her hand down the side of the nearest moonshine barrel. The wood was faintly green, as if grass stained.

'Just like mom and pop used to make,' Shelly said. Her smile lingered somewhere between pride and disdain.

Dana looked back at the barrel. It was almost the height of her. 'Is this the one you gave me the bottle from?'

'No,' Shelly said. 'It's a new batch. This one is still fermenting.'

Dana looked back to the barrel, curious. They were much bigger than Dana had envisioned.

'Can I see inside?' she asked.

Shelly shook her head. 'Open it too early, and the whole batch is ruined.'

'Do you brew it by yourself?' she asked.

Shelly ran a sisterly hand up and down Dana's arm. Dana flinched away.

'You're shivering,' Shelly said, moving her bandaged hand to Dana's back, 'Come on. I've got to keep it cold out here to keep the kegs,' she guided Dana to the door in the corner, 'Let's sit inside here, it's warmer.'

The curtain swooned aside, plastic beads hitting each other like hailstones. The dissonance between the two rooms was so startling, Dana wondered how sober she really was.

It was as if she were stepping inside a jewellery box, or a fortune teller's tent. A pink cloth—draped over a lamp like a scrap of tossed aside underwear—made everything warm. There was a low couch, with silk-poly blend cushions the colour of Valentine's Day, and a round coffee table. It was bedazzled.

But it was the bright, astonishingly single white bed at the centre of the room that Dana's eyes were fixed on. It was narrow and dusted with a layer of fine white crystal, like snow.

'Don't worry, officer,' Shelly said from the doorway. 'It's nothing scandalous.'

Dana licked the tip of her pinky finger. She dipped it into the crisp surface. It crunched. Salt.

'What's it for?' she asked.

'Magic. Obviously,' Shelly said.

Shelly crossed the room and opened a wooden box on the table. Two tall white candles were beside it, along with a cracked open pomegranate glistening like a cow's heart and a framed photograph of Sandy Ackermann.

Shelly lit the candles and unwrapped a deck of cards, too big for games. As she shuffled them, Dana saw flashes of red hearts, blue cups, silver swords, their gold edges catching the candlelight. Sure, Dana had heard of wicca, witchcraft, whatever, but this was all pretty silly.

'Tarot cards. I can do it all. Palmistry, reiki, séances,' she smoothed out the cards into the shape of the crescent moon. 'Do you want to know your future?'

'Is it real?' Dana asked.

Shelly smiled. It was tight and tired. The gash on Dana's hand was still bleeding sluggishly, dripping on to the carpet, but Shelly seemed to have forgotten about the first aid kit.

'I don't know,' Shelly said. 'To be honest with you, I'm beginning to wonder if it's just a way to sell candles.'

Dana was disappointed by her answer.

'Then why do you do it?' Dana asked.

Shelly didn't reply. She held out her hand, the bandaged one.

'Because of you,' she said. 'Come over here. I'll tell you your future.'

Dana stayed where she was, close to the door. 'Another time. You probably need to get back to the bar, right?'

Shelly shook her head. 'It doesn't matter.'

Dana backed away. 'I have to go. I need to find Sera.'

Shelly looked at her. The exhausted desperation that had been lurking, deep out of sight, leapt to the surface.

'She's a liar, Dana,' Shelly said. 'Why can't you see that?'

No one knew Dana was here, did they?

'That's not true,' Dana said.

'Yes it is!' Shelly said. She hit the surface of the table with the flat palm of her hand. The cards jumped with Dana. 'You know it's true.'

Shelly had closed the door to the basement behind them, Dana remembered. Had she locked it too?

Shelly bit her lip. She stood up, but kept her shoulders crouched, making her smaller.

'I'm sorry, Dana,' she said, eyes wide and bloodshot. Dana met them, though she didn't want to. 'It's not your fault you can't remember.' Shelly shook her head. 'What did she do to you?'

Remember what? Dana wanted to ask. But she wasn't sure she wanted Shelly to remind her.

'Did you know Jerome?' Dana asked, mouth dry.

'Why don't you ask him yourself?' Shelly said. 'And Sandy, and Anthony, and Cathy?' Dana didn't reply. 'I know you saw them. The four of them,' Shelly came closer. 'I knew you'd be able to.'

Dana's legs wavered under her. She was drunk after all. If this was real, then it meant it was all real, and the things she had buried inside her to rot were not fears but realities.

'They're dead,' Dana said. It was only half a question. 'But I saw them.' She looked at Shelly. 'Why can I see them?'

Shelly took her hurt hand. 'You know why, Dana.'

Dana didn't answer, didn't move: her body locked with dreaded familiarity.

'No, I don't,' she said.

Shelly squeezed her hand, comfortingly. 'Remember that party in high school, at the Enckles' house?'

Yes, but only in the way she remembered her dreams. The white house, the fire, the stars dancing, distorted by the water—

'No,' Dana said. 'I don't remember.'

Shelly stared at her for a moment. The pupils of her eyes were small, like the end of a dart. Before Dana could move away, the grip on her hand became painful, and she was pulling her to the table.

'What are you doing?' Dana said, trying and failing to break free from her grip. Her knees hit the floor painfully as she was pulled down; under the carpet it was just concrete.

'If you can't remember, I'll help you,' Shelly said, forcibly running Dana's hand over the cards, *twack, twack, twack.* 'Pick a card, any card!'

'Let me go!' Dana shouted, breaking her hand free. As she pulled it away, a card came with her, caught on her finger, and flipped over.

A hooded figure on a bone white horse. Death. It lay between them on the table hushed.

'Pick another one,' Shelly said, breathing hard.

'Doesn't mean anything,' Dana said, getting to her feet. 'I

don't believe any of this crap.'

'Pick two more. Turn them face up on the table,' Shelly said, pointing. 'And I'll tell you why you can see them.

Dana wasn't sure if this was a game to her, a scene she was re-enacting. But even if it was, Shelly was standing between her and the door.

And Dana wanted to know why.

Dana pulled out two more cards. One from the middle. One half-hidden, at the very end. She turned them face up.

Death and Death.

'Past, present, future,' Shelly said, coming closer. 'Do you know what that means?'

Dana shook her head.

'You can see them because you're already dead,' Shelly said. Dana's heart thudded as if in protest. She closed her eyes, trying to shake off the memory of wet mud sliding down her bare back, then recoiled. Shelly was touching her face.

'Do you even know how special you are?' Shelly asked.

She traced her fingers over the purple hollow underneath her eyes, the small bones of her nose.

One hand went to Dana's hair. Dana flinched, anticipating it would be grabbed. But Shelly stroked it slowly, the way you'd stroke a dog before putting it down. 'How lucky you are?'

Her face was needy. Dana couldn't look at her, but gazed at her ear, as if this wasn't happening.

'Did it hurt? You must have been scared,' Shelly asked. 'You can tell me.'

Over Shelly's shoulder, Dana could see the photograph of Sandy Ackermann, the wavering flames reflected in the glass. Shelly couldn't hurt her, Dana tried to remind herself.

'I have to find Sera,' Dana said, like an automatic response.

There was an outraged pause. Then, Shelly's hand moved quickly but clumsily towards Dana's hip and her gun holster.

Dana pushed Shelly away from her. Surprised, she fell back easily and hit the floor, knocking over the table, spilling the cards, the candles drowning in their own wax.

Shelly looked up at her from the ground, startled tears in her eyes, the cards pooling around her. In the fall, some of them had flipped. Death, Death, Death.

'Please don't go, Dana,' Shelly said, a drop of blood on her lip. She bit her tongue in the fall. 'Stay with me. Stay with us.'

'I'm not dead,' Dana said.

Dana ran back into the cold, up the stairs, Shelly shouting after her. Dana found the cuts at the back of her lip, opening them with her tongue, reminding her what was real. She had to get out. She had to find Sera.

The back door: locked. Shelly was still calling for her, the same two words over and over. Running the other way, Dana pushed a door, it opened on to the bar, bursting around her like a firework; neon lights, laughter, music, life.

Anthony Dorhamer was propped up on the bar, mid-story, crossed legs. Sandy was grinding to the music, one arm sliding around Cathy's waist, the old lady's head tipped back. At the back, Dana could see Jerome. He was no longer looking for her, lost in a kiss.

Sera.

Gasping into the night air, Dana let the door slam shut behind her, and ran to the road, Shelly's voice ringing in her ears *Not yet! Not yet!* as twin headlights roared towards her.

♦ ♦ ♦

It felt like he'd been waiting a long time, but when Gary checked his phone, only twenty minutes had passed. Missed call: dad. Missed call: dad. Missed call: dad.

It was late. He was probably mad.

Is this seat taken? He'd been asked this more than once as the bar continued to fill, becoming hot with human skin and breath. Eventually, without his permission, the seat was taken by a man his father's age. Joe's jacket slipped off the back and pooled on the floor.

Shelly was nowhere to be seen. He wanted to be the kind of person who could drink alone in a bar comfortably; he wasn't. His empty plastic cup in one hand and Joe's suit jacket folded over his arm, he went to check the men's room.

No Joe, but the cramped space was full. One guy peed against the wall —why, Gary wasn't sure, as the urinal was right there—two of his friends were leaning over the sink. They stood up straight quickly. Gary had the sense he had interrupted something.

'Hey, man, aren't you going to piss?' the peeing guy said

over his shoulder as Gary made to shuffle back out.

'Uh, no, I'm okay,' Gary said. 'I was just looking for someone.'

As he left, one of them said, 'In the men's room?'

Back inside, a couple of men had piled behind the bar, laughing as they uncapped bottles of Rolling Rock and handed them out to the crowd egging them on.

Someone should stop them, Gary thought.

In the parking lot, Gary looked around for Shelly, or Stan, or Joe. They weren't there. Just parked cars like sleeping houses, the trees rustling in the wind and the noise from the bar behind him.

Shocked by the concrete into sobriety, Gary shivered. He put on Joe's jacket. It felt like slipping into snow. It was later than he thought, and home was a long way to cycle in the dark. He put the plastic cup he was still holding on top of the ashtray on the wall. It was the closest thing to a trashcan he could see.

Taking out his phone, called Dana. It rang out half-heartedly a few times, then stopped.

Gary wished, very suddenly, that Ariel were here.

His phone came alive in his hand.

'Dana?' he asked.

'Gary, it's dad.' His voice was so distorted, it sounded like they was standing at opposite ends of a very long tunnel. 'Where are you?'

'Don't worry,' Gary said. 'I'm just with some friends.'

'Gary, where are you right now?' his dad said urgently.

'I'll come and pick you up.'

'It's okay, you really don't need to do that.'

'Gary, I saw the tape,' he said. 'We need to—'

Numb, Gary hung up.

He needed to get away.

Rounding the corner to the back of the bar, Gary veered backwards. The guys from the bathroom stood with the red-faced man Shelly had kicked out earlier. He held a spray can, his handiwork still drying on the wall.

WHORE.

Gary didn't know what to say.

'Hey fagg-o,' the pissing guy said. 'Nice jacket. Did your boyfriend give it to you?'

It was so stupid, Gary started to laugh. He laughed, even as one of the others came towards him.

The first weak punch surprised him even as it slung him out on the ground. He had not expected to get hit. It was not something that usually happened to him.

Someone kicked him in the stomach. There was no room for thoughts, except, *Please stop.*

The air shifted and turned to salt.

♦ ♦ ♦

The first thing she'd said, after the car's wheels had stopped spinning and she'd opened the door to run towards Dana was, I was looking for you everywhere.

They didn't make it back to Brussels, and were still close

enough to the road that Dana could smell the tire rub and petrol, when she put her shaking hand on Sera's shoulder, feeling the thrum of the pulse in her neck. Sera's hair was tangled, her eyes wild.

'Are you alright?' Sera asked, not for the first time. 'Dana?'

Dana didn't know what to say, so screwed her eyes shut and kissed her. Their teeth clacked together—more like a bite—but Dana kept pressing her lips against Sera's.

Sera let this continue for a handful of seconds, before pulling back.

'Dana,' she said, and then again, 'Dana.' Her hand curled around Dana's own, as if she might either remove it from her shoulder or hold it. 'Do you want me to kiss you?'

Dana's embarrassment shot hot through her. What hadn't been clear?

Sera's hand stayed warm where it was. 'I want to kiss you,' she said, calmly. 'I want to hold you. I want to fuck you. But I need you to tell me what you want.'

In defiance of her shaking legs, and the part of her which wanted to run, Dana nodded.

'Yes,' she said, when Sera still didn't move. Dana didn't want to say it. 'Please,' she said.

As she closed her eyes, she saw Sera moving in on her. Dana was unsure how to lead, but she could follow. Sera opened her mouth. Inside, she felt that kind of searing white cold jolt that could burn or freeze. Her tongue and lips sensitive where they had been bleeding, but Sera touched her wounds in a way that was addictive, a bruise Dana wanted her to press again and again.

It was so cold that Dana couldn't stop shaking, held between a tree and Sera's body, arms wrapped around her, warming her slowly.

Sera covered her on the forest floor, lips spilling hot wine. Dana took Sera's hands and put them where she wanted them, skating up limbs threatening to drift apart, holding them with her hand like a stitch. Sera undressed her. Dana could see the vast expanse of her own skin, moonlight making it white as a sheet ghost. Her shirt and bra were gone, she could smell herself, ripe, Sera reached for her trousers and Dana cringed, legs coming together.

Sera took her hands away immediately.

'Sorry,' Dana said. Numb, she lay on the ground, like a half-hunted animal in the dirt. Sera sat back on her hunches. Her eyes were alert, watching Dana, waiting. She had always been waiting.

Dana didn't know how to explain. She wasn't scared. Her body was. She wanted this.

'We don't have to do anything,' Sera said, averting her eyes. It was almost funny. She'd never seen Sera shy. 'We can stop.'

But they couldn't. Because, wrecked car or not, tomorrow Sera would be gone.

Dana stood, so she could see Sera's face clearly, see more than just the whites of her eyes. Her expression was muted, at odds with her swollen mouth, the twig in her hair. She made as if to move, but Dana held out a hand. Wait.

Dana pushed off her boots first, stuffing her socks inside them. They were steel toe cap. Regulation. The first week she'd worn those boots, she could barely walk without flinching by Sunday. It had felt as though instead of breaking them in, they'd broken her. She unbuckled her belt, dropping her trousers and underwear at once like ripping off a band-aid, her naked body an injury.

On the ground in front of her, Sera was still fully clothed. Her eyes on Dana's body—gooseflesh and shivering—legs splayed. Dana sank between them, the denim rasping on her skin. Sera's lips were still at first. So, Dana kissed her, moving her lips as if she was mouthing something across a crowded room, praying to be understood.

Sera began to kiss her back, holding her tongue in her mouth. Dana wasn't cold anymore, but she was still shaking, shaking as she held the two fingers Sera offered in her mouth, as she led them, wet, between her legs, holding on to Sera, burning all around her, barefoot in the mud.

Chapter Sixteen

> The habitat of angels is equally perplexing. In the opinion of Aquinas, angels cannot occupy two places at the same time (theoretically it would not be impossible for them, being pure spirits, to do so). On the other hand, they can journey from one place to another, however far removed, in the twinkling of an eye.
>
> *A Dictionary of Angels (Including the Fallen Angels),* Gustav Davidson

They were still naked in the woods when the day began to breathe. Even in the dark, Sera had been warm. Even in the dark, Dana had seen her. The hollow scar on her shin, the shape and size of a thumb print. A stuttering tattoo on her shoulder, ink shot with age. The thatch of dark hair on the back of her thigh.

Her own body felt good, but strange. Like she'd been broken down and put back together differently. Sera's fingers were lightly running down her arm; her skin thrummed awake.

'The first time I ever saw the ocean,' Sera said. Dana's head was resting on her chest, so she could feel the buzz of her voice under the skin. 'I wrote you so many letters about that.'

Their skin was still crushed together. She used to dream about this.

Sera licked her chapped lips. 'Come with me,' she said.

Dana looked up into her eyes.

Every time she had a part of Sera pinned down, mapped out and measured, she either came to a dead end, or a doorway where there had been a wall.

'Why did you leave?' Dana asked. 'Back then.'

Sera's eyes fluttered away, birds in the trees. Dana waited.

'You know that my family found out about you and me?' Dana nodded into her. 'Well, I thought they were going easy on me, or that they'd given up trying to change me. Turns out they were just waiting. The night I turned 18, they told me the time had come for me to carry on the divine bloodline.'

Dana pinched her brows together. What did she mean?

'They were going to inseminate me,' Sera continued, in Dana's confused pause. 'With an offering from another descendent.'

Dana didn't know what to say. 'Sera—I'm sorry.'

'It's okay. I mean, it's not, obviously.' Sera's fingertips drummed her freckled arm like she was playing a piano. 'But it's over. Anyway, before that, Father Enckles said I had to be cleansed. We have a—well it's kind of a pool, in the basement.'

'I remember,' Dana said. Finally, she did.

Sera met her eyes and nodded, as if she saw something she'd been waiting for there.

'Anyway, I had to get in and tread water. Dad used to make us do it for hours when we were bad. Try not to drown, with everyone watching, my brothers and sister...' she closed her eyes. 'I saw the tube in my mom's hand and something in me died. I knew they would never let me go. Never let me be. I couldn't do it anymore. None of it. I wished I was nothing, that I didn't exist,' she stopped, 'And I let myself sink.'

A bird sang in the trees.

'What happened?' Dana breathed.

'I opened my eyes in a river in Wisconsin. Naked as a baby,' Sera smiled. 'That's the funny thing. I'm a descendent of Raphael—concealment is my right. But the first time it ever worked that way for me, was when I wanted anything but a descendent.'

Sera looked down at Dana. 'I'm sorry. For all of it.'

Dana moved her head, as if she were pressing deeper into her chest. 'You don't have to be sorry. I'm glad you survived.'

Sera breathed in deeply. 'Come with me?'

Dana held her gaze.

'Stay,' she said, simply. 'Fight.'

Sera closed her eyes. The sigh.

'I'm not as strong as him. Look at last night.'

Last night could refer to so many things.

'I'm not talking about your Houdini thing. Concealment. Whatever you want to call it,' Dana said, pushing through

Sera's attempt to interrupt, 'Just stay. We can figure this out.'

'You're better without me,' Sera said.

'No,' Dana said. 'I'm not.'

Sera sat up, dislodging Dana. Her spine curved underneath her skin, like the bones of a fish. She reached for her clothes.

The car was fixable. Dana watched as Sera hitch the trailer to it, shining silver in the early morning sun.

Then she watched her leave.

♦ ♦ ♦

People called it the Jesus-Loves-You Motel, because the turn-off for it was about a minute down from the Jesus Loves You billboard. That sign had lasted through rain, snow, time, and so had the joke; it isn't just Jesus' love people go there for, if you know what I mean.

Gary had always wanted to stay in a motel, but the Jesus-Loves-You didn't live up to his expectations. The room was small, all grubby white furniture and old fabric. The 'attached kitchenette' was a microwave and a mini fridge.

But the lady on reception had taken one glance at the two of them—Gary bruised, with a split lip, Ariel, hair tucked under a baseball cap and wearing sunglasses at night—and hadn't batted an eye, so he wasn't complaining.

He was sure he hadn't slept, but at some point he opened his eyes and it was light again. His face still hurt, but his cuts were clean. Ariel had wiped them with a hot, damp towel before pulling back the sheets on the bed and looking at him in a way that meant, *get in.*

Eyes cracked open, Gary saw the same towel lying on the floor. It was red. Blood. His blood. Joe's jacket hung off the back of the single chair, Gary's phone weighing down its pocket like a stone. Ariel, standing in the corner, watching him.

Gary wished he could hide under the covers, pretend he wasn't awake after all. When the kicking had stopped, and Gary had seen what was going on, he'd almost been more afraid.

'Uh, morning,' he said.

Ariel blinked. She turned and picked up a can of Sprite and a Twinkie, putting them beside Gary on the bed. There was a pile of snacks on top of the microwave. Gary wasn't sure where they came from, but he suspected they had the wallet Joe helpfully left in his jacket pocket to thank, yet again.

He sat up in bed, wincing as his stomach protested. Ariel loomed over him, still watching. Nervous, Gary picked up the Sprite and cracked it open.

Wiping his mouth, forgetting about his still fresh cut and wincing, he said, 'Thanks. For this, and for, uh, saving me.'

Ariel blinked.

Gary continued. 'My dad knows about you. We can't go home. I don't know what to do.'

Ariel blinked.

'I really don't know,' stuffing half the Twinkie in his mouth, he continued, chewing. 'I don't know what we're going to do. I don't have a car. I could take Dana's but...' Gary blinked rapidly. 'She'd be so mad. My dad is probably—' he swallowed.

Gary started to cry.

'I fucked it all up,' he confessed. The salt stung. 'This is all my fault.'

The weight on the bed shifted as Ariel sat down beside him. Gary opened his eyes. Her cold hand was on his chest, right over his heart. He grabbed her forearm and held on, tears splashing.

'I'm sorry,' he said, sobbing.

There was a knock on the door. Gary jumped, startled enough to stop crying. He looked at Ariel. She didn't blink. He didn't breathe, didn't move; if he didn't do anything, they would go away.

They knocked again.

'I know you're in there, Gary,' a voice said—Shelly's voice. 'Open the door, unless you want me to tell the sheriff about your friend.'

♦   ♦   ♦

There were six men on the Town Council.

Principal Graham, who had halted assembly to tell her to pray harder last year. Sheriff Wormwood, who pulled her over for speeding a handful of times. Mr Ackermann, the owner of the grocery store. Mayor Spinner; Ed Spinner's uncle, similarly big and broad and proudly stupid. Father Enckles.

Then there was her dad. He was the minute taker for this meeting. His pen went slack in his hand as she walked into the room.

The men sat around a long table. The mayor had a wooden gavel in his hand, like Judge Judy. There was coffee. There were doughnuts. Dana sat at the seat near the end of the table, mouth dry.

'Next item on our agenda is an audience with Miss Dana Fisher,' Mr Ackermann said, reading from a sheet of paper, eyes straining behind the slim reading glasses perched on the end of his nose. 'Welcome, Miss Fisher, and my goodness don't you look like your daddy?'

'She's the spit of you, Francis,' Principal Graham said, a smile she'd never seen him wear before on his face. He waggled a finger at Dana, light bouncing on his bald head. 'Though I have to say, she's not as big a fan of the books as her old man.'

The men all laughed. Dana smiled. She didn't really find it funny, but she didn't want to be rude.

'Well, Miss Fisher,' Mayor Spinner said with a smile. 'Why don't you tell us why you're here?'

Dana knew what she'd seen. Over the Christmas break, she'd snuck over to the Enckles house, hoping to see Sera. There had been snow on the ground. The lake had been frozen.

The family had been outside, a circle around Sera.

Dana had read once that prey animals hide their pain, so they don't make themselves a target. It had made her think of the fear Sera hid in her silence, the way she'd cracked the ice with her ankle before walking in, head held high, naked.

Shivering, breath cold in front of her face, Dana had watched her tread the water for hours, until the sun had set, Michael watching her from the pier.

It was Sera's face she held in her mind as she'd quickly hidden the bruises on her arm in the changing room. The way she'd said, *nothing much,* when Dana had asked her what she'd got for Christmas.

Finished, she breathed, eyes on the pink sprinkles. Father Enckles was silent. She was ready for a fight; ready to scream.

'Young lady,' the Mayor said, 'I have to confess that I'm not entirely clear what the basis of this meeting is. What, exactly, are you trying to say?'

Dana licked her lips before she spoke.

'I'm not sure. I don't know too much about the law. But it seems to me that punishing your kids like that isn't right.'

'It might seem strict, but the Enckles kids are keen swimmers, even in winter,' Mr Ackermann said, eyes kindly blue. He looked around at the other men. 'Now if I saw my kids doing anything like that, I'd just be glad they got off their lazy butts.'

It warranted a few titters. 'Don't blame you for getting confused, but it's nothing for the law to get involved in, right Al?'

Sheriff Wormwood was not smiling.

'No. A little bit of swimming isn't unlawful.' He hesitated. 'If someone was hitting her, that'd be different.'

Father Enckles was still silent.

Dana thought. 'I did see the bruises on Sera's arm, sir,' she said.

'Could have been anything,' Principal Graham said. 'Gym can get a little rough from time to time.'

'They were shaped like fingerprints,' Dana said, 'Like someone grabbed her arm and squeezed.'

'Even so, I'm not sure what you're saying,' Principal Graham said. 'It's likely to have been a boyfriend.'

'Sera doesn't have a boyfriend,' Dana said.

'Girls that age keep secrets,' he told her, 'Even from their best friends.'

'She doesn't have a boyfriend,' Dana said again.

Her dad made a movement in the corner of her eye, but Dana didn't catch it.

'But you and Michael Enckles dated for a little while,' Mayor Spinner said. 'Right?'

Dana's body flooded with cold water. She had thought telling them about the night of the party, but she didn't know how. Words like assault and rape sometimes crossed her mind, but she didn't feel that she could reach out and grab them. They didn't belong to her. They belonged to people who'd been really hurt.

'Miss Fisher?' one of the men said: she wasn't sure which.

'Yes?' She responded to her name, and then again. 'Yes. I mean, we dated for a little while. But this was years ago.' Dana woke up a bit, as the coldwater shock abiding. 'And it's not why I'm here. I'm here for Sera. Maybe he's the one hurting her, but it could be someone else.'

'Who?' Mayor Spinner said, triumphant. 'Who exactly are you accusing?'

Father Enckles still hadn't said a word. His fingers were laced together. Dana knew what they were thinking. *She wouldn't dare.*

Raising her shaking hand, she pointed it at Sera's father.

'Him. He's the one hurting her,' she said. 'He's the one who made her get in the water.'

Father Enckles gazed back at her, unmoved.

'Dana,' the sheriff asked. 'Did he physically force Sera to get in the water?'

She forced herself to look at him. There was something purposeful about him. He had the body of a retired dancer.

'No,' she said.

'And the bruises on Sera's arm,' the sheriff said. 'Did she tell you her father hurt her?'

Mayor Spinner opened his mouth to interject, but Father Enckles held up the flat palm of his hand.

'I can't remember,' she said. It was the truth. Recently she found herself reaching for memories and finding them missing.

'Yes or no?' the sheriff asked.

'No,' she said.

Some emotion appeared in the sheriff's eyes before he hushed it. For a moment, she felt she had disappointed him.

'Dana, if you're going to report a crime that you were not a witness to, you have to be able to tell us what happened,' he said.

'Not waste our time with insinuations about good people,' Mayor Spinner said, mouth stretching into a cheap smile.

'I'll talk to your friend, just to make sure there isn't some boyfriend around causing her trouble,' the sheriff continued, 'Though I'm sure this is all a misunderstanding.'

'But he'll make her lie,' Dana said. 'Don't you understand—'

'Very convenient,' Principal Graham noted, unemotional. 'Miss Enckles can speak for herself, don't you think?'

Dana felt insane with fury. She wished that she could be so rational about someone's life.

'He won't let her!' Dana shouted, pointing at Father Enckles again. 'Don't you see that family is evil?'

There was a crash as a heavy sheaf of papers fell to the wooden floor.

Francis Fisher stood, pen still in hand, fingers blue, skin red and stretched over his face. The only part of his body that was still were his eyes, black pupils huge and swallowing the thin blue line around them. He was almost vibrating with contained fury, his words slipping out like steam underneath the lid of a boiling pot.

'Dana,' he said, 'Shut your mouth.'

Dana could feel her cheeks grow cold as the blood drained from them. He had never raised his voice to her like this before. She didn't know what to do.

'Please believe me, dad,' she said. 'I'm not lying.'

It was as if she hadn't spoken. Smoothing his pants, he

sat down again, and the Council decided with her consent to strike the audience from the record.

'The Lord forgives,' Father Enckles said as she left. His voice was low like thunder. 'No matter how lost, you can still be saved from the fire.'

Fire? Dana thought. If I burn, I'll take you with me. I'll burn this whole town to the ground.

♦ ♦ ♦

There was no mob outside the Sheriff's Department, just fresh flowers and white tealights burning on the steps of the church opposite: it was quieter than it had been in days. A memorial, where before there had been a riot.

At the morning briefing, Deputy Boldry mumbled through a vague welcoming speech. *This isn't what any of us expected.* Graham and Coops clapped Michael on the back, big and meaty. Mel sweated over the fax machine. The phone lines were still glitching, patches of cell service available in random spots.

There were doughnuts. There were not usually doughnuts. Sheriff Wormwood had high standards of hygiene. Dana doubted he'd approve of anything so sticky. Out of loyalty, she didn't take one. If she told the sheriff what she'd seen last night, would he believe her? Would anyone?

Michael didn't wear the uniform, but he was dressed differently. No suit, just ironed denim jeans, a sweater, a gun. He wasn't wearing the hat, but he had found a five-pointed silver star and pinned it to his breast.

Last night, she'd walked with the dead, somehow this was worse.

Only Stan looked how Dana felt, face drawn behind his flashing glasses. He had sat in the empty seat beside her but didn't meet her eyes when she said hello.

The sheriff was concerned not just about *the situation*, but about vandalism. There had been complaints from concerned citizens of teenagers running wild night, spray painting vulgarities on to businesses. Officer Wu and Officer Fisher would handle the removal of this graffiti as soon as possible; after all, we're talking about people's livelihoods here.

'And finally,' he said with a smile, 'We had quite an unusual anonymous call this morning. Mel, do you want to tell everyone about it?'

Mel stood up straight like a gofer in an arcade game.

'We got a call this morning from a gentleman who claimed to have been attacked by a UFO,' Mel said.

Michael raised his eyebrows, as if to say, Go on. Laugh. Some of them did. Mel, emboldened, continued.

'He said that it was little and grey. It flew and made things fly around with its mind.' Mel was now trying hard not to laugh. 'That it beat him up and…stole fifty bucks from his wallet.'

Michael was so indulgent. 'And where did this gentleman claim this alien attacked him, Mel?'

Mel was grinning now. 'Behind Nyx.'

Even Deputy Boldry laughed.

'Sounds like too much moonshine to me,' Jacob said.

Michael shrugged, blue eyes twinkling. 'You said it, not me.'

'Shouldn't we dig a little deeper?' Stan said. The laughter stopped. 'Initially, Sheriff Wormwood thought Nyx was a potential site of interest. We even searched it and confirmed the alibi of the owner. It's weird, but just because the guy was drunk, doesn't mean it's a complete fantasy.'

Dana thought of the future. She could team up with Sheriff Wormwood and Stan, a rag-tag gang of heroes and friends. It wouldn't be easy, but together they'd find the bodies and enough evidence to arrest Michael. He'd spend the rest of his days somewhere far from here in a cell with a stainless-steel toilet and a thin bar of soap, and the sheriff would get his job back.

Without him, with the Enckles family cycle broken, the town would change. All kinds of people would move here and feel welcome. Her father's work would flourish. Stan would never endure another racist comment. Kids like Gary would grow up with a future. Kids like Jerome would grow up.

Someday, when the sheriff retired, she'd take his place and his wide-brimmed hat. Lake in the Woods would be a beautiful place to live, where no one would ever die alone.

Sera would come back.

'Yeah,' Dana said. 'Stan's right. Besides, what are we going to do about these bodies? Wouldn't searching for them be a better use of our time than cleaning off some spray paint?'

'I understand your frustrations, Officer Fisher,' he replied, with the same bland politeness he showed everyone. 'The senior officers—by that I mean, Deputy Boldry and myself—will be handling the search. What I'd like you guys to focus on is morale. Think of the town as a herd,' he suggested. 'We're the shepherds.'

Dana glared at him. Michael expected respect the same way people expected to wake up in the morning and expected to breathe.

'Whatever,' she said.

In a sick way, Dana had hoped that Michael would acknowledge the animosity between them. That he would ask her for a private word, threaten her. But when the briefing finished, she was simply dismissed along with the other junior officers. Michael and Deputy Boldry went to the sheriff's office. He met Dana's eyes as he passed. He nodded. She ignored him. They closed the door.

In the bathroom mirror, she gulped water from the tap. She hadn't been home since the night before. Dana wondered if she could get Stan alone. She owed him an explanation. She owed him a lot of things.

Everyone was in the office. She couldn't get to the evidence locker, and Stan was talking with Jacob. She wasn't sure if that made things easier or harder.

Mel was on reception. He didn't have time to say hello, before Dana had pulled out her gun. Cold metal looked so incongruous amongst his paperclips and rolled up copy of *Christian Youth*.

'I have a message for Michael,' she said, dropping down

her badge, her handcuffs and keys to the patrol car. Shocked, Mel still picked up a pen and paper. 'He's full of shit. I quit.'

♦ ♦ ♦

Now that school was over, it was harder to meet. The Enckles house was off-limits, of course, but so was Dana's after the meeting with the council. Town was dangerous. Kids from school liked to hang out there aimlessly, drifting with brown paper fast food bags, translucent with grease. Coopers and skateboarding by the closed stores, tipping cows at night. A thousand eyes.

That left the woods. They walked for so long that their routes became desire trails. When it got too cold, they got into the parked car, talked for so long their breath steamed up the windows.

It wasn't the thing adults did, and Dana wondered if their time was running out. Sera was busy, and when they were together she was quiet.

Dana hated Sera quiet. She wanted to reach inside and grab on to the part of her that threatened to outgrow this.

If Sera left, Dana could cope. If Sera said to her, thank you and goodbye, Dana could handle it. But she didn't want to be a joke. She didn't want this not to be real.

So, she drove. Dana drove at breakneck speed, past the border of the town and into the night, waiting for Sera to say, *you're going too fast,* but she never did.

She called the Enckles house, let it ring three times and

hung up, to say, *I'm here.*

She worked at the carwash. She saved a thick wad of one-dollar notes underneath her bed, held together with an elastic band. Saving for something she refused to admit to herself.

Despite all this, it was Sera who asked the question in July, the month before her birthday.

'What if we didn't go back?' she wondered in the hot night air of the car. 'What if we kept driving?'

After Sera was gone, Dana would count the money and try to remember what she had been saving for; park the car on the edge of town, look out and wait.

◆ ◆ ◆

In the shower, her body was someone new in town. There was dirt inside her ears, on her scalp like fleas, but even the sore bits were magical, the full-body ache of exhaustion somehow surmountable as it had never been before.

She could solve this.

Still wet hair dripped onto the T-Shirt she wore, her uniform crumpled on the floor with her phone, still dead from last night. If Michael had killed Ariel—and increasingly Dana found herself believing that he had—it was unlikely that he had excavated the bodies. The missing had been on their way to being forgotten, now their lives and deaths were being held under a microscope.

There's no way the person who murdered Ariel would

want their deaths to be scrutinised like this. Michael was afraid, Dana realised with a jolt of pleasure. That's why he was doing his best to control the investigation.

Which led Dana to conclude that—weird as it was—whoever had uncovered the bodies hadn't done it to help him. They'd done it to expose him, expose the family. Which meant not only would they be close enough to know there was something to expose, but they might be an ally.

There were only two possible suspects; Shelly Ackermann or Joe Enckles.

Shelly fit the bill almost perfectly. She had been Joe's teenage girlfriend, so she'd had a close relationship with the Enckles. Maybe she had seen more than she should. She also knew several of the missing; Anthony, casually, Sandy, intimately. Then, there was the tarot card in Jerome's locker.

She was also, clearly, unwell.

But Shelly had an alibi for all but thirty-five minutes of that evening. Nyx was close enough to the graveyard that she could have walked there, but there was no way she could have uncovered and successfully hidden five bodies in thirty minutes.

Sheriff, Stan had asked, *Is it possible they weren't all moved on the same night?*

Dana thought about it. The only body that could not have been moved prior to that evening was Ariel's, and thirty-five minutes was still not enough time. It ruled Shelly out, but something in Dana hesitated. Shelly was confused, maybe even unstable, but she had to be involved in some way.

Dana shivered. The shoulders of her T-Shirt were soaked through. *Not yet.*

It sounded like a threat, but what if it was a warning?

She started to towel dry her hair. The evidence against Joe Enckles was much thinner. He was connected to Jerome and Ariel, both intimately. Obviously, he had insider knowledge of the Enckles home.

What did a cult look like? Dana wondered. Maybe it just looked like Sera's blank eyes.

Sera had told her that Joe's abilities opposed her own—whatever that meant. They seemed close, Dana thought. Sera said Joe was the one who had told her to leave. How far was she now?

Dana hadn't expected Sera to ask her to come with her. Whether she wanted to or not seemed irrelevant. She had the feeling that if she were to leave Lake in the Woods, she would disintegrate into the wind, and whatever was left behind would be unrecognisable.

She flopped back to stare at the ceiling, damp hair spreading a slow, cold patch on the blanket. Could Joe and Shelly both be involved? It would make sense. Joe's alibi was that he'd been home with his mom all night, but even if she wasn't lying, Dana knew that didn't count for much in terms of reliability. It was possible he moved the bodies, and Shelly stored them somewhere in Nyx.

Why else would Jerome have led her there?

There were still holes in this theory. Namely, the sheriff had already searched the premises. Besides, what about

Cathy Copeland? Neither Joe or Shelly knew her. But then, no one seemed to.

Dana was close, but she was missing something. That was fine, she repeated to herself, chewing her thumbnail. It was good. Knowing it was missing was already a start—now, all she had to do was figure out what 'it' was.

Something in her had been unlocked, or perhaps broken. Either way, new memories were spurting out: first a trickle, but they were steadily becoming a flood.

Just part of the truth wasn't enough. Dana had to know it all.

She got up and picked her uniform up off the floor. No point putting it in with the laundry. It could just go out with the trash.

♦ ♦ ♦

In the light of day, Nyx was dull as an off-season carnival attraction, cigarette butts speckled over the brown grass outside like dead confetti.

The back door was open. Nothing was in the office except the two glasses from last night, a bottle of yellow nail polish and a cigarette butt on the table. The tip was cold.

'Shelly?' Dana called.

The basement was empty. Without the candles the red wasn't warm, but horrifying, like a day-old murder scene. Dana opened drawers and boxes, but the things she found meant nothing to her; funny coloured stones, dried herbs, paperback novels. Maybe Dana should re-align her chakras, whatever they were. Pulling up the carpet to pull at the floorboards with her blunt nails, she thought this was becoming increasingly like a game of hide and seek.

Upstairs, Dana's shoes stuck to the bar floor. Glasses were stacked in the sink, or still sitting on tables, as if waiting for their owners to return.

A CD was still spinning in the player, silent and stuck on the last track. Dana popped the top. *The Immaculate Collection.*

Something was wrong. *Not yet.*

There had been a car in the parking lot. Shelly had to be here, somewhere.

The trees behind the parking lot breathed in the wind. Someone had told her once that the Ackermann's moonshine was made from apples. Maybe it was true, the branches back here were heavy.

At first, she thought the cut rope was a broken branch, flirting back and forth in the wind. Shelly lay below it, the other half of the fraying noose still around her neck. Crouched over her, hands hovering, was Ariel Enckles. Looming over them both was Gary, a shovel shaking in his hands.

Chapter Seventeen

> Rebekah said to me once, 'there are no monsters in these woods, except for you and me.' I remember it clearly. I laughed and turned away from her. Back then, I looked away from things that frightened me.
>
> *Lake in the Woods: A Complete History of an American Miracle*, Francis Fisher

Cathy's family were all dead, but she saw her grandmother every time she looked in the mirror. She knew she hadn't aged prettily, lips too thin and nose too large, a mean woman moustache, white skin.

No, grey. She had grown into a grey woman in this empty house, a forgotten cupboard in this town where she prayed alone. At least, where she used to pray alone.

Ariel was incongruous in her sitting room, trying to get the cat to come closer. She was pretty, Cathy admitted. In a cheap American way.

It was the things she said that lingered in Cathy's mind.

Once Ariel started to help her with her groceries every week, Cathy had wondered if this was a mission. It was a little too late to convert, she told Ariel. Don't you waste your time on me, pet.

But Ariel had said that she was not trying to convert her. She hoped they could be friends.

It was a young person's concept, friends. There was your family, and the people that lived around you, and husbands. Ariel was none of these things.

Perhaps she was a grandchild. Ariel loved hearing stories. They would both pretend Cathy was telling them for the first time, Ariel appropriately awed. She told her the story of her namesake, Catherine of Siena, over and over. Each time it became more real, until it enthralled Cathy herself, until she could smell the broken rose petals.

Perhaps Ariel was like a friend that Cathy might have had in another life.

'We have another life ahead of us,' Ariel said, though Cathy couldn't remember saying this thought aloud. 'A better life.'

♦ ♦ ♦

Dana pushed Ariel out of the way and opened Shelly's mouth. Finding Shelly's breastbone, she fit the heel of her hand into it. She laced her fingers together, shoulders over her head. Push. Push. Push.

There were songs for this situation, she thought, feeling Shelly's rib crack. That was okay, that was good. Why couldn't she remember any of those songs?

Gary was yelling something. Dana screamed without looking at him—*Call an ambulance*—before pressing her open mouth to Shelly's. She could taste the snot under her nose.

Not yet. Please, not yet.

♦ ♦ ♦

'No, not until marriage,' Sera said finally. 'I mean, not ever. We can't do it ever.'

Dana squinted at her, confused. 'What do you mean?'

'Not ever,' Sera said.

Dana waited for the black part to come and rewrite what had happened next. It didn't. She remembered.

'But I did it with Michael,' Dana said. 'At that party. I think.'

Sera looked at her. In the sun, her legs were long and brown. Dana wondered if it was too late to take back what she'd said.

'You think?'

'Well, I can't really remember.' Dana laughed. She pulled her knees in, and hugged them. 'Probably for the best. I must have been bad at it, seeing as he broke up with me right after.'

Sera's face was still.

'He shouldn't have done that,' Sera said, her lips barely moving.

Dana felt shame so often, that her embarrassment at Sera's words was barely noteworthy.

'Yeah, yeah, I know,' she said, rolling her eyes. 'I'm not good enough for your brother. Message received.'

'What he did was wrong,' Sera said. Something about her burned. 'You were drunk. You can't even remember.'

'It's no big deal,' Dana said, easily, though she wasn't sure what it was. If she said it was alright, maybe it would feel alright. 'Really, it's not. I wanted to.'

Sera looked out on to the water. After a moment, she spoke.

'It can be difficult to force people to do things they don't want to do. It's easier to convince them that they want to behave that way.' In the hazy light, her dark eyelashes caught gold. She suited this, Dana thought. She suited the sun. 'Because, even if it's not what you want, when you're doing the things that you think are right, you feel right. Good,' she frowned. The tip of her finger was trailing through the dirt. 'So you keep wanting to be good.'

This was one of those times when it felt like Sera's brain ran so hot she hummed, and Dana felt lukewarm in comparison.

'I think you're a good person,' Dana said.

It was a shot in the dark that didn't quite land; a look passed under Sera's face, something moving in the deep. But, with effort, she smiled.

'Well, I think my brother is an asshole,' Sera said.

She got to her feet, brushing the twigs from her summer dress.

Dana hid her face. For some reason, the sound of the word *asshole* in Sera's steady voice made her grin.

'I'll be right back,' Sera announced. 'Stay here.'

Dana watched her melt into the trees, skinny brown legs picking through the grass. She felt lighter. This truth had existed under her skin. It hurt, but it was a relief to have pulled it out into the open.

Out on the water, Ariel's red head was bobbing like a seal as she swam back. When it got shallow enough to walk, she stood up and waved, underwear soaked through.

'Hey Dana,' she said, grinning, freckled in the sun. She was holding something in her hand.

It was a fish. Yes, it had been a fish, Dana remembered it wriggling in her hands and then suddenly stopping as she'd killed it. Ariel had looked at it dead on the shore, then had looked at Dana sadly and said something like, You're just ordinary after all, aren't you?

'Come here for a second,' Ariel said.

♦ ♦ ♦

Places without people always smelled different. Dentist's waiting rooms, supermarkets, and libraries, places were people just passed through, didn't live in—they smelled like mint or plastic or paper.

Cathy Copeland's house smelt like dust, like something forgotten. Despite the lack of housing in the town, it had lain empty for years—an inheritance dispute, or something. She'd had no family when she was alive, and too many after she was dead.

'Is she going to make it?' was the first thing Gary asked when Dana arrived.

'What do you think?' she snapped.

They were waiting in the living room, with the plastic wrapped couch and crystal Celtic cross on the mantel piece.

Ariel sat like a limp doll in the corner, one arm raised up to be tied to a radiator.

Gary had argued. Dana suggested they inquire if there was any room in the sheriff's department holding cell. Gary done as she had said.

He hovered near Ariel, worrying his thumb. Dana had the impression he'd been sitting beside her on the carpet before she'd got here.

She held out the ice pop she'd bought in the gas station; it had been the coldest thing she could find, but it had already started to melt in the lingering September heat. Gary stared at it, eyes blank.

'For your lip,' Dana said. 'What happened to you?'

After he continued to stare at her, she pointed to his face.

'Oh,' he said, touching his bruised mouth. 'I forgot.'

He took the ice pop and held it to his swollen lip.

Dana forced herself to look at Ariel. She should take her pulse or something. Verify what she was seeing. But she just looked, unmistakably, so dead.

Dana didn't want to touch her. She should, but she couldn't.

'She can't talk much,' Gary said, quickly. 'She's still getting better. Recovering.'

Lucky her. Shelly still hadn't been breathing when they

loaded her in the ambulance. Dr Wu had asked Dana if she wanted to come with them, but the hospital was miles away.

'Is she going to make it?' she'd asked, as he was closing the bright back door. Dr Wu hadn't replied.

When she looked back to Gary, his eyes were already on her. He was scared. Not of Ariel, she realised. Of her.

'Come on,' she said, walking into the kitchen. He followed her, quiet.

In the kitchen, there was a large cat scratch post that hadn't been packed up. It looked expensive, with little ledges for the cat to perch on, and a tunnel for it to walk through.

'What happened?' Dana said.

'Shelly saw us last night. She said we had to come with her, or she'd tell the sheriff about Ariel.'

'When?' Dana said. 'What time did she see you?'

'I don't know. Late.' Gary mumbled, looking at the cat scratch post instead of Dana.

Super helpful, Dana wanted to say. Thanks.

Had Shelly tried to take Dana's gun to threaten her with? That's what Dana had assumed. Now, she wasn't sure.

Dana folded her arms. 'Did you know what she was going to do?'

'Not at first. But when I saw the rope, I...' Gary paused. His eyes were wet. 'She said that Ariel would heal her. That she'd be fine. I tried to stop her, talk her out of it—but she said she'd call the police.'

'If you'd let her call them,' Dana said. 'This wouldn't have happened.'

He looked like he was going to be sick.

Good, Dana thought.

'Why is Ariel with you, Gary?'

'I found her,' he said. 'I thought I could help her. She—she's been staying in our house.'

Dana stared.

'In our house?' she said. 'Are you serious?'

He didn't reply. The hair fell into his eyes. The more pathetic he looked, the angrier she felt.

'Did you even consider how easily you could have gotten me and dad arrested?' Dana knew she should soften up, but she couldn't. 'You know what, don't answer that. Obviously, the only person you've been thinking about is yourself. Have you seen the other bodies?'

Gary didn't look her in the eye. 'No. Just her.'

She wanted to shake the truth out of him.

'Gary,' she said. 'I can't protect you if you lie to me.'

His head shot up, angry for the first time. 'I'm not lying,' he bit back.

Dana had to admit, she felt a little relieved.

'Well, you're clearly more adept at deception than I thought, so excuse me for not taking you at your word,' she said. 'If you want me to trust you, tell me everything.'

'I think Ariel was murdered,' he said.

Gary told her the whole, moth-eaten theory. Dana filled in some of the blanks. Her mind drifted back to Shelly; she couldn't help it. She was probably dead by now.

When they both finished, Dana asked, 'Are you okay?'

He looked at her, frayed at the edges. 'What do you mean?'

'What Shelly did in front of you...' Dana said, tailing off, unwilling to say it clearly. 'Are you okay?'

He nodded his head, his hair lank with grease bobbing along with him.

'Yes,' he said. 'Yes, I'm fine.'

♦ ♦ ♦

In the bathroom, Gary admired the way the tap washed away the dust and wondered what had changed. Before, the thought that Ariel had been murdered had given him a rush of—not joy, but some kind of satisfaction.

It wasn't that he'd wanted her to have been hurt. Of course not. But he'd wanted to save her. He still did.

When he'd explained everything to Dana, he'd waited for the *got ya!* moment, the pleasure of knowing something she didn't. It never came.

Was Shelly going to die? He'd cut her down, but had it been too late?

No, he couldn't think that way. It hadn't been his fault, anyway. It hadn't been Ariel's fault. Shelly was sick. What could he have done?

Drying his hands on his jeans, he pulled out his phone. Missed Call: dad. Missed Call: dad. Missed Call: dad. Missed Call: Mr Dale.

There were two voicemails. He deleted the first one

without listening to it. Another call from Mr Dale interrupted the second one. Sometimes, Gary wished he could turn himself on and off again.

When he walked back into the living room, Dana was still questioning Ariel. Ariel didn't even blink, didn't breathe. Dana was standing over her, staring down, but a couple of feet away. Far enough that Ariel couldn't reach her, even if she wanted to.

Gary should ask if they could untie her again.

Dana looked around at him. 'What's wrong? Is it Shelly?'

He didn't know how to say it.

'No, it's just,' he said. 'Mr Dale saw Sera's trailer getting towed into town by a police car. I think she's been arrested.'

Dana blinked. Ariel's fingers twitched. Gary wondered if she recognised Sera's name.

'Oh,' Dana said. Then, seeing something in his face, she asked, 'What else?'

'Nothing,' he said. It felt like the wrong moment to mention he'd just been fired.

♦ ♦ ♦

Stan opened the door right on time.

'Five, ten minutes max,' he said, his face tired and tense as he ushered Dana in. 'I know it's not much, but it's all I can guarantee. Michael's just gone out to talk to the crowd. Knowing our luck, today will be the day he'll finally get sick of the sound of his own voice.'

The first bolt heaved with a jolt. The door to the holding cell swung open and he turned to face her.

'I'll go out to reception. If I see anyone coming, I'll set off the smoke alarm—if you hear it, run like hell out the back door.'

'Thank you so much.' She'd tried to say it like she meant it, but it came out so sincere it sounded sarcastic.

Stan shrugged. 'I'm not doing it for you,' he said. 'I'm doing it because I hate that man's guts.'

Things had changed.

'No arguments there,' Dana said.

Stan thrust a beige paper folder into her hands.

'Phone records of Nyx,' he said. 'You're not a cop anymore, so I guess you might as well have them.'

There were other things she wanted to say, but Stan was gone too soon to say them.

Sera was sitting on the holding cell cot under the too-bright light. She wore the same clothes she'd left in, white t-shirt grey. Her body was still, her eyes blank. She almost looked like Ariel. Or—whatever Ariel had become.

Dana was relieved when she looked up, and the resemblance stopped.

'Dana.' Sera said the word slowly, stretching each of the two syllables. She rose to her feet and came close. Sera always stared without embarrassment, but this was next level; every part of Dana was being drank in. Sera smiled. 'I was saving you for my one phone call, but I have to admit, it's good to see you in the flesh. Even under these circumstances.'

Inexplicably, Dana remembered the taste of other circumstances.

'No uniform?' Sera said, when Dana didn't reply.

'I quit.'

She laughed. 'You quit?'

'Yes,' Dana said, defensive. 'I thought you'd be happy. You said you hate cops.'

Sera shook her head. 'I do, but I can't deny that it'd be useful to have one around right now.'

'Can't you just…' Dana waved her hands around, miming something she didn't have the words to describe, '…you know.'

'No. Michael won't let me,' she said. 'How did you get in?'

'Stan,' Dana said. 'We haven't got long. Look, you're not going to believe this, but Ariel is alive.'

The word didn't quite fit. It didn't act like Ariel, and it certainly wasn't alive. Dana hadn't wanted to leave Gary alone with it. She'd made him promise to keep it handcuffed to the radiator.

Sera stared at her through the bars, still as an animal in the dark.

'I know it's crazy,' Dana started, 'But you have to believe me—'

'I do,' Sera said. 'You don't need to convince me.'

Dana expected a thousand questions; Sera only had one. 'What did she tell you?'

'Nothing,' Dana said. 'She can't speak. She can't do anything, really. If it wasn't for the fact she's walking around,

I would say that she's dead. No heartbeat, no reactions. I don't know how else to explain it.' For the first time since she'd seen Ariel, Dana felt like she could let her fear out. It would be safe with Sera. 'She really is dead,' Dana said. 'It's horrifying.'

Sera broke eye contact and looked away, thinking so quickly that Dana could almost hear her brain whirring.

'What did Michael do to her?' Dana asked.

'I'm not sure,' Sera said, 'that Michael did this.'

'That's what I thought,' Dana said. 'Why kill her just to bring her back? I think Shelly might have done something.'

Sera didn't answer. Dana said her name several times.

'Sorry. This is a lot.' Sera ran her hands through her hair, agitated. 'I mean, it shouldn't be possible, even for us.'

Her face was pale. Dana didn't know how to make this easier.

'Raising the dead doesn't run in the family?' she asked.

Sera looked at her. The clock ticked.

'You're having an easier time accepting this than I would have anticipated,' she said, at last.

Dana thought there was a question underneath those words, but she wasn't sure what it was.

'Not much debating with cold hard evidence. Literally.' Sera didn't respond. Dana didn't know what to say. They were running out of time, and she didn't know what to say. 'This is good, right? If we can make her better—if I can get her to talk—I can figure out where the other bodies are. Then I can get you out of here.'

Muted cheering could be heard from outside the station. Sera reached her fingers through the bars and grasped what she could of Dana's hand.

'Dana. Listen to me,' she said, low and urgent. 'Take Ariel to Joe. He'll take care of that. Then, forget us. The whole family, everything. As if we never met.'

Her words were steady as always, but her eyes weren't: fear was unfamiliar on Sera.

'Inside a cell and you're still bossing me around?' Dana said lightly, looking down at their hands. Sera couldn't push her whole hand out and Dana couldn't get her whole hand in, but they twined together what they could—the first two knuckles, the nails.

'No. I'm pleading,' Sera squeezed her fingers tight. 'I'm sorry I'm not better at it.'

'I have to get you out,' Dana said. 'You don't deserve to be locked up, and if he killed Ariel, he could kill you too.'

'Deserve?' Sera said. 'Even if people got what they deserve, I'd get this.'

Dana didn't like that, and Sera knew it. Her fingers fluttered in Dana's, as if she were trying to soothe her. 'Dana. There's nothing more you can do.'

At the platitude Dana went cold. Oh god, she thought. Oh god.

'If you really can't disappear, then I'll break you out.' Dana clenched her jaw and began looking around the holding cell. There had to be something she could break it open with. This wasn't it.

Sera's grip on her hand became vice like. 'Dana. Leave me. Forget me.'

Dana was shaking. 'No.'

Sera let go of Dana's hand. One by one she slipped her fingers back into the cage. She stood back, and hardened.

'Do you remember the night we met?'

In Dana's experience, fears didn't fade over time. In the dark, they fermented.

'Michael,' she said.

'Yes,' Sera said. 'He hurt you. But you don't remember everything about that night.'

Dana could feel the hard plastic of the tarot cards underneath her fingers. *If you don't remember, I'll show you.*

'Stop it, Sera,' she said.

'You drowned,' Sera said, ignoring her. 'Michael left you alone and you vomited in your mouth.'

'Don't,' Dana said. 'Stop.'

Sera ignored her. 'You were unconscious, you couldn't spit it out. You choked on it.'

Each word was an arrow. They were just meant to wound her, Dana knew, they didn't mean anything real.

'He came to the house to get me. I was the one who cleaned up his messes. He was crying,' Sera frowned. Her eyes were drifting. 'Not over you, I think. He was afraid of what would happen to him, to us.'

'But you saved me,' Dana said. It was the only thing that made sense.

Sera shook her head.

'No. Michael took your legs, I took your hands, and we threw your body into the lake. I suggested we weigh your pockets down with stones, but Michael thought it would be better if we let it be found.'

By *it* she meant her body. Dana's dead body. On the inside, she felt unsteady and wet.

'Ariel,' Dana said. 'She saved me?'

'I used to think it was one of her stories,' Sera said. 'She'd just done CPR or we'd got something wrong. But I—'

The alarm rang, piercing. Sera was saying something, but Dana couldn't hear her, the alarm bleating over and over like a wounded animal.

'Not yet,' Dana shouted. The words made no sense and she knew Sera couldn't hear them over the alarm. *Not yet*, it didn't mean a thing, it might not be true, but it was something to say.

The back door clanged behind her. She ran as fast as she could, past the car park, chain link fencing broken. Beside a sleeping patrol vehicle was Sera's car and Airstream trailer. A fire burned from inside it, black smoke choking up its small windows and spilling out. The tires had been slashed; *murderer* printed onto its silver side.

Jesus wept.
See how he loved him!
But could he not have saved this man from dying?

Chapter Eighteen

The cabin smelled of wet wood and the air inside was the same as the air outside, green and pressing on Dana's skin like open mouthed kisses. There were only two cups. Gary had insisted he was fine, Ariel hadn't acknowledged the offer, so Dana was left to punctuate the silence with her sips while Joe paced.

'The water is siphoned straight off the lake,' Joe explained, staring at Ariel, his one green eye wide and intent as a tennis ball. He'd only taken one sip of his coffee, before pulling out a hipflask and glugging something stronger into it. 'The moss and stones filter it. I think it's pretty iron-rich, that's why it tastes rusty.'

It was like mud. 'Thank you,' Dana said.

'This place is awesome,' Gary said. 'Did you build it?'

He sat on the floor, legs folded like a child. Beside him were several open books; Joe had told him to feel free to look through his collection. *Awesome* was generous. Aside from one pot, one pan, a damp couch and a bed, the place was all paperbacks and dead citronella candles.

Joe continued to pace, eyes settling back on Ariel every few seconds. Beside Dana, she was still. When Dana didn't look at her, she momentarily forgot there was anyone there.

'Nah. Got a friend of mine to do it. I don't like getting my hands dirty, if I can help it.'

'So, you live here?' Gary said. 'That's cool.'

Joe laughed.

'No, no, I don't live here. It's just my getaway. For when I need to reconnect with nature.'

Sounded like a hook-up hideaway to Dana. At that thought, she tried not to get riled up at how readily he'd invited Gary over when he'd called. The jacket was not that nice.

'Sera told me that this,' Dana gestured to Ariel, 'was impossible. Even for your family.'

'She did?' Joe's eyes were still on Ariel. 'I wonder what she meant by that.'

Dana glared. 'Drop the act. I know what you guys are. About your little cult.'

Joe laughed, again. He did that a lot. For the hell of her, Dana couldn't figure what, exactly, there was to laugh about.

'Nobody knows what we are. Josh and Pam liked to think that they did. Angels! Here to protect the good lord's flock!' He waved his cup, and a smatter of coffee hit the ground with the shards of sharp wood. 'But you know what? There's more angels in the Qu'ran than there are in the Bible, and it was Rabbis who gave us names.'

Gary leaned forward, eagerly. 'So maybe you were around before Christianity?'

When Dana had told Gary about the Enckles' bullshit,

Gary had smiled, nodded, and said, That makes a lot of sense.

'For sure. Well, our ancestors were. Grandpa Gabriel and the gang,' Joe said. 'Sometimes I've even wondered about the Greek gods—they had supernatural abilities. They gave mortal heroes messages, guidance, commands, a stone's throw away from Bethlehem, you know?'

When Sera was nervous, she was quiet; Joe was the opposite. Dana had to grab ahold of this conversation before it galloped off for good.

'But resurrection,' she said. 'That's new, right?'

Joe looked at her, his brown eye a little dark moon. Dana didn't know what she wanted him to say.

'More or less,' he said.

'Or less?' Dana pressed.

'Well,' Joe said, 'There's Jesus. Heard of him?'

Gary turned, looking over his shoulder at Ariel.

'You're unique,' he said, soft.

Dana thought, just for a second, she saw Ariel's fingers twitch.

'If she could do this,' Dana continued, 'Couldn't she bring back other people?'

She hoped Joe would see the hint and take it, but he just shrugged.

'I wouldn't be hoping for a miracle for Shelly, if that's what you're getting at.'

Either, he didn't know about that night, or he was a good liar.

Or, Sera had made the whole thing up. Sera's face behind the bars replayed in Dana's memory. Her words had been stolen by the sound of the alarm. She could have been saying anything, but the more Dana thought about it, the more it looked like she'd been saying, *I'm sorry, I'm sorry.*

'Shelly's not dead,' Gary said, strained.

'Not yet,' Joe said.

'You two were friends, right?' Dana asked, carefully ignoring Gary. 'Why do you think she did it?'

'Fuck knows, but I wish she hadn't,' Joe said, dumping his cup in the metal basin that passed for a sink. 'Dana, give me a hand for a sec? I've got something in my car that might make Ariel a little more chatty. Gary, put on more coffee, will you?'

Joe's car was parked in the woods like a key jammed in the wrong lock. He leaned against the trunk and lit a cigarette, turning his face up to the night. The sky was clear. The storm Shelly had predicted hadn't come after all. Maybe it never would.

'What's on your mind?' Joe asked, still looking up.

Where to start? The phone records Stan had given her had shown that someone had called Nyx the night before Ariel's death. The call had been short, three minutes twenty seconds. Nyx had made several outgoing calls to that number on the day after Ariel's funeral, but they'd all dialled out—no one had answered the phone.

Dana didn't know the number off by heart, but Stan had circled it and written *Enckles home phone.*

Stan was still helping her. She didn't deserve it.

Dana wondered if she should start with the easy question, or the hard one.

'Did you call Shelly the night before Ariel's death?' Dana asked. Easy.

Joe looked bewildered.

'Maybe,' he said. 'I don't know, we talk pretty regularly. We're still friends, you know.'

The present tense hovered in the air.

'I really don't remember,' he said. 'You can check my cell phone if you want.'

The call was from a landline. It had been Michael. Dana was sure of it.

Now time for the hard question.

'You knew Jerome,' she said.

Joe looked at her, eyebrows raised. 'Yeah. So?'

Dana didn't know how to say it. 'So, do you think he killed himself?'

His teeth flashed white in the dark: another impossible smile. 'Yeah, detective. I think he killed himself.'

The scales tipped from annoyance to dislike.

'First of all, I quit,' she said. 'Second of all, Sera said Michael could control people's thoughts. I think he—'

'Murdered him?' Joe looked back at the fingernail moon. 'You've got quite an imagination.'

Dana felt a twig snap under her boot. It didn't matter if she didn't like Joe; they could trust him. Sera wouldn't have sent her here if she couldn't trust him.

Unless, a nameless voice hidden in her head told her, she couldn't trust Sera, either.

'You don't think he's capable?'

'No, Michael could kill someone if it was part of the plan,' Joe said, laughing a little. 'But there's no big conspiracy. Jerome was just some sad guy. He killed himself because he was poor, and no one loved him.'

Didn't you love him? Dana thought. Didn't you ever love him?

'I think Michael killed those people,' Dana said. 'Shelly was working with him—I don't know why, maybe she was threatened—and he killed her to remove the evidence.' Dana took a deep breath. 'I think he's going to kill Sera next.'

Joe snorted, but his face was grim.

'He doesn't have to. This town will do it for him.' For the first time, Joe's expression became unhappy, shifting over into something close to accusatory. 'If she'd left when I told her to, she'd be safe now.'

'If you care about her so much, why don't you tell Michael to let her go?' Dana snapped.

'You still don't get it, do you? He wouldn't, even if he wanted to.' Joe was still laughing as he stubbed his cigarette out against the bark of a tree. 'Why are you here, Dana?'

Had Sera really helped cover up Dana's death that night? Or had she lied, hoping Dana would abandon her? The first was impossible. Neither were easy.

It was times like these when Dana envied Christians. They were always able to flip to the back of the book and find the answer.

'To save Sera,' she said. 'If we find out the truth, find evidence, they'll have to release her.'

Joe popped the truck and pulled out something long and wrapped in a black trash bag.

'What's that?' Dana said.

'Ariel's sword,' Joe replied cheerfully. 'I was planning to pawn it, but I guess I should check if she wants it back first.'

♦ ♦ ♦

Gary put a glass of water in Ariel's hands. It tasted of moss, and Gary thought it was slightly brown. She didn't raise her hands to drink, but her lips were cracking.

'Are you alright?' he asked her, dipping his finger into the cup and dabbing a little onto her mouth.

Their eyes were together. She leaned forward and let her forehead touch his. It was cold. The sword lay on the ground like a piece of driftwood, where Ariel had let it fall.

Dana and Joe were still arguing.

'You failed once, so you're going to give up?' Dana said. 'There must be something else you can try.'

'I told you, it's pointless,' Joe said. 'If she doesn't even remember how to hold it—'

'Don't do that,' Gary said. It came out louder than he expected. 'Don't talk about her like she's not here.'

'I'm not sure she is,' Joe said.

Gary felt unsteady. He didn't look at Ariel, but he could

smell her faintly, the barest hint of salt.

'What do you mean?' he replied, eventually.

'Maybe she didn't come back all the way,' Joe said. 'I did say this was impossible. Even Christ only came back for a couple of days. Maybe she's winding down.'

Gary stared at him, oddly betrayed. Joe was Ariel's brother. Why didn't he want to help her get better?

Dana's eyes were on Ariel, uncertain. Her expression reminded Gary of something.

Ariel's eyes were unfocused. They had been unfocused all day. Gary brushed the back of her hand. After a handful of seconds, she blinked.

'She does talk,' he said, appealing to Dana. 'She's just been quieter recently.'

Dana bit her lip, and Gary realised she used to wear the same expression when he would ask her, when's mom coming back?

Joe walked towards the couch and crouched down until he was at eye level with Ariel. He gently took her immobile hand in both of his. As the underside of her arm unfolded, Gary watched Joe's eyes trace her wounds, as if he was reading them.

Ariel didn't move.

'Ariel. Listen. If you need to go, it's alright.'

Dana and Gary's mouths both opened, but it was Gary who got their first.

'Are you telling her to just *die*?'

'Gary, look at her,' Joe said, still holding her hand. 'She's practically dead already.'

For some reason, Shelly popped into Gary's head. The way she'd looked at him as she slipped the rope around her neck. The way he had stood there and watched her do it.

Dana gave him a significant look, but he wasn't sure what she was trying to say.

'You can do...magic, right?' she said.

'Magic?' Joe said, as if the word was distasteful. 'If that's what you want to call it, I guess.'

Dana looked like a big part of her was fighting the urge to roll her eyes.

'Is there a way we could use magic to speak to Ariel?' she said. 'Or work out if she's in there?'

Joe didn't reply right away. Now that he was closer, Gary could smell the stale liquor on his breath.

'Sera told me your abilities were the opposite of hers,' Dana pressed. 'So, if she could conceal things—or whatever—can't you reveal them?'

They both stared at Joe. He still held Ariel's hand.

'Yes,' Joe said. He shook his head. 'Maybe.'

'Yes,' Dana said, teeth gritted, 'Or no.'

'There's a way, but it's dangerous,' Joe stood up, letting Ariel's hand slip away. It dropped, lank in her lap. 'It might work, or you might give yourself brain damage.'

'But we'd be able to talk to her?' Gary said.

He glanced at Ariel, guiltily. He'd slipped into it; saying *her* as if she was *it*. Ariel's eyes flickered like a projection stuttering as he brushed his elbow against hers in a silent apology.

Joe nodded.

Gary's mind was made up; it was worth it if they could help her, if she could be safe.

'Whatever it takes,' he said.

'It won't work with you,' Joe said. He pointed at Dana, like a Game Show Host announcing a lucky winner. 'It might work with you.'

When Gary looked at Dana, her eyes were on Ariel.

'I'll do it,' she said.

◆ ◆ ◆

Shivering in her T-shirt and underwear, Dana folded up her pants at the base of a tree, shoes underneath, socks tucked inside. From the other side of the tree, she could hear Gary huffing as he dragged the copper tub closer to the cabin, and then the hard splash of the water from the outdoor shower beginning to fill it. She hoped it was cleaner than it had tasted.

Her cell phone was in her hand. Missed call: Francis Fisher ICE. Missed call: Francis Fisher ICE. It went on.

Citronella scented the air: Joe had said there would be candles. Part of Dana pushed against the convenience store casualness of using whatever was around. It didn't seem very legitimate.

She dialled. After a couple of rings, the call went live.

'Hello?' her mom said. 'Hello, this is Rebekah speaking.'

Dana didn't say anything. The wind blew the smell of the

gasoline and orange candles closer. The line hitched.

'Dana?' she said. 'Dana is that you?'

'Yeah, it's me,' Dana said, wrapping her arms around herself, pimpled in gooseflesh. 'Hi, mom.'

'Hi, Dana. It's—so good to hear from you.' She hesitated. 'Is everything alright? Your father and Gary, are they...'

'They're fine,' Dana said, wiping her face. 'Everything's fine. I just wanted to hear your voice.'

'Are you alright?' Rebekah said. The line cracked. Where was she? Dana couldn't remember the name of the state, but it was far. Maybe even a different time zone. 'Are you in trouble? I can send you money—or come get you. Whatever you need.'

'Mom,' Dana said. 'I'm sorry we never thanked you for the stuff you sent at Christmas and our birthdays. Dad hid them all. He didn't do it to hurt us. I think he just thought it would be easier.' The sound of water had stopped: the tub must be full now. 'He still misses you, I guess. So do I. Sorry I never called.'

'Oh, it's okay, baby,' she said. Her voice was fainter, a ghost in Dana's ear. 'I love you very much. I'm happy— you—'

'Mom, does it stop?' Dana asked. 'Do you ever stop missing people? Because I can't do it anymore.'

'Sorry—the line isn—*na.*'

The call clicked off, phone silent in Dana's ear. No service.

Dana turned it off, and tucked it in with her socks.

The rocks of the salt circle crunched underneath her bare feet. Already shivering, she got into the deep tub quickly. The night air was cold enough that the water wasn't a shock, but still she pulled her knees in tight, holding them while she could.

'Comfortable?' Joe said, leaning over her.

'No,' Dana replied. 'What's going to happen?'

'Probably? Nothing. You'll be cold. We'll all have a good laugh.'

'And improbably?'

Ariel sat on an upturned bucket nearby. Gary was beside her, speaking to her quietly.

'On the off chance it does work, you'll be able to speak to Ariel.' He frowned. 'Because you won't be in a "real" place, your mind will kind of have to fill in the blanks. It's easiest for people who don't have an imagination, so I'm sure you'll do fine.' Discreetly, he added, 'Are you sure you want to do this?'

Dana nodded.

He sighed and passed her Ariel's sword.

She held it down her body carefully, hands crossed over the handle like an ancient king.

'Don't get lost,' he said, standing.

Gary leaned over her, smiling, worried. Past him, Dana could see the stars.

She took a deep breath. Then, she sunk into the tub until her head hit the back of it.

Beyond the water, everything shimmered. Joe guided Ariel's hand to rest on Dana's foot. A couple of pinpricks of blood into the water. They danced red and drifted.

Dana closed her eyes. Her lungs were already shifting and uncomfortable.

Gary took one last look at Ariel. Her face was reflected on the water like a distant moon.

Joe nodded at him. *Ready.* Gary submerged his hands, and held Dana under.

Chapter Nineteen

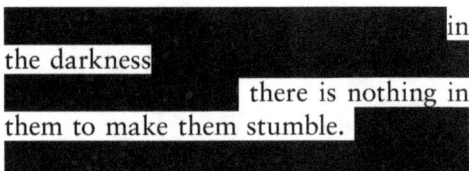

> in the darkness there is nothing in them to make them stumble.

The queue at Green's Grocery store is always slow. Stan jokes that it's because Lake in the Wood's senior citizens shopped there exclusively rather than the Walmart; they liked to remind themselves of the good old days when supermarkets were new and exciting.

Dana shifts the weight on her feet, trying to fight that hot day feeling that leaves her feeling glued down, green plastic basket in the crook of her arm. The queue is always slow, but this was ridiculous. Didn't these people have anywhere to be?

'Excuse me,' she says, tapping the shoulder of the woman in front of her. 'Could I cut in front of you? I'm in a rush—police business.'

Bright hair swishes over her shoulder like a shampoo advert as she turns. Dana curses inwardly—she hadn't realised who it was.

'Oh, sure, officer,' Ariel says, recognition hovers in her eyes, and then indecision. 'Go ahead!'

Dana is relieved that they have mutually decided not to know each other.

'Thank you,' she says, stepping in front of her to unpack her basket on to the belt.

Each *beep* is like a tick. The check-out girl's hair is in a skinny braid and she wears clip-on earrings; she scans each item with care and attention. Dana thinks, as she always does in these moments, of Sera and how grief is never finished.

'Would you like your receipt?' the check-out girl asks.

Dana can't quite hear her over the tannoy announcement, *Welcome to Green's Groceries. This is your Manager Ariel speaking.*

'Uh, no thanks,' Dana says, squinting at the girl's name tag, '*Ariel.*'

Ariel smiles.

'Have a lovely day,' she says. Dana can tell that she means it, but then she always does.

As Dana leaves the store, she looks behind her. Queuing-Ariel is handing some folded ones to Check-out-Ariel. The line is long, impatient, jostling; the line is all Ariels.

Dana wanders into the sunshine, the cobbled walkway that leads to the town square, and people watches. Baby-Ariels being pushed by Mom-Ariels. A Teenage-Ariel is getting a ticket from Officer-Ariel, with a pot belly and a moustache, Sunday-Best-Ariels looking on in disapproval. It is a lovely day.

The town square is heaving with Ariels; Ariels gossiping with each other, hands covering their mouths, Ariels handing out coffee in Styrofoam cups and Ariels shaking signs. Sheriff-Ariel in a wide-brimmed hat, hair in a bright ponytail down his narrow back, is arguing with Mayor-Ariel, smiling in a neat little suit. The Ariels are different, but none of them are old.

On the steps of the church was a Dead-Ariel.

Dana drops the bag of groceries, and oranges bounce and roll. Milk spills. It smells sweet. Dana heaves Ariels slack body into her arms, but her neck lolls; she is definitely dead.

Oh right, Dana thinks. Michael is the sheriff, Sera is in a jail cell, she's drowning in a bathtub, and Ariel's dead, that's why she's here.

'Hey, Ariel,' she yells into the crowd, still holding Ariel's body. 'Who did this?'

The Ariels stare back at her, expressions ranging from polite bemusement to blank stares. One Ariel, dressed in a boiler suit, points at another Ariel, this one around seven-years old.

'She did it!' Boiler-suit-Ariel says, grabbing her cruelly. 'Let's get her!'

The Ariels move like a school of fish, converging on Seven-year-old-Ariel. All except for the Dead-Ariel, still in Dana's arms, and the person coming towards them.

At first glance, she looks like Ariel, too. On second glance, she looks *like* Ariel—as in, she and Ariel could both be actresses auditioning for the same role—they were of a type.

'She's confused,' the newcomer says. 'I don't think she wants to talk.'

As Dana looks closer, she thinks that, actually, this person looks like Ariel to someone who only had a vague idea of what Ariel looks like; like Ariel to someone who had only seen her once, only knew her from a handful of photographs; she looks like Ariel except she has no red hair, no colour at all in her skin, her eyes only approximately blue; she looks like Ariel except she doesn't, not at all.

'Who are you?' Dana says. 'Are you the real Ariel?'

Behind her, two of the Mom-Ariels are tearing apart Seven-Year-Old-Ariel with their teeth, while the crowd cheers.

'Um, I don't think so? I'm not sure,' Not-Ariel says, shifting. 'You're not Ariel, and I'm not you, but…besides that, I don't…really know?'

Dana doesn't know what to make of that.

'Okay,' Dana says. 'Well, do you know which of these is the real Ariel?'

Not-Ariel blinks rapidly. In between blinks, her eyes are empty, as if they'd forgotten for a moment to be blue. It's creepy, but Dana doesn't have time to stand around pondering the depths of Ariel's subconscious.

'Um, they're all real,' Not-Ariel continues, 'But these Ariels don't know much of anything.'

Dana whirls around at the sounds of screaming. Seven-Year-Old Ariel lies in pieces. The pieces are being set on fire.

Her hand hovers at her belt; Dana found she was wearing her uniform again, gun and all. She can smell the meat. Some of the Ariels are cheering. It's not real, she reminds herself.

Sera is real.

Dana looks around. Beyond the square, the opposite direction from the supermarket, the streets are ugly and overgrown, streetlights filtering light through dark trees.

'This way,' she says, to herself more than anything else. If Ariel with the answers is hiding, Dana knows where she'll be.

'Can I come with you?' Not-Ariel asks, already following her.

'If you want,' Dana says. 'Since you're not Ariel, do you have a name?'

Not-Ariel doesn't smile, but her face flickers like a TV changing channel.

'You can call me Gary,' she says.

♦ ♦ ♦

As they walk through the town, its population grows more and more dead. Dead-Ariels dance in the road and drink dead beer on the sidewalk, they lie under the trees like roadkill, eyes open and staring. They don't answer Dana's questions.

When they finally arrived at the Enckles' house, the party is in full swing. Streamers hung from the porch, clusters of balloons fluttering in the wind. The air smells of cake and candles. The house wasn't just white, it was the moon.

'Wow,' Gary says. 'I've never seen it like this.'

The party is Hawaiian beach themed, and full of Ariels.

Drinks are being poured and left on top of the piano, sticky.

'Is this what parties are like? I thought they'd be less uncomfortable.' Gary says, watching a cluster of Ariels play spin the bottle. 'Hey, I think that one looks like you!'

On the sofa, Dana-Ariel is beside Michael-Ariel, laughing.

It is. This isn't exactly how it happened, but Dana gets the gist.

Dana flinches from that night. She wants to see it. There is no in-between. Either, she can pretend it didn't happen, or she needs to know every detail.

Sometimes, she thinks there's something wrong with her. Maybe if she can figure out what it is, untangle the hurt and comb it through, her heart would beat smooth again, and she'd be complete. But that's not why she's here.

The lights shuddered. Dana looks out the window. The streetlights outside that led them here flick off, one by one, until all that's left is the house.

'She's dying,' Dana says, letting go of the curtain.

'No,' Gary replies, uncomfortable. 'You are.'

Dana-Ariel and Michael-Ariel are holding hands. If she sticks around, maybe she can watch him hurt her; she can watch herself die again.

Dana takes a last look, and walks into the kitchen.

Underneath a dull, direct light, is an Ariel, sitting at the kitchen table. This Ariel is twenty-three. She is dressed like the ones who told her *I just wanted it to be over.* Her eyes glitter in a *they deserved to die* way, but her hair says, *I was murdered.* This girl is a god. At least, she thinks she is.

Dana sits down. She can feel Gary-Ariel hovering behind her. On the table is a mud-stained manila folder and a tape recorder. This Ariel is waiting. This Ariel is ready to talk.

'Ariel,' she says. 'Why did you kill yourself?'

It's not the question she had planned to ask, but it's the right one. Ariel's smiles. It's honey bright on her skin.

'I wanted to see if I could come back,' she says. 'Did I do it? Did it work?'

Dana thinks of the empty body sitting on Joe's couch.

'I don't get it,' she says, instead of answering. 'Why did you need to come back at all?'

The tape recorder churns slowly, filled with water. The kitchen floor is wet, too, lapping over the tops of Dana's shoes.

'To see if I was really divine,' Ariel says. The *duh* is silent. 'I brought you back, but once is nothing—it's just a miracle. I had to try again, to know if I was really…well, you know. An angel.' She leans forward again. 'Did it work?'

Dana doesn't want to answer that. Once she had found a baby bird that had fallen out of its nest. It was featherless; Dana knew it would die soon.

'Yes,' she replies finally, mainly because it seems to be what Ariel wants to hear, mainly because of Ariel's empty funeral. 'It worked.'

The ceiling is dripping: fat, cold drops of water than slide underneath Dana's shirt and make her shiver. Water is running underneath the closed basement door, flowing down the steps like a small waterfall.

'Then it was worth it,' Ariel says, eyes bright. 'It was all worth it.'

'And the others?' Dana says. 'Anthony? Cathy? Sandy? Jerome? Was it worth it for them?'

Ariel's answering expression is bland.

'I didn't kill them,' she says.

'No,' Dana says. She thinks of fish bone and blood. Of tasting chlorine in her mouth before Michael had finished saying, *Jump in the pool.* Of all the things she had convinced herself she'd wanted. 'You didn't have to. Why get your hands dirty?'

Ariel stares at her. She is defiant.

'They were just human,' Ariel shrugs. 'And they were so unhappy. They wanted a better life. Shelly said she preserved them, anyway. Now I've ascended, we can try again. Don't you get it, Dana? I can try again.'

For a moment, Dana sees the missing returned, and it's wonderful.

But it's not real. Dana still feels Shelly's ribcage under her hand. Ariel—the dead Ariel, the Ariel that was left—hadn't been able to help her. That was real. That was all there was.

'They're dead,' Dana says. 'Just because you came back, it doesn't change that. They're still going to be dead.'

Ariel shrugs.

'There's always sacrifice. At least this way, I gave them a chance to be holy,' Ariel says. 'Be more.'

'You could have just helped them be,' Dana says, standing up.

'Where are you going?' Ariel asks, eyes wide.

'Dana,' Gary says, 'I think you should go back now.'

Dana shakes her head; hand poised to open the door to the basement, she hesitates. Ariel shouts after her, but Dana ignores her.

'Why not? You're scared,' Gary says. 'I can feel it.'

Dana's trousers are wet, water creeping upwards through the denim. Even Gary looks damp.

'Oh yeah? What does it feel like?'

Gary wrinkles. 'Itchy.'

'Sorry,' Dana says. She can hear it; water pooling in the belly of the house. 'There's nothing to be afraid of, right?'

'Oh, no,' Gary says, 'You should be afraid.'

The door wasn't locked. The water runs down the steps, and tries not to slip.

Sera is waiting in the water at the bottom. Her white tights are translucent, the water knee deep and creeping higher.

She reaches out for her.

'You found me,' she says. 'I always knew you would find me.'

She's not real, Dana thinks. Still, she walks towards her, kicking through the water.

When Dana reaches Sera, she is seventeen, she is still a girl. Her eyes aren't as hard.

'Dana, it's a trick,' Gary calls from the stairs. 'It's just Ariel again!'

Dana holds her, wraps her arms around her thin body, water rising. Sera tucks her face into the corner of Dana's neck.

'Stay with me,' Sera says. 'Promise you won't leave me.'

Dana can feel Sera's anxious brain humming. Her skin smells of soap. She holds her tighter, presses her nose into her face, breathes in her hair. Even her hair is precious, even her bones.

'Alright,' she says, cupping the back of Sera's head with one hand.

'Dana,' Gary says, voice muffled, 'Dana you have to go—'

'We'll die together, won't we?' Sera whispers. Dana can feel her breathing.

'I promise,' Dana replies. She is still trying to decide if she means it when water fills her mouth. Her feet leave the ground; at once her arms are empty. The white house sinking, wood rotten through.

◆ ◆ ◆

Dana began to thrash about a minute in: face twisting, eyes still closed, splashed water putting out some of the candles. She was almost still now, almost there, just making small aborted movements.

Gary kept holding down her shoulders.

'This isn't going to work,' Joe said abruptly. 'Gary, get her up, before she really drowns.'

Gary didn't move, eyes focused on Dana's hairline, so he couldn't see her eyes.

Joe pulled at his shoulders. 'Didn't you hear me? You're killing—'

♦ ♦ ♦

Dana swims, her body heavy and difficult. There is no finesse to it. She keeps swimming up through the house, lopsided and dogged. The rooms are drowned, bed and sheets floating beside her like a deep-sea creature. Dana swims out an upstairs window. The water is black.

She is seized by the scruff of the neck and pulled up. The absence of water is shocking for a moment, and she splutters on her hands and knees, drenched clothes dripping all over the tiles. She's on the roof. It's the only part of the house left.

It isn't Gary. It's an Ariel. This Ariel is fourteen or so, wearing jeans and a scrunchie. Her feet are bare on the yawning roof; as if the flood had taken her by surprise, and she had no time to put shoes on.

Around them is just water. Even the trees are covered. This Ariel is no different than the others Dana has met, except that she is the last one.

'Did it work?' Ariel asks.

Dana nods, but this Ariel doesn't smile as the other one had. The water is coming over the roof now; they are already knee-deep. Dana takes her hand, scrambling on the sliding tiles, she grabs a hold of the TV aerial, holding her tightly.

Ariel stares at her, blue eyes wide. The water was licking Dana's elbows, and somewhere in the house she can hear wood splintering. It groans.

'Are you mad at me?' Ariel asks.

Dana is crying. At this point, it seems stupid to be

embarrassed about it.

'Yes, Ariel, I am,' Dana said. The water was at Ariel's chin now, threatening to lap into her mouth. 'I'm so, so angry with you.'

Only Ariel's eyes were above the water now, helpless. The lake swallows her, consuming her red hair last like a match spluttering out. She's gone.

Dana is floating in the water, feet unable to find the ground, face tilted up. She can't swim: she won't. Still crying, her tears are lost to the flood, the house is crashing down around her, it's going to crush her. It's okay. Dana is ready to be crushed.

Gary's voice vibrates through the water, like a whale song or an earthquake, thunder miles away. She is too far to hear him.

Dana doesn't want to go back. It's dark here, and things are much more simple. She opens her mouth to say as much, but then something cracks. It's just Dana dying like she wants to.

It's bliss.

But her legs don't know how to die. Despite herself, she kicks, pressing her face towards the surface. Though the air is almost gone, she kicks. It's painful to take that last breath of air but she takes it and then another. And then she kicks even though there is no more air and she is submerged, she kicks.

Chapter Twenty

When she woke up, it was not Gary she saw over her, but Joe. She was on the grass, and his hands were hovering over her, green eye worried, brown eye observant.

After she'd finished coughing enough to trust herself to breath, Dana had grabbed the collar of his shirt and whispered harshly into his ear, 'She killed him. Not—not literally.' She could feel the brush of his stubble against her lip. 'She pushed them to do it to themselves.'

His face barely moved as he replied, 'Why?'

Gary appeared above them both, wringing his wet hands. 'Dana, are you okay?'

Joe poured them all a drink—for the shock—while Dana towelled herself off. Gary sipped it gingerly, alcohol still a novelty to him. Maybe this was his first-time drinking moonshine. Maybe his first time drinking at all.

Ariel—Ariel's remains, as Dana had come to thinking of her—didn't drink. She just held the glass limp in her lap as Dana told them an edited version of what she'd seen in the dead town.

They six of them all made a suicide pact. It was Shelly's idea, maybe, she wasn't sure on the details, but nobody murdered anybody. We are all responsible for our own choices, aren't we?

Gary stared at her intently and open. 'Why would they do that?'

Dana shrugged. 'They thought they'd come back to life. All this angel bullshit clearly messed with Ariel, and it must spread from there.'

Joe's gaze was on her. Why are you lying? He seemed to be asking her.

Because Gary loved Ariel. That much was clear.

'But it worked,' Gary said.

Dana blinked and looked away from Joe. 'What?'

Gary's mouth opened and closed. 'It's not bullshit. It worked.' He looked at what was left of Ariel. Then, as if he was afraid he'd lose his courage if he waited a second later, he seized her hand and held it. His heart was in his eyes. 'She was right. I mean, look at her.'

Yes, Dana thought. Look at her.

Maybe she needed to tell him everything, after all. But she had other things to do. Nothing she'd seen in the dead town had told her where the bodies were.

She still didn't know how to clear Sera's name.

Dana stood, dropping the blanket Joe had draped around her. She drained her glass. It burned her already hoarse throat. She tried not to retch and, suddenly, she knew.

'I have to go,' she said.

Gary blinked at her, confused. 'What?'

Dana looked at Joe as she swung on her coat, skin still damp.

'You take care of this,' she said, not gesturing to Ariel, but not having to either. 'I'll take care of Sera.'

Joe nodded, once. Dana looked at Gary and Ariel. Gary's hurt was hardening into something else; Ariel was still dead. He'd get over it, she told herself as she drove through blueing woods.

♦ ♦ ♦

Ariel sat in the back of Joe's car, back in her baseball cap and sunglasses. Gary crouched beside the open door, night air crisp and breaking. Morning was coming.

'Lake in the Woods isn't safe for her,' Joe said, again.

'I know,' Gary said. Again.

'I'll take her away, just for a while. Maybe we'll dye your hair,' Joe pointed: *hair*. 'Would you like that?'

Gary winced. Maybe he was just tired, but it annoyed him that Joe spoke to her so loudly, as if she was hard of hearing rather than being a reanimated corpse.

Ariel stared balefully at him, as if she felt similarly disdainful. This reaction gave Gary a secret thrill. If it had been him, she would have at least twitched.

'Well,' Joe said, unwillingly. 'I better make sure all the lights are off and the place is locked up. So, I'll let you say your goodbyes, alright?'

Gary couldn't look at her. He couldn't believe that this was goodbye. Gary thought Joe's cabin was the perfect place for Ariel. He'd thought he could visit her there, help her keep getting better. He didn't understand why she had to leave at all, but Joe was her family, and he said she did.

Gary didn't know what to say; he was already starting to cry.

Something stopped his tear before it fell. Ariel's thumb, splayed on his cheekbone. It was cold and stiff, as if she'd positioned her hand in this shape before lifting; a doll whose parts were only partly moveable.

He smiled.

'It'll be alright,' he said, with confidence. 'We'll see each other again.'

Ariel nodded. Behind her sunglasses, her eyes were grey, greyer all the time.

It was only when the car was packed up and ready to go that he realised he was still wearing Joe's leather jacket.

'Oh,' Gary said. He took it off, and shivered. 'Um, here.'

Joe shook his head. 'Look after it for me,' he said. 'Don't call us. It's not safe,' he added, before moving to close the car door.

'Joe,' Gary said before he could. 'The shapes on her left arm. Do they mean something?'

Joe's smile didn't reach his eyes.

'No,' he said. 'They don't mean anything.'

Gary watched Ariel's face until it disappeared, watched the car until the headlights winked out in the night like a star dying.

Gary supposed he'd better go. It was a long walk back into town. Dana was gone. She'd barely stopped coughing up water before she jumped in Brussels; no explanation, no time.

Where was he going, anyway? It was a Tuesday. Usually, he had a shift on Tuesday mornings. Of course, that was over. He couldn't go home, could he? Dad was angry. Everything was different now.

Gary sat down on the ground. His phone was in his hands, but for the life of him he couldn't think of anyone to call.

♦ ♦ ♦

Dawn was just cracking over the lake, a golden yolk splintering into a black frying pan. Somewhere, a hundred miles away, men in jumpsuits climbed masts strung between the trees to fix wires.

Dana waited in the basement of the Enckles house. It hadn't changed much. But the swords on the wall were child-sized, and the painting of four angels had faded.

Her eyes lingered on the angels on the left and right. One was blowing a trumpet. Opposite him, his brother was pressing a finger to his mouth: *shh*. Raphael, Sera had said, the angel of concealment. Of hidden things.

Raphael is always making me forget, Mrs Enckles had said.

Above her, she heard footsteps. Mrs Enckles was in bed. Whoever had put her there, whoever had cleaned the kitchen, was gone. These footsteps were steady and sharp, so Dana heard clearly when they paused; when Michael saw that the basement door was open.

Dana waited in the dark, Ariel's sword sweating in her hand. She stood with the pool of water behind her, the devil's pulpit. While she waited, she had dropped a quarter into it, but it never reached the bottom. Now the water was still.

'That doesn't belong to you,' Michael said, pausing at the top of the stairs.

Dana didn't move.

'I'm here to return it,' she said. 'Come here. I'll give it to you.'

'Trying to threaten me, Dana?' Michael laughed lightly. 'That's not the way to get your job back.'

'No, Michael,' she said. 'I'm here to save you.'

He moved deeper down the stairs. His silver gun and his badge in the dim white light, ready for a day at work.

When he reached the bottom, Dana put the sword on the ground. The gold paint left flecks on her hand; spray painted or something.

Michael looked at it frankly, as if he had not expected her

to put it down. He bent down, eyes on her, and picked it up. After he had placed it back on the wall, she spoke.

'You're a liar,' she said. 'You know that Sera is innocent. She has no idea where the bodies are and neither do you,' Dana clenched and unclenched her empty hand. The splinters and alcohol still burned. 'Without them, this will never be really over.'

Dana wanted to smile like Michael did, but she couldn't manage it. 'But I know where they are, and I know who put them there.'

Michael raised his eyebrows. 'Oh? And do you have any evidence?'

Dana held something woven between her fingers. A silver cross, identical to the one Michael wore himself.

'That's Ariel's,' she explained needlessly, holding it out to him. 'Evidence. I'm sure she won't mind.'

Michael stepped closer. He took it from her, fingertips brushing the palm of her hand. He did not step away as he examined it.

'What do you want?' he said, apparently satisfied it was the genuine article.

Dana wanted many things. Not all of them were good, fewer still were possible.

'I have three conditions. If you can meet all of them, I will tell you where the bodies are.' Michael opened his mouth to speak, but she continued. 'I won't take any of the credit. It will be your win,' she continued. 'First, you let Sera go and drop all charges.'

Michael looked thoughtful.

'If you have evidence that someone else is responsible, the law certainly will play out that way,' Michael said. 'Why don't you come upstairs, and we can talk more about it?'

Dana ignored him.

'Second, you hand in your resignation—both as Mayor and sheriff—and reinstate Sheriff Wormwood.' She ploughed on before he could protest, her heart hammering, 'Third, you tell me exactly what happened that night.'

Michael looked at her, puzzled. 'What night?'

Dana's mouth was dry. She suddenly missed the sword. This conversation would be much easier if she was holding a weapon, no matter how stupid.

'The night you sexually assaulted me,' Dana said.

Michael was an expert at reacting to truth as if it were impropriety.

'Excuse me?' he said, shocked, stepping back from her.

Dana stepped towards him.

'If you want to know where the bodies are, you'd better start talking,' she said, as coolly as she could manage.

Michael held his hands up, as if to say *don't shoot*. 'I don't want to embarrass you,' he said.

Dana didn't reply.

'Why is this relevant?' Michael said, expression mild. 'Surely, if you really think my sister is innocent, that should take precedence over this high school stuff. The past is the past, right? We both want the same thing.'

I am stone, she thought. I am stone.

'Anyway, if you want the truth—though I don't see why it's important—you threw yourself at me,' he smiled, sheepishly. It wasn't my intention to lead you on, so if I did so, I apologise. I'm a Christian man, Dana.'

She shook.

'And when you found my unconscious body? Can you tell me why, instead of trying to resuscitate, you decided to hide the evidence—'

'I think you need to calm down,' Michael said, 'You've broken into *my* home—'

'—why you left me for dead?'

The words echoed around the white, windowless room. Dana's heart was beating wildly. Behind her, she could hear water.

'I don't know what you're talking about,' Michael said.

'I just want to know what happened,' Dana said. 'Please, just tell me what happened that night.'

'You must be crazy,' his hand itched towards his belt, even as he cowered away, 'You must be crazy.'

Before she'd thought it through, she taken two steps forward and seized the gun from his belt. Throwing it to the ground, she grabbed a firm hold of his shirt, the polyblend bunched in her hand. Then, she swung him around and held him over the edge of the pool.

'I'm not going to tell the police, Michael,' Dana said. His eyes were wide; the water behind him black. 'I'm not going to kill you. I know your parents brainwashed you, but they're not in charge now. You are. You can start over. You can be someone new. I'm giving you this chance,' she shook him, and his boots stuttered on the rocky edge, unsteady. He was heavy; if she dropped him, she would probably fall too. 'I just need to know what happened to me. I just need to hear you say it.'

Michael opened his mouth over and over again, gaping like a fish caught on a hook, but his eyes were oddly blank.

Dana had hoped he would confess. Hoped it would let her tuck that night away in a box and bury it.

'I'm a Christian man,' he said, over and over. 'You must be crazy. I'm a Christian man.'

♦ ♦ ♦

That morning, she'd shivered in the cool basement, watching her own breath in the cold air. She still felt half-awake.

Once, she started, it was easier. Dana scrabbled at the barrels with her too-short fingernails, trying to pry the hammered wood away. Exhausted, she stumbled, only letting go of the wood too late. She hit the cold concrete. The barrel above her tottered, thinking about it for a moment, before giving in. It fell.

Dana pulled her legs in close to her body, narrowly missing the barrel. It made a sound like the crack of an egg, wood splintering, fluid rushing out. Instinctively, Dana covered her eyes, even as the liquid reached the underside of her legs.

The smell tanged the air, somewhere between vinegar and vodka. Dana knew she would have to move her eyes. She didn't want to look. She'd die if she didn't know what it was.

Slowly, she put down her hands, eyes averted. Took two deep breaths. She looked.

Between the snapped shards of wood, something white was in there, folded up like something sea-dwelling in a shell. Dana breathed in and out, and she got to her feet. If she was going to look, she was going to look thoroughly.

So, she unwrapped him. Pulled the wood away, piece by piece, as more liquid poured out. His body was wrapped in a white cloth, edges of it rough and fraying. An old bedcover, she thought, cut into strips. Dana did not pull it all away. She left enough that his dignity was maintained, but his face was exposed. It was slightly bloated, but he hadn't rotted in any way she could tell. His eyes were disjointed, like a broken doll: one closed, one half-moon open.

Dana cradled the Jerome Smolinski in her arms, torso in the hollow of her body, neck against her forearm. Greenish liquor spilled from his open mouth like a drunk.

Dana knew she shouldn't hold him. He wasn't the friendless man who lived in a basement anymore. He was evidence. But the two of them were there together, and it wasn't like anyone could see her.

She brushed the wet strands of hair off his forehead, away from his eyes and looked.

♦ ♦ ♦

Joe thought that the Fishers were good people, but they were not the kind of people Mrs Enckles would have suggested that they befriend. They were good but they were not always nice, and niceness can always be relied upon.

The road whiled away beneath them; the radio sang; in the passenger seat, Ariel gazed out the window. His knuckles were cold on the steering wheel. No reason to turn back; Dr Wu had said he'd look in on his mom. Last he heard from Dave, Shelly was hanging on, but she wasn't going to make it. If he changed direction now, he could make it in time to say goodbye.

Ariel reached forward. Hands stiff, she changed the station clumsily until it became all ugly static. Joe rolled his eyes.

No reason to say goodbye, wouldn't change anything.

'If you've changed so much,' he said to Ariel, slapping her hands away, 'How come you still break my things?'

As she moved her arms, Joe's eyes fell to the names she had carved on them. It had always been her habit to write down the things she didn't want to forget on her hand. *Cathy Copeland. Sandy Ackerman. Anthony Dorhamer.*

Jerome Smolinski.

Joe had thrown his phone out the window a few miles back. He hadn't left Michael a message. Joe knew his brother. He'd be lonely. He'd be worried. He'd also tell Joe that they should kill Ariel.

Looking at her from the corner of his eye while he tried to fix the radio, Joe couldn't quite convince himself it wasn't the best solution.

She killed them, was what Dana had said after she woke up. At least, she pushed them to kill themselves.

Ariel still had grave dirt in her lungs. Besides, if the situations were reversed, she would do the same. Joe thought it was lucky the situations weren't reversed.

The radio blared; static, static, static.

'Damn it!' he shouted, slamming his hand on the top of the dashboard. It stung. He was tired. He'd been driving for so long the trees were thinning. 'Why did it work for you and not him?'

Ariel didn't reply. He didn't expect her to. Even if she could speak, there was no answer.

Finally, the radio switched back to a station. It was a vaguely familiar voice.

'18-year-old male, six foot 3 inches, light brown hair,' Deputy Boldry said. 'Again, I'll repeat, please call if you've seen this young man. Gary Fisher is missing, and we'd like to talk to him in connection …'

Joe turned it up.

'…with the recent events. Gary, if you're listening—'

Another voice broke in. 'Gary, it's Dad. Everything's okay, son. Just come into the station,' he continued. 'It's all going to be alright.'

When they were kids, Joe had always known when one of his siblings had the jump on him; he liked to think all older brothers had this instinct. In this case, he was a beat too slow, only taking his hands off the wheel to stop Ariel when she was mid-swing.

The car didn't spin so much as veer. She seized the wheel and stilled it. Joe was slumped over, but his breath steamed the glass of the mirror she held under his nose. His pulse thrummed.

She'd cracked him over the head with the heaviest thing in arm's reach—a Bible in the back seat.

She opened the car door. She started to walk.

By the time she had reached the sheriff's department, quite the slack-jawed crowd had amassed behind her. None of the officers were there. Len was watching the tape again at the Fisher's house, waiting for Gary with Francis Fisher. Stan, Coops and Graham, along with the fire department, were at Nyx, trying to figure out if they should take the rest of the corpses out of the moonshine barrels, or roll them to the station as they were.

The only one there to receive her was Mel. The pen he was chewing dropped out of his mouth, damp, when she walked through the front door. No idea how to react, he did as she asked, and arrested her on the spot.

♦ ♦ ♦

Secretly, Stan hated receiving anonymous tips. He knew he should be intrigued by the mystery. Dana always was. They did sound exciting if you liked true crime.

But in Lake in the Woods, it was all well-meaning kids reporting this or that friend for smoking weed, or ladies whose voices he recognised from church, spotting a stranger on their street. Generally, he ignored both of these and—in as polite a manner as he could muster—suggested that they give minding their business a try.

As he pulled the folded-up note out from under his windscreen wiper, he had to admire the panache of it.

Inside, were three words.

In the moonshine.

♦ ♦ ♦

Dana closed the trunk of her car. Across the lawn, the sound of voices spilled out as the Triegers' front door opened. Dana wondered if it was too late to hide.

They had a guest. Mr Trieger was too busy manfully slapping someone's back to notice her, Mrs Trieger saying goodbye. *Come any time, come any time.* Dana couldn't hear the reply, but she recognised the voice.

The sheriff stepped into the street. Well, the man who used to be the sheriff. He looked different out of uniform, smaller without his hat, but just as sharp.

His footsteps slowed as he saw Dana.

'This is my dad's house,' she said, before he could ask.

He looked at it, hands on his narrow hips.

'So it is,' he said. Mr Wormwood. She would never have the nerve to call him *Al*. 'Everybody knows everybody in this town. Is he home?'

She shook her head. Her dad hadn't been home all day. Neither had Gary. They must be together; whether at the station or with the press she didn't know.

'You knew Jerome?' she asked. You knew about Jerome, was what she meant.

'Yes.' Dana waited, but he didn't elaborate. 'You did a good job finding him and the others.'

'It was Stan,' Dana said. 'I didn't do anything.'

'Yes, you did,' Wormwood said. Somehow it sounded like an accusation rather than praise. 'The barrels—I should have thought of that.'

Dana wanted to apologise. More accurately, she wanted to be forgiven.

'From the outside, your hunch made more sense,' Dana said. 'The only reason I knew it was the barrels was because she didn't want to get rid of them. She wanted to preserve them. They might have got washed away in the lake.'

'That damn lake,' he sighed. 'Nothing's getting washed away there. Real lakes have rivers, they go somewhere. That lake is stagnant. It's manmade.'

'Dad said records show that it's an ancient well, that goes underground,' she said. 'The pilgrims came here from Europe to find it. They thought it was a gateway—'

Wormwood laughed: a real laugh, that went back all the way to his gold fillings.

'Baloney. Nothing in this town is carbon dated before 1800.'

This was too big a fiction. Their town was historical. One of the oldest settlements in America. Why else would it have cobble stones?

'But the records confirm it,' she said, confused.

Wormwood nodded.

'True, that's what the historical records say,' he was still smiling a little, 'But records are only as accurate as the people who write them.'

Chapter Twenty-One

> What did the angel tell you? I have been asked this question countless times. I've yet to come up with an answer that satisfies, because, the truth is, I did most of the talking.
>
> *Lake in the Woods: A Complete History of an American Miracle*, Francis Fisher

The phonelines were working again by the afternoon and a real news station had already picked up the story.

'Officer Wu, did you ever drink this moonshine?' one reporter asked the hero of the hour, a slim twinkle in her eye.

For the moment, it was a backwater joke, a conspiracy waiting to be unveiled. These small-town hicks were really hoodwinked into thinking that the dead were walking, can you believe it? The liquor barrels, corpses folded up into them in the local dive bar, was the macabre cherry on top.

Stan's glasses flashed in the camera light, his mouth a grim line. 'Ma'am, I don't take the lives of these four citizens lightly. I'd count myself as a friend to all of them, I think most of us here would.'

The square was swarming and furious. The town was hungry for blame, as if, were it unassigned, it would pick itself up and attach itself to them instead. No one cared who was coming out of the back. So, when Sera came out the fire escape door, she and Dana were alone.

Her long hair was dirty. She ran her hands through the temples, peaking it back from her face. She wore her faded grey jeans and a borrowed white t-shirt. Her only possessions, now. At the sight of her, Dana felt scraped away inside, raw with relief.

When Sera saw her, she smiled. It was brief, and quickly tucked away again.

'I guess I have you to thank for my freedom,' Sera said.

'You have your sister to thank,' Dana said.

Dana didn't know how to feel about it. Joe had said that they shouldn't feel sorry. Jerome made his choice. Shelly made her choice. Ariel made her choice. It was so easy to extract herself from these choices, Dana found herself wondering if choice had anything to do with it at all.

'That's not my sister,' Sera said. There was only one holding cell. Sera had seen Ariel as they led her out. Her bare scalp had been shockingly white, with veins like a river map to be followed with your fingertip. 'It's something new.'

Unsure how to express the magnitude of the loss—for the possibility of Ariel alive to have been there, and then gone again—Dana just said, 'I'm sorry.'

Sera looked at her. It was tired, and heavy with things

that were done.

'Don't be sorry for us,' she said. 'We aren't worth it, Dana.'

The dead town still felt so real. When Dana looked at Sera, she saw her dying. She couldn't fix this in one night, but she could try and beat back the current.

'Well then,' she said, 'I'm sorry about your trailer. It was ugly as sin, but it didn't deserve to die like that.'

Sera actually laughed. They both looked over in the direction of the car park. Behind the chain link fence was what was left of Sera's home, blackened and burnt. The shouts of the crowd were dim.

'Michael is a petty man,' she said, smile grim.

The two of them began to walk.

'I forgive you,' Dana said, because some things were too important to be unsaid. 'By the way.'

Sera looked forward. Her hands twisted into each other.

'Why?' Sera said, sighing. 'You don't have to. I'm not asking you to. It seems like a stupid thing to do, if I'm honest.'

'Well, you know me,' Dana said. 'I can't help being stupid.'

'Not that you listen to me, but I'd rather you didn't,' Sera insisted.

'Too late,' Dana said, because it was. If nothing else, it was far, far too late.

'I don't deserve it,' Sera said. It wasn't said with pity; it was said like a fact.

'People don't get things because they deserve them,' Dana said. 'See? I was listening.'

They reached the road. Brussels was parked under a streetlight that had just flickered on. The sun had set. Dana's heart began to pound.

'Can you give me a ride?' Sera said, looking a little awkward. 'To a motel or something?'

'I have another idea,' Dana said, unlocking the car. 'How far is the ocean from here?'

♦ ♦ ♦

Their white faces were plastered on his mind like billboards on the highway. His dad's wide-open eyes, as he lied. I was worried about you. Ariel's closed expression, watching him from the window being led to the cell.

He should have said something, done something. But he hadn't. That was his problem, wasn't it? Shelly had told him she was going to kill herself and he had to play along. And he had, hadn't he? And she was dead. He'd killed her, just by standing by and doing nothing, he had killed someone.

His converse and jeans were wet. No one had seen him in the square as he left the station to become just another face. Now that they had Ariel, he wasn't important: an innocent bystander. No one, really. At the gas station, Dirk hadn't said hello, as if he didn't know who he was.

In the crowd outside, he'd seen one of the guys who'd beat him up that night. A kid he'd went to school with, holding up a sign with Ariel's face on it that said SHE-DEVIL and, in smaller letters, fags go to hell. Their eyes had met, but he hadn't recognised him. In school, Gary had thought he was a nice enough guy; he hadn't had as many opportunities as Gary had; but still Gary hopes he burns.

The tanks of gas were heavy, so he tried to lift from his legs, pour it down the stairs like rain. He'd thought Lake in the Woods was his home. But it was as if a rock had been overturned, and underneath it was a swarm of ants.

There was something evil in this town, in this house as white as bone, in this stolen land. He didn't know what it was, he couldn't taste or smell it, but it was there, and it had its roots. He poured out the last tank on the piano, soaking the strings through. Dana said justice could be bloodless, that nothing was worth throwing your life away for, but Gary knew what Shelly knew, what Ariel knew, that some things couldn't heal, that the wound would only fester; you had to start again, you had to transform; that some things you had to cauterize and some things you had to cleanse, but for some things only fire would do.

Gary wasn't Ariel. He wasn't the fire, but he could be the match.

This is what he thought, over and over as he lit the match, as he dropped it, until it didn't mean anything. He was nothing. She'd saved him, but he'd failed her.

The time it took the fire to spread from the piano, the living room, the kitchen, was too long, time for many thoughts.

What should he think about? he wondered. What was a suitably meaningful last thought to round off his life with?

His eyes swam, pricked red, he blinked to clear them, his

lips began to peel.

Coughing, he made his way to the hallway, watching the flames make their way up the staircase; a grand entrance, like Prom Queen, the house roared in approval. It sounded like someone saying, Gary, do not be afraid.

He tried to hold Ariel's face in his mind, but it kept slipping out. Mom. Dad. Dana. He couldn't settle on a memory to focus on, it was so hot, he felt like he was already burning, what would they say at his funeral? What was there to say? Not much, nothing at all—

He tripped and fell to the ground, eyes swimming in black smoke. It was like he was coughing up half a lung; it was like there was a pillow pressed over his mouth. Michael would know, he'd know why he did this, people would see, they'd understand, and he'd be remembered, but he'd be dead.

The floorboards were hot, but the front door wasn't far. He could crawl there on his hands and knees and make it onto the porch before it caved. His hair fell into his eyes, he couldn't keep them open, they closed.

He was going to die here. This place was going to kill him either way—this way, he'd die on his terms.

It's easy, Shelly had said, before she'd killed her body. It's worth it.

He was going to die here.

In his pocket, his phone vibrated. He pressed it to his ear, hearing just faintly over the fire, it was so loud, his eardrums were burning.

The line was dead, but Gary was sure he could hear

someone, somewhere breathing.

That white wooden house with all its secrets was splintering, falling into the water, flames reaching into the sky like hands reaching for god. Black smoke filled the black sky in the rear-view mirror, but in the passenger seat, Sera rolled down the window to feel the cool night air on her face and taste the thunder.

Come back soon!

Pushing under the shadow of stone, Dana's eyes were on the road ahead, headlights crawling up one stretch at a time.

CAST (NOT IN ORDER OF APPEARANCE)

The Fishers

Rebecca Fisher, born in the town

Francis Fisher, married into the town, historian

Dana Fisher, officer at the sheriff's department

Gary Fisher, employee at Dale's Gas Station

The Enckles

Father Joshua Enckles, formerly the town's preacher *(deceased)*

Pamela Enckles, mother

Michael Enckles, eldest brother, now Mayor, briefly Dana's high school sweetheart

Sera Enckles, eldest sister, Dana's ▇▇▇▇▇▇ *(deceased, legally)*

Ariel Enckles, youngest, Green's Groceries check-out girl *(deceased)*

Joe Enckles, cousin by blood, more like a brother

Hanna Enckles, sister to Joshua *(deceased)*

The sheriff's department

Sheriff Alvin Wormwood

Deputy Len Boldry

Officer Stan Wu

Officer "Coops" Cooper

Officer Jacob Spinner

Melville, intern

The missing

Jerome Smolinski, lover of Joe, given away by birth parents *(deceased)*

Anthony Dorhamer, husband to Martha, alcoholic *(deceased)*

Sandy Ackermann, wife to David, mother *(deceased)*

Cathy Copeland, former Irish Catholic novitiate *(deceased)*

The town

Father Thomas, preacher

David Ackermann, owner of Green's Groceries, widower

Shelly Ackermann, Nyx bartender, sister to David

Sloppy Sal, mechanic, blues lover

Hilary, editor of The Lake in the Woods Declaration

Lena Trieger, the Fisher's neighbour

Wu Wei-Ting, doctor, good in a crisis, Stan's father

Mr Dale, owner of Dale's Gas Station

Miss Boldry, High School teacher

Ed Spinner jnr., popular

Ed Spinner snr., former Mayor

Principal Graham, high school principal, member of Town Council

Lynda, Dale's Gas Station employee, gossip

Dirk Dale, Dale's Gas Station employee, slacker

Brussels, Dana's car

Acknowledgements

Writing needs time and focus to flourish, and my participation in the Creative Writing MLitt program at The University of Glasgow from 2018-19 was incredibly helpful to finishing *Jesus Freaks*. I am both lucky and privileged to have been able to study my passion. Thanks to my mum for financially contributing to my attendance and encouraging me to write, even though I suspect you will probably hate this resulting book. Thank you to my tutors and peers, hope you're all still writing. An additional thank you to Will, Adam and Kathleen for letting me crash with you that October.

Thank you to Lena Hofbauer, Emily Rose and Shaun Patterson for being my first readers. Your kindness at that time is still so appreciated. Thank you to Katy Simmons for your friendship and the tarot card reading, although the final version here—thankfully—doesn't resemble it at all. Thank you to Tánička Gersiova, Marianne Docherty and Ren of Paperxclips bookstore in Belfast for your time and encouragement in the last leg, and to my sister for putting me in touch. Much appreciation to James Fenner for the perfect cover—I'm still swooning over it—and Liina Koivula for the incredible typesetting job.

Many thanks to my fellow writers Ruthie Kennedy, Anjeli Caderamanpulle, Felicity Anderson-Nathan, Siobhan Mulligan, MJ and Billie for your valued feedback and all the silly jokes. I hope we will reunite soon, demons included. A special thank you to Ciara Maguire for always believing in and loving *Jesus Freaks*. You are literally the most important dyke in the world.

When I started this book, I felt like I had nothing to live for. Thank you to the counsellors, mental health professionals, helpline volunteers and nurses who helped me throughout that time. Thank you to the doctor who said, keeping taking medication if that's what you need. Thank you to the people I shared group sessions with, and to everyone over the course of my life who has believed me when I've told them, I'm suffering and I need your help. Unfortunately, mental illness is turning out to not be something I've checked off the list and will never deal with again, but I'm still here. A win is a win!

Jesus Freaks would not have been finished without my dear friend River Ellen MacAskill gently telling me to get on with it (so if you didn't reading enjoy it, blame them). Thank you for not letting me give up, for your astonishing compassion, and for the thousands of cups of under-appreciated tea.

I can't wait for the rest of my life!

Content warnings

These warnings include spoilers.

Suicide

It is a major plot point.

The act itself is not described 'onscreen', but the aftermath is described in detailed physical terms in Chapter Two, Chapter Three, Chapter Thirteen, Chapter Sixteen and Chapter Seventeen.

Sexual assault

The victim is assaulted at a party by her boyfriend.

The assault itself is not described, but alluded to most heavily at the end of Chapter Five.

Dead bodies

Described in detail in Chapter Three and Chapter Twenty.

Homophobia

A homophobically motivated assault happens in Chapter Fifteen.

About the Author

Born in Belfast on Valentine's Day, Suki Hollywood is a writer and poet. Her work has been featured in *Gutter, Clav Mag, The Selkie* and *Spam*, and she is a graduate of The University of Glasgow's Creative Writing Program. *Jesus Freaks* is her debut novel.

Find out more at www.sukihollywood.com.